TENOCLOCK
SCHOLAR

TENOCLOCK SCHOLAR

A Johnnie Baker Mystery

JOHN MILES

WALKER AND COMPANY

NEW YORK

First published in the United States of America in 1995 by Walker
Publishing Company, Inc.

Published simultaneously in Canada by Thomas Allen & Son Canada,
Limited, Markham, Ontario

Library of Congress Cataloging-in-Publication Data
Miles, John.
Tenoclock scholar : a Johnnie Baker mystery / John Miles.
p. cm.
ISBN 0-8027-3273-9 (hardcover)
1. Women detectives—Colorado—Fiction. 2. Sheriffs—Colorado—
Fiction. I. Title.
PS3563.I3719T46   1995
813′.54—dc20   95-30752
CIP

Printed in the United States of America
2 4 6 8 10 9 7 5 3 1

TENOCLOCK
SCHOLAR

..

1

IT HAD NEVER occurred to anyone around the resort town of Tenoclock, Colorado, that they might become the object of a scholarly research project.

Of course, it had never occurred to them that there was any truth in the old stories about an Anasazi curse, either.

It had been a very long time since any of the white people around town had so much as thought about the legends of a curse on the area. Probably nobody except a handful of poverty-stricken Ute descendants isolated in the farthest southwest corner of the county had mentioned it in decades.

Especially when Tenoclock began to boom in the 1980s, the idea of a curse seemed absurd. Things were going fine: the tourists and celebrities started flocking in, and a lot of the locals got far too busy making money to ponder nonsense.

Mention of the curse was restricted to vivid tales in any number of "authentic history" booklets sold in the souvenir shops. Some of the yarns might have been near historical truth. But only tourists believed such stuff.

Then, however, in a one-week period that fine early spring, an African lion walked down Main Street; a horrendous fire razed the courthouse annex, killing an elderly night watchman and destroying almost all the county's old legal documents and land records; some south-end sheep men swore they felt the earth tremble in the night; and a stranger was found by the side of the west road, killed by an antique Indian arrow driven through his throat.

A few of the old-timers began to frown.

Sheriff Johnelle "Johnnie" Baker, appointed to her office only seven months earlier, had no time to think about tales of the curse. She and her tiny staff just ran from crisis to crisis, trying to keep up.

Despite her blond good looks, Johnnie was one-sixteenth Choctaw, and she had gone to a great deal of trouble to prove it to the nation's leadership down in Oklahoma in order to get an official card. For that reason, among others, she had a profound respect for the native American culture and its legends. But she did not put much stock in talk of an ancient curse said to date back millennia, to a fabled time when the Anasazi—"the Old People"—lived nearby even before their first great migration far to the southwest, to distant Mesa Verde and beyond.

She saw no curse in any of the weird things that happened that week. As bad as they were, she figured she could somehow get them all sorted out, eventually. But then the other things started to happen.

THE ANCIENT BANJO-CLOCK on the scabby south wall of the sheriff's department in the courthouse had just made a shuddering sound as it did every hour when it tried—and failed—to chime. Midnight: the start of a fine new day for law enforcement in Tenoclock County, Colorado. Another Monday, and this week had to be better.

At the front reception counter, which also served as the two-way radio desk, Johnnie stifled a yawn. One of her deputies,

Dean Epperly, had the midnight-to-eight shift in the office. Intelligent, but not intelligent enough to be scared of much, Epperly also had the advantage of being unbelievably good-looking. Walking around town in his gray uniform, he was grand PR for the county. Johnnie would have considered him all-around satisfactory if he did not hold the world's record for laziness. He always made it a point to be late—just a wee, tiny bit late, as much as he thought he could get away with—whatever shift he happened to be on.

Johnnie, who had been on since a little before 6:00 A.M. Sunday morning, more than 18 hours now, had a headache that wouldn't quit. She reached for the battered gray Motorola hand microphone on the desk to yell politely on the sheriff's frequency and inquire in vague cop-type terminology when in hell Epperly planned to honor her with his presence.

As she did so, however, headlights flared brilliantly across the dirty glass of the high basement windows that looked out toward the back parking lot. At the same time she heard the roar of Epperly's big pickup-truck engine. Then the lights went out, and so did the noise of the engine; seconds later, upstairs, came the sound of the rear steel security door slamming.

Johnnie stood, brushed pizza crumbs off the front of her wrinkled jeans, straightened her dark red flannel shirt, and tried to feel philosophical while she waited. The rest of the sheriff's department stood vacant, two rows of crummy olive-drab metal desks and some dented filing cabinets under a low ceiling of acoustical tile that had once been white, before several major water leaks and the smoke from a million cigars turned most of it varying shades of yellow and brown. One of the overhead fluorescent light fixtures flickered and fluttered, making a nearby dark tan water stain appear to squirm.

One of the opaque-glassed back doors swung open, and Dean Epperly strode in, every hair in place and his hundred-kilowatt smile on full power. "Morning, Sheriff!"

"Dean," Johnnie began, coming around the counter. "Dammit—"

She got no further. The radio behind her, almost always silent at this time of night, squawked loudly, "Sheriff's unit two to base." It was veteran deputy Butt Peabody's gravel voice, no mistake possible. But he had gone off duty at 7:00 P.M.

Johnnie hurried back around the counter and grabbed the mike. "Unit two, headquarters. Go."

The old radio squawked again, Peabody's voice over the howl of his truck engine moving at high speed: "Code two for the Eastside Tavern, Johnnie. Picked up the ambulance call on the scanner at home. Got a fracas, one subject maybe in bad shape, couple others hurt some."

"Oh God," Johnnie murmured in dismay. The office scanner had been broken for over a month, and the commissioners had already told her they couldn't afford to buy her a new one.

On the other side of the counter, Dean Epperly eagerly slammed his Stetson on his head. "I'll go too!"

Johnnie lunged across in time to catch his arm and haul him back. "No, you won't! You'll stay right here."

"Aw, Johnnie—"

She keyed the microphone. "Butt, is the city PD on this one?"

"Negative." The roar behind Peabody's flat, disgusted voice sounded as if he must be pushing his big Ford just as hard as possible. "They can't respond at this time. All units working a seventy-six at Denver and Stockwell, plus they got one cruiser down for a tire change and another one in the paint shop."

Johnnie bit her tongue to hold back the expletive. She knew the Eastside Tavern was almost ten miles out in the country on State Highway 127, the route to the Anvil Mountain Resort and a link to the road south toward faraway Del Norte. Strictly speaking, that put it outside city jurisdiction and in her lap. But once there had been a lot more cooperation in situations like this, and the city wouldn't have allowed a 76—a traffic accident without injury—to prevent helping out. They wouldn't have had one of their badly needed cruisers out of service for a flashy new paint job with smiley faces on the fenders, either.

But that had been before the understaffed city police department was saddled with walking-beat public relations appearances, officers out of cars and on horseback to add to the local color, and static salaries that had decimated the force. So far, both city and county had gotten away with pinchpenny law enforcement budgets and extra public relations chores that took away vital time from meaningful work. But Johnnie knew it couldn't last forever; one of these days there was going to be an outbreak of violent crime, and Tenoclock—city and county alike—would not be equipped to handle it.

The bizarre events of the last week or so had been enough to make her wonder if the breaking point wasn't at hand now.

This, however, was no time to think about any of that.

She keyed the mike again. "You still south of town, Butt?"

"That's affirmative."

"Okay. I'm a lot closer. I'll head out now, maybe get there first."

"Ten-four."

She put the microphone down, easily vaulted the end of the counter, and hurried into the back room, where the locked gun cabinet was. A moment later she strode back into the office as she punched waxy red 12-gauge shells into the magazine of the shotgun. Dean Epperly stood by, looking sad and forlorn.

"Dean, stay close to the radio. Call the city on the phone and tell them we're code two to the Eastside Tavern on Onetwenty-seven. Call Billy Higginbotham at home and let him know what's going on, in case we need to call him in on overtime later tonight. Tell Jason, back in the jail, what's happening, too. We probably won't need you or Billy either, but if we do have to call you out, Jason will have to be ready to take over desk duty up front, here."

Epperly's face twisted. "I was going to go get me some coffee and a doughnut or something."

"Sorry," Johnnie flung over her shoulder as she ran for the back doors. "Stay put!"

Before he could whine something in response to that, she was out of the office and on the stairs leading up to the back security door. Seconds later she shoved the steel door open and hurried out into the cool April night, hoping her old Jeep wouldn't pick this time to be temperamental again.

It started up at once, belying its advanced age and the 206,000 miles on the odometer. Johnnie flicked on the headlights and the roof-mounted red rotator and gunned out of the parking slot to head for the exit ramp. Less than five minutes later she was out on 127, headed east as fast as she dared to push the old heap, the hood ornament pointed straight toward a sliver moon hanging low over distant Anvil Mountain.

THE EASTSIDE TAVERN, a rambling, broken-down log building sitting across the road from a small convenience store on an otherwise deserted stretch of 127, had never been one of the county's better establishments. Minor fights and injuries out there were common enough, and this seemed to attract a regular clientele of high school dropouts, mildly retarded oil field workers, and drifters who seemed to have an uncanny knack for locating their own kind. The tavern's rooftop lights threw a pink glow up against the sky that was visible to Johnnie almost two miles before she crested a slight rise in the scrub-country valley floor and actually got the location in direct view.

The convenience store parking lot across the road from the tavern was vacant under its bright security lights. The Eastside, however, had plenty of business. The usual collection of battered pickups and older-model cars clogged its gravel lot. Close to the battered shingle front porch of the tavern, the city hospital's Emergency Medical Services van sat with its red-and-blue rotators flashing on top and light flooding out from opened back doors. As she wheeled in, Johnnie caught sight of two technicians shoving a gurney into the back of their unit; they had a skinny boy strapped down on it. A clot of Eastside patrons stood around on the porch, watching with great interest. A couple of them had towels or cloths of some kind to their heads. Between the van and the porch, two other figures—bulky men—lay prone on the gravel.

Johnnie braked sharply to a halt, cut lights and engine, and reached for her hand microphone. "Sheriff's unit one to base."

"Go ahead, unit one."

"Out of the car at Eastside." Without waiting for Dean Epperly's response, she piled out, shotgun in hand, and ran toward the ambulance.

A burly figure with a pale apron around his thick waist lumbered down the porch steps and intercepted her halfway there. Louis Mack, owner of the Eastside, was shaking and sweaty. "It all happened before I could stop it, Sheriff! Goddammit, you know I do my best. It wasn't my fault this time!"

"I know, Louis," Johnnie snapped. "You're all choirboys out here. Excuse me?" She pushed by him.

One of the two paramedics had just slammed the back doors, leaving his partner inside with the injured boy. He turned a grim face to Johnnie. "Beat up some. Not as bad as we first thought. Life signs stable."

"Hi, Jerry. Did you get an ID?"

The young paramedic pulled a small notebook out of the breast pocket of his white jacket and glanced at the first page. "Henry Burlingame. Ute, probably. High school ID card: junior. DL says he's seventeen. Home address Rural Route Six."

"Six? That's down in the Big Gully area."

Jerry shoved the notebook back in his pocket. "Need to roll."

Johnnie stepped back. "Go."

He hurried around to the driver's side and climbed in. The engine had never been turned off. The big van lurched into motion and pulled out onto the vacant road, siren starting to wail.

Johnnie turned and almost bumped into the rotund, nervous Mack. "He said he was eighteen, Sheriff, I swear to God. He looks eighteen. He showed me a card, said he was eighteen."

Johnnie stepped around him and walked briskly over to the two males lying facedown on the gravel near the steps. Both were older than the boy who had just been taken off in the ambulance, mid-twenties perhaps, and thickset. Both were wearing the required uniform for places like Eastside: faded jeans, cowboy boots, dirty white T-shirts sticking out below the bottom of frayed Levi's jackets. But what really engaged Johnnie's attention was that both men's wrists had been lashed painfully behind their backs with what looked like white rubber tubing. Another glance showed their ankles tied the same way.

"You guys conscious?" she asked, squatting beside the nearest one, who was slightly thinner than his companion.

Both of them squirmed and rolled their heads to see her. Their eyes looked twitchy, dazed. With dismay, she recognized them. "You two again?"

The nearer one, a faint glint of vicious intelligence coming into his eyes, bared tobacco-stained teeth. "Led us go, we ain't done nothing."

"Looks to me like you've had a small riot here, Tim."

"Fug you."

Tim Riley's brother, the other captive, groaned. "That guy hurt us, he hurt us real bad, I was tryin' to make peace, Sheriff, I really was—"

"Shut your stupid face, Billy!" Tim snapped.

"Just because he beat me at pool—"

"Shuddup, I said!"

Johnnie stood. "Just cool it, both of you."

"Damn Indian kid cheated us. First them Utes kill a guy by

sticking an arrow in his neck, and you don't do nothing about it, and then this kid hustles us at pool. We should of killed the little—"

"Tim," Johnnie warned, "You'd better be quiet."

She felt irritated and not entirely capable of adopting a philosophical attitude. The Riley boys were regular troublemakers. There had already been vague racist rumblings since the arrow murder, and she didn't need any more incidents.

Behind her came the roar of Butt Peabody's truck. She heard gravel spray as he hit the lot and braked hard.

She stood, still holding the shotgun over her shoulder, and surveyed the crew on the front porch. "Does anybody want to tell me what happened here?"

"It wasn't anybody's fault," Mack said. "The boys had words, you know how boys will be, and then they went outside and the fight started—there was no way *we* coulda known anything was going on clear out here—"

"Louis," Johnnie said, "hush." She turned back to the gawkers on the porch. "Now. Let's try again. What happened?"

As she spoke, Butt Peabody crunched up to join her. Six feet tall, still powerfully built despite his middle age, he was wearing baggy corduroy pants stuffed into his boot-tops and an ancient leather jacket over a Denver Broncos sweatshirt. Shaggy gray hair stuck out around the edges of his shapeless black Stetson. Small, metal-framed eyeglasses halfway down his bulbous nose might have made him look vaguely professorial if he hadn't been sporting a two-day growth of gray stubble on his face. A half-burned cheroot, dead, stuck out of the corner of his mouth.

Peabody had a revolver in his hand that looked big enough to kill an elephant. Rapidly taking in the situation, he shoved the weapon into a leather holster on his right hip and examined Johnnie's face with keen, narrowed gray eyes. "I passed the ambulance. What happened?"

"That's what I'm trying to find out." Johnnie turned back to the loafers on the porch. "Who wants to talk first? Or do we make ten trips back and forth to jail, and talk at our leisure back there?"

"The kid started it," a white man with a densely bearded face said.

"No, he didn't," another man grunted. He was short, thickset, and possibly Indian, although the wide brim of his hat made it hard to tell.

"Tim Riley caused it," another voice said from the back.

On the gravel, the older Riley made a hissing sound. "You'll be sorry you ever said that, Arch!"

"Be quiet, Tim," Johnnie ordered. "Now: who else?"

Another, older man spoke. "They argued about pool, and the kid left, and they follered him outside and got into it out here."

There was a general grumble of agreement to that.

Butt Peabody stared at one of those holding a towel to his head. The towel appeared to have blood on it. "What part did *you* play, buddy?"

The man jumped. "None! Nothing at all!"

"That was a different fight," someone else put in from the back.

"That's right," another voice chimed in. "Harry and Bill got into it about the fishing deal, and then—"

"I was trying to break it up," one of the others, holding something to his head, interrupted. "Goddam, you start swinging a pool cue around—"

"Yeah," the bearded man cut in. "But none of that had anything to do with these two guys and the guy in the rubber suit."

Johnnie started. "The *what?*"

"The guy in the suit! The guy in the rubber suit, with the fins on his feet and all that shit!"

Johnnie exchanged baffled glances with Butt Peabody. This, she thought, was not going to be easy.

AS A MATTER of fact, it took over an hour to get the story sorted out.

No one could agree about the exact nature of the argument between young Henry Burlingame, now in the hospital emergency room, and the two men who squirmed and twitched in the gravel at Johnnie's feet. There was general agreement, however, that young Billy Riley had come in alone at first and found Burlingame playing solo pool. Billy got into a game with him, and then another and another, for five dollars a game. Billy won all of these, and then the teenager talked him into one final game for a hundred dollars. Billy, giggling like a maniac, thought he saw easy money. Unfortunately, the high-schooler ran the table on him.

It had been about this time that the older Tim Riley appeared, face already dark with the kind of manic rage he sometimes showed in public.

Sharp words had been exchanged. Finally Billy Riley had paid up. When the Burlingame boy swaggered out, however, Tim followed him. Then Billy followed his brother. The next thing anyone knew, there had been shouting in the parking lot.

No one had seen the start of it, that they would admit. However, several patrons had peered out through the front window to see what was happening. What they saw—and there was agreement on this, too, allowing for minor variations in accuracy of observation—was the Burlingame boy on the ground, evidently unconscious, Tim Riley kicking him and Billy trying to stop it. A couple of men went outside at that point to try to break it up before more harm was done, but they had proceeded at something less than a breakneck pace because the brothers were known far and wide as poison if crossed.

A few words had been exchanged between the Rileys and the would-be intervenors, at which point the other man—the one in the rubber suit—clomped across the road from the convenience store. His Ford pickup with a camper shell on the back was parked at the gas pumps, and he had been fueling it or something when things got hot and heavy. Everybody who had seen this part agreed the stranger had been wearing a skin diver's wet suit, flippers and all, and a glass mask.

The skin diver had walked up to the Rileys and said something polite, trying to get them to stop kicking Burlingame. Tim had then hit the stranger in the face, knocking his mask off and putting him down in the gravel. The stranger had then scrambled to his feet and fled back across the road to his camper.

The gawkers on the front porch had at this point resumed trying to reason with the Rileys, but were getting nowhere when the skin diver fellow came back across the road again, this time with a coil of some kind of tubing over his shoulder and some kind of a *thing*—not a weapon, exactly, but this long tubular *thing* in his hands. He had walked up to the Rileys again and said something, and Tim had said something back, at which point Billy lurched at the skin diver as if to attack him, and the skin diver pointed his weapon-thing at them and knocked each brother half-unconscious and flat on his back with it.

"An underwater stun gun," someone put in helpfully at this point. "I seen one on the Discovery Channel once."

The skin diver guy had then rolled the stunned Rileys over on their bellies and neatly trussed them up with the tubing he had brought along. Coming face-to-face with tavern owner Mack at this point, he had cheerfully advised him to call the authorities. Then he had clomped back across the road again, his rubber flippers making a funny racket, gotten into his pickup, and driven away, headed south, in the direction of Killdeer Mountain.

"Did anybody know this guy?" Butt Peabody demanded.

No one spoke.

"Did anyone get a license plate number?"

No one spoke.

Johnnie took down a lot of witness names. Someone said he felt pretty sure the skin diver's truck had an Oklahoma plate. Butt Peabody got the two still-dazed Rileys into the back of his pickup. Then Johnnie's Jeep wouldn't start, and Peabody jumped it for her. And then they headed back toward Tenoclock.

"Very strange, Johnnie," Peabody said over the radio.

She didn't answer. What else is new? she thought.

2

BY THE TIME they got back to the courthouse, it was almost 3:00 A.M.

Dean Epperly was asleep at the front desk. He jumped badly when Butt Peabody nudged him with the toe of a boot.

"I was thinking about a case!"

Peabody nodded, phlegmatic. "Got a couple of prisoners out in the back of the truck. Fetch Jason from the jail, and the two of you take them over to the emergency room, get 'em checked out. I don't think they're bad hurt. Have them checked and treated if necessary, then haul 'em back here to the lockup."

"Wow," Epperly muttered, rubbing his eyes. "You apprehended the perpetrators, eh? They're hurt? What happened to them?"

"We think they got an electrical shock from an underwater stun gun."

Epperly's eyes went wide. "They were *under water?*"

"Never mind. Go."

Epperly hurried out. In a few moments, coming back from unloading and locking up the shotgun, Johnnie heard the back doors slam as he and Jason Ramsey went out. She looked around. Butt Peabody, filthy old hat parked on the counter, had started to build a fresh pot of coffee.

"Good idea, Butt. It looks like we'll be here a while longer tonight."

Peabody's weathered features crinkled in either a grimace or a smile. "Oh joy, oh rapture."

Johnnie crossed to the nearest desk, picked up the telephone, and punched the button for the special direct line into the hospital ER.

"Emergency Room, Thelma Dodson speaking."

"Thelma? Hi. Johnnie Baker. How's the teenager doing? The one who was brought in from the Eastside Tavern?"

"Hi, Johnnie. Well, they're still checking him over. The X rays didn't show any skull fractures or anything, and it doesn't look like there's any brain swelling. He's got some broken ribs and missing teeth, and we'll be keeping him overnight, but I guess he's going to be okay."

"Great. Listen, we've got another couple of customers on the way over with two of my deputies. They each had a severe electrical shock. Rileys, Tim and—"

"Oh, no," Dodson groaned. "Them again?"

"Afraid so."

"They had been good a long time this time."

"Yes," Johnnie said wearily. "I guess they were due. Look, Thelma. Check them out and pass the word that my deputies will bring them right back here to the hoosegow if they're essentially in one piece."

"Will do, Johnnie. Wow. You guys have been working overtime lately."

"Tell me about it."

Dodson's voice became cheerier. "I guess you can look at the bright side."

"That being?"

"Gosh. This kid isn't dead, anyway."

Johnnie hung up and walked over to watch Butt Peabody shove the coffee basket into the maker. "Kid's going to be all right."

"Good," Peabody rumbled.

"What do you think we ought to charge the Riley boys with?"

The older man thought a moment, his forehead becoming massively corrugated. He had been sheriff here for a long time, when Johnnie was much younger, and only political chicanery by the opposition had ever put him out of office. Johnnie's first act, when she was named interim sheriff seven months earlier, had been to appoint him her chief deputy despite the howls of protest from some local politicos. She liked him. More important, she needed his experience at times like this . . . among others.

"I guess we could file a drunk and disorderly," Peabody told her now. "Assault, too. That's about it."

"I'll have Jason book them on those charges, and see what the county attorney will file in the morning."

"Family might cause a furor. Dad's a surgeon, you know . . . pals with the mayor and all."

"I know."

Neither of them spoke for a minute. The wall clock made one of its agonized noises. Johnnie blurted, "Butt, what do you make of this stuff about a skin diver?"

"Well, I think there was one. I mean, I don't think any of those old boys are smart enough to make up something that weird."

"We really ought to talk to him, if we can find him."

Peabody's face wrinkled in a different way. "Yeah. I'd be real interested to know why he needed a wet suit in a convenience store."

"I wish we'd get a quiet night for a change!"

"Hey, girl, we're just starting the summer season. All the good fun is still ahead of us."

"This strange murder we just had, and all the other stuff, are quite enough for me right now. Thank goodness you had your own scanner on a few hours ago. Otherwise, how long would it have taken for us to know what was going on out there?"

Peabody eyed the dead Bearcat scanner on the shelf beside the radio counter. "Got to get a new unit for in here."

Johnnie nodded. "I'm going to Radio Shack tomorrow and buy one with my own money."

Peabody's eyes narrowed. "Watch it. Next they'll have you paying 'em rent for the sheriff's office."

She had no reply to that. Turning, she walked to her desk, first in the row of army-surplus units nearest the counter, and sat down dejectedly. Nothing about the job had turned out as she had hoped it would when she reluctantly took it in the wake of the murder of Sheriff Jim Way. Once the initial shock had worn off and Way's killer had been found, she had expected to make some long-needed changes in the way the little department operated. But she had not counted on the county commissioners.

They had installed her half as a publicity stunt in the first place, and would not have paid for any new departmental costs whatever the state of the county budget. The fact that the county was teetering on the edge of fiscal disaster just gave them an additional reason for saying no to everything Johnnie asked for.

It all became clear early on, when she assumed the county would supply her with a cruiser and instead the commissioners authorized an expenditure of up to $65 to have a gold star painted on each door of her personal Jeep. On sober reflection, Johnnie had seen then that she shouldn't have expected much more.

Tenoclock County really was virtually broke.

A decade earlier, when commissioners had floated the first bonds to build a fine ski lift and new airport capable of handling celebrity jets, the risky venture had worked: the first movie stars appeared on cue, a piece ran in a national newsmagazine saying Tenoclock was destined to become the new Vail, and the tourist trade exploded as little people flocked in to gawk at big ones.

Encouraged, especially since each of them had quietly invested in property now appreciating in value at a rate of 40 percent a year, the commissioners decided to press on and make things better yet. First, Wal-Mart was given a piece of county land on which to build a superstore, plus what amounted to a ten-year dispensation from property taxes. Then more bonds had been floated to build the new hospital and start repaving county roads in all directions. Then, when Eddie Bauer inquired about locating a retail outlet, someone got the bright idea of promoting Packer's Alley, a previously shabby retail block between Gunnison Avenue and Silver Street. Eddie Bauer was immediately given a tax and retail licensing break by both the county and the city, and while carpenters were still nailing up his false front, along came Sharper Image, Victoria's Secret, Hallmark, Radio Shack, J. C. Penney, J. Crew, and The Limited, among others, all on the same kind of free tax ride.

Longtime local merchants, of course, got no such break, which put some of them out of business. But they were not glamorous anyway.

Unfortunately, the result of a shrinking actual tax base and expanding population had added more and more demand for improved infrastructure, everything from still more roads to new bridges and fire protection. Commissioners had had no choice but to order a general belt-tightening, along with a promise of a turnaround in three years or so.

The turnaround hadn't happened yet. That was why Johnnie made do with a law enforcement staff that included only herself, Peabody, Dean Epperly, Billy Higginbotham, jailer Jason Ramsey and his part-time assistant, and office clerk Hesther

Gretsch. It was far from enough. So far they had been lucky.
Now she wondered if the luck hadn't just run out. . . .

THE LION INCIDENT had been the first crazy thing to happen. That had been just a week ago. In some ways it seemed like a
year. But, thinking back, Johnnie remembered everything about it.

It was just past midnight on a fine, clear, cool April night,
and Johnnie had finished her coffee and was just getting ready
to leave the all-night Pick & Shovel Cafe not far from the courthouse when the telephone behind the counter jangled and the
night cook answered it, raised his eyebrows, and signaled that
the call was for her.

He stretched the coiled cord to the limit to let her take the
call from her counter stool.

"Sheriff Baker speaking."

"Sheriff! Sheriff! Get right down here! There's a lion walking
down the middle of Main Street!"

Johnnie came off her stool. "Who is this? Where are you?"

"It's Skivey, Skivey Toole, and I'm in my shop here at
thirteen-oh-one, and oh, Jeez, there he is out there, walking
along—"

"A mountain lion? I hadn't heard any reports—"

"No! No! Not a mountain lion! Me and Harrigan, from next
door, and these few tourists that're still out, we can all see him
plainer than hell! He ain't no mountain lion, Sheriff. He's an
African lion, he's got a mane and everything, and he's walking
down the street right in front of us right now, this very minute,
and he looks bigger'n a moose!"

Main Street was just a block from where she was wheeling
her Jeep through the alley. She came out onto Main within a few
hundred feet of where Skivey Toole's curio shop was located.
She looked that way and felt her entire nervous system go cold.

A dozen or more people stood transfixed on the board sidewalk in front of Toole's shop. A couple of others were rooted on this side of the street, too. No one was moving an eyelash.

Walking down the middle of the street, passing them, was a big yellow male African lion.

He seemed to be sauntering along, paying no attention to anyone, moving with such weary slowness that it almost looked as if he had sore paws. Head down, he looked as though he might be headed into the darkness at the far end of the block, where the old-fashioned streetlights stopped. At the rate he was traveling, it would take him a minute or two to go out of sight.

Johnnie grabbed her Motorola microphone. "Unit one to base."

Butt Peabody's growl came back promptly. "Unit one, base. Go."

Thank God it was Butt on the boneyard shift tonight, Johnnie thought, again keying her mike. "Butt, find Clint Fredrickson, fast. If he's not at the game ranger station, get him at home. Tell him we need him and his tranquilizer gun down here on Main in front of Skivey Toole's, *now*. We've got a situation."

"Ten-four. Does officer need assistance?"

"Affirm. Get down here fast. Call Dean or Billy to come in on emergency duty—no, call one and tell him to call the other, and both of them get to the office, fast. Then come on. Bring two rifles. Bring Jason, too."

"Ten-four," Peabody's voice rapped back without questions. "Headquarters out, assistance on the way."

Johnnie tossed the microphone onto the passenger seat and hauled the old Springfield bolt-action rifle out of the side-window bracket. Working the bolt to chamber a round as she climbed out of the vehicle, she trotted up the street in the direction of the onlookers and the lazy-looking lion. She had no idea what she intended to do. But she had to do something. Lions— unless she had been badly misled all her life—ate things. Sometimes the things were people.

Moving fast, she started to close the gap between herself and the animal.

"Watch out, Johnnie!" somebody called shrilly from the sidewalk.

Evidently hearing either that or her footfalls for the first time, the lion suddenly stopped plodding south, away from her. He turned with considerably more speed than he had shown before.

Johnnie stopped just as fast and froze.

The lion looked at her. Head-on, he appeared about four times larger than he had going the other direction. His mane stood on end with surprise or fear or something—she hoped it wasn't anger—and his golden, green-flecked eyes gauged her with jungle wisdom that she could only guess about.

"Just take it easy, boy," she crooned, feeling really stupid.

The lion opened his mouth and made a hoarse, coughing roar. Saliva drooled off fangs as big as a Ford hood ornament.

"Nobody's going to hurt you," Johnnie told him, her voice choked. What did she do next? Ask him to surrender?

The lion stared at her another long minute. She held the old rifle ready at hip level. If the lion charged, she would start firing as fast as she could. She figured she might have time to get off a second shot before he was all over her. Two shots were not going to do it. If he decided she posed a threat requiring defensive attack—

Apparently the lion decided otherwise. The sparkles of venom died in his eyes. He opened his mouth, but this time it was in a yawn.

He turned away from her and started sauntering up the street again, back end swaying wearily.

Johnnie held her position. She didn't want the lion to walk into the darkness up in the next block, where a few poverty-level houses hid among falling-down storefronts, but she didn't know how to prevent it, either. She did not want to fire because she didn't want to kill the beast if that could be avoided, and she had no confidence she could bring him down anyway. Anything she did might just spook him into a killing rampage.

The lion kept on plodding south. She moved cautiously in pursuit. The people on the sidewalks yelled encouragement or something—she was much too nervous to listen.

Behind her a block or so came the screech of the brakes on Butt Peabody's truck, mixed with tire-skidding sounds. She heard a truck door slam and Peabody's guttural voice barking orders to someone, probably old Jason Ramsey, her venerable black jailer, who did a shufflin' Mose act for the public and read Homer in the original when he was at home alone. Then footsteps pounding on the pavement closer behind her made her turn to see Peabody and Ramsey, each with a rifle, their eyes glazed with surprise.

"Holy shit," Peabody exclaimed, his barrel chest heaving for air. He moved in close, protectively, on Johnnie's left side. "Is that a *lion?*"

Jason Ramsey limped up to take his place on Johnnie's other side. His eyes bulged, never deviating from their quarry almost at the end of the lighted block. "Take it from me, Mistuh Peabody. My people has known lions in the olden days, an' *that* is a sho nuff lion, fo sho, fo sho."

"Can the crap, Jason," Johnnie snapped. "Have either of you got any ideas?"

Ramsey's lazy tone changed. "Attempts to subdue could result in bodily harm to onlookers as well as to ourselves. Discharge of our firearms might only provoke, unless first shots felled him. Where did he come from?"

"Don't I wish I knew. Butt? Any ideas?"

Peabody, too, couldn't seem to drag his eyes away from the animal now moving into the twilight beyond the last streetlight. "I got Clint. He was in the sack, but from where he lives he can be here inside ten minutes. Maybe he'll have an idea."

"What if he doesn't?"

Neither of the men answered that.

"Well," Johnnie said warily, "nothing to do in the meantime but keep him in sight. It wouldn't do to have him get away now."

"Leetle late, boss," Ramsey muttered. "*Lee-tle* late."

Johnnie turned back to stare up the street again.

The lion had vanished into the dark.

JOHNNIE TOOK A deep breath. "We'll wait for Clint. He'll know what to do. In the meantime, let's try to get these folks off the street in case Mr. Lion decides to come back looking for a snack."

She led Peabody and Ramsey over to the board sidewalk along the part of the block where Skivey Toole's place stood with all lights still blazing. "Okay, everybody, you'd better move along, now."

The dozen or so onlookers jostled around, not eager to miss more fun. The tall, slender figure of an old man hove into view from where he had been standing back in the small crowd. Long gray hair braided down his back, he wore a battered felt hat, faded flannel shirt and jeans, and a well-worn leather vest. His face was as dark as mahogany, and he bore himself with great solemnity. Johnnie knew him; his name was Abner Wakinoki-man, and he was as close to a spiritual leader as most members of the fragmented, sometimes-feuding Ute community had.

He spoke slowly and gravely, in a rumbling bass. "The walking of strange animals is said in the tradition of my people to be a first sign of fruition of the Anasazi curse."

"That's all we need around here, Ab," Butt Peabody said disgustedly. "Somebody bringing up that old stuff."

"You cannot say that this was not a strange animal, walking amongst us, just as the curse is said to predict."

Somebody in the crowd—possibly Skivey Toole—piped up behind him: "What's *your* version of the story, Ab?"

Wakinokiman turned, his classic profile granitic, and started to repeat word-for-word the tale Johnnie had heard him relate on two earlier occasions, years ago. "It is said that in the longest-ago times, when the earth was still new and only the People—the Anasazi—walked in the land, there was a great chief. As a child he was crippled from a fall down a cliff, and some believe he may have been the model for Kokopelli, the sacred hunchback flute player so common in the art of the Old People, or Anasazi as they are called today."

"So," another voice called out nervously, "what's this about a curse?"

Wakinokiman cleared his throat before resuming: "The great and crippled chieftain is said to have gone into the mountains alone on a great spirit quest. While there, he fell into a deep sleep and was carried on the back of an eagle to a place so high above the world that he could see into the future. He saw a time when others—people of pale skin and barbaric customs—would drive the People from this valley, cheat them out of their land. He saw the rivers defiled and the air itself turned foul. He saw most of the descendants of the People gone to another place, and the few who remained ill and with little to eat, and without hope. Even the sacred burial mounds would be defiled.

"The great chieftain pronounced a curse on this valley, one that would be visited upon it at a time when his vision of the terrible future had come fully true. He said strange animals would walk among the inhabitants, and death would come, as would great and killing fires, and the earth itself would tremble."

Wakinokiman turned back toward the street, where everyone else had been watching fearfully all along, waiting to see if the lion reappeared. "It could be, as I said, that this beast marks the beginning of the fulfillment of the ancient one's pronouncement of a curse."

For an instant no one spoke, and it got extremely quiet on

the street. Johnnie felt the fine hairs rise on her arms. Without thinking, she hugged herself.

The sound of an approaching pickup truck broke the spell.

Driving up the street to where the three of them stood without a good idea of how to proceed, the tall, hatless Fredrickson piled out of his gray government truck with a big battery-operated portable spotlight in one hand and his ugly dart-shooting tranquilizer gun in the other. He had a vest slung over his shoulders, and Johnnie saw extra drug darts in its pockets.

"Where did he go?" Fredrickson panted.

Johnnie pointed. "That way."

"A lion? An honest-to-God African lion?"

"Yes."

"Are you sure?"

She thought of trying to say something funny, then decided against it. She was too worried about the unsuspecting people up the street. "I'm sure, Clint."

Fredrickson nodded, set his mouth in a grim line, and turned on the spotlight, which hurled a blinding beam up the street. "Let's go, then."

Johnnie was dumbstruck for an instant. "Now?" she finally demanded.

Fredrickson had already taken two long strides away from them. "Sure."

"Don't we formulate a plan first?"

The ranger's forehead wrinkled, puzzled. "What's to plan? We find him. I shoot him. We haul him back to my place and put him in that sewer-pipe bear trap I've got in the backyard."

"Oh." She felt deflated. "Fine."

They joined Fredrickson, forming a parallel line with him as he moved on up the street. A couple of onlookers called encouragement. They sounded gleefully excited. Easy enough for them to be enjoying this, Johnnie thought.

They reached the end of the block, where the streetlights

played out. Fredrickson moved staunchly a few paces ahead of them, the beam of his spotlight jerking back and forth over broken fences, weedy yards, and boarded-up storefronts.

Butt Peabody moved slightly nearer Johnnie. "If that critter comes at us, Johnnie, I want you to get behind me, pronto."

She didn't reply. She knew he meant well, but she knew she wouldn't do it. Her heartbeat felt heavy in her throat, and sweat stood cold all over her body, but she wasn't going to duck behind him or anyone else, if it came to that.

They moved farther up the street. By now the streetlights were well behind them, and they seemed to be in pitch blackness except for the blinding white ray of the spot wielded by Fredrickson.

Suddenly, as he swung the beam far to the right, the ranger stopped. "Uh-oh!"

Johnnie and her deputies edged up beside him again. "What is it?"

"Look."

Off to the right about thirty feet, broken fencing marked the demarcation line of a weed-choked front yard. Another twenty feet beyond the fence stood an old frame house that looked deserted and about to fall down. The house had a rickety wood front porch. Lying on the front porch, right paw crossed over left and eyes fearlessly reflected in the beam of the spotlight, was the lion.

Fredrickson shoved the spotlight at Johnnie. "Okeydokey, here's the deal. Keep the light on him at all times. Don't any of you move. I'm going to slip off here to the left and come up on him from the side, in that next lot over there. I'll have a lot better angle from over there, might be able to get pretty close before I shoot him right in the ass."

"What do we do if you miss?" Peabody asked quietly.

Fredrickson sounded aggrieved. "I don't miss. I'm a trained professional." He moved off into the darkness without waiting for more conversation.

Johnnie kept the spotlight beam centered on the lion on the porch. The lion continued to stare back with unblinking attention.

Beside her, Butt Peabody worked the action of his rifle. "Jason, if he goes at Clint, we open fire, and we keep firing until he's down or gone out of sight again. If he starts this way, we do the same thing. You can't run from something like that. He goes after us or Clint either, we've got to bring him down; there's no alternative. Johnnie, that old Springfield might be the best piece we've got out here right now against an animal of this size. If we don't down him, it might be up to you. If that happens, you'll have to let him get close—give yourself a sure shot. Aim low, below the chin. Try to get a chest shot. You might be our court of the last resort here."

Heartbeat hammering in her throat now, Johnnie said nothing. Neither did Jason Ramsey. They waited. The lion did not move. The circle of brilliant light quivered against the wall of the deserted house, Johnnie's hands shaking slightly. Off to the left they heard the sounds of Clint Fredrickson moving closer through the waist-high weeds of the adjacent yard. The lion didn't seem to notice.

Suddenly, back in the direction of the last lit block of Main Street, headlights glared. A big truck of some kind barreled down past Skivey Toole's and through the empty intersection where the darkness began. The headlights flared across pavement and illuminated Johnnie and her companions, halfblinding her.

"What the hell—!" Peabody yelled angrily.

Brakes squealed. Truck undercarriage howled and rattled. The truck, engine thrumming, humped to a halt not ten feet from where they stood. The windshield of the cab lit up for a second or two as a short, skinny man with tangled dark hair climbed hurriedly down. "Where is he? Where is he?"

"Get outta here!" Peabody bawled. "We got a wild animal back here, you idiot!"

The little man rushed up beside them. He was almost totally out of breath and smelled of sweat, tobacco, and whiskey. His Levi's and T-shirt looked as if they hadn't been changed in a month. He had close-set eyes and buckteeth, and he was shaking. "Where is he?" he repeated.

Then his eyes followed the beam of the spotlight. "Oh, dadgum, there he is!"

Then, before anyone could move to stop him, he loped away from them, heading straight for the lion.

"Hold it, you fool!" Peabody yelled.

From the next yard came Fredrickson's cry: "Wild animal! Get back!"

The little man clambered over the remains of the fence and walked straight up to the front steps. The lion looked up at him with what under other circumstances might have been described as a sheepish expression. The man said something they couldn't hear, then reached into his pants pocket and pulled out a short, rolled length of leather. He reached down and hooked one end of the cord into the lion's mane—or perhaps into a collar.

He stepped back, tugging on the leash. "Get up, you lazy old fart! Haven't you caused me enough trouble already?"

The lion coughed and wearily heaved himself to all fours. The man led him back through the yard and to the rear of the big, dirty white truck. He opened the rear doors and hauled down a metal ramp and kicked the lion in the hindquarters. The lion loped up the ramp into the interior. The man slammed the doors, turned, and limped back to Johnnie and her companions.

"I'm terribly sorry about all this," he told them. "It really wasn't my fault. Really!"

3

BY THE TIME Johnnie had finished her coffee and notes for her report on the trouble at the Eastside, Butt Peabody had made a few telephone calls to night clerks at the major area motels, seeking information about a possible resident with skin-diving equipment.

"Struck out," he told her morosely.

"Maybe there wasn't a skin diver."

"Right." Peabody's furrowed, weather-beaten face wrinkled more deeply into the frown of a fond but disapproving parent. "And the cow jumped over the moon. I've told you before, Johnnie girl: don't indulge yourself in wishful thinking. Wishing won't make it true, not in this job. All it might do is give you an ulcer, and you're a hell of a lot too pretty for that."

Johnnie grinned back at him and was about to ask how being pretty squared in any way with your stomach or duodenum. But before she could, the sound of a vehicle penetrated the old building from the back parking lot. Moments later she heard the back door slam, and footsteps on the back stairs, and the door of the jail section hammered back against the wall the way it always did because a hinge was broken.

"Let me go make sure everything is okay," she said, and strode out of the office, leaving Peabody hunched over his desk.

In the receiving room behind the jail section doors she found Dean Epperly scowling at the Riley boys, standing disheveled and in handcuffs in front of Jason Ramsey's desk. The black jailer had one misshapen manila envelope on the surface in front of him and was just putting a big wristwatch and billfold into another. He licked the flap, closed it, bent down the little metal locking tabs, and put it on the desktop with the other one.

Rising to his feet with a deceptively lazy look, the elderly man made a twirling motion with one hand at the Rileys. "Aw right, gentlemen, kindly turn around and face the wall."

Tim Riley, face smeared with dirt and mud and dirty curly hair wet with sweat, went redder in the face. "You're not searching me, you nigger bastard."

"Tim," his larger brother moaned. "Don't cause no trouble."

"Just shut your face, Billy!"

"My, my," Jason Ramsey murmured, reaching for the older brother's arm.

Face flaming, Tim Riley hawked up a gob of spit and let it fly. It hit Ramsey in the face. Dean Epperly moved with amazing speed and considerable brutality, slamming his weight into Tim's back and driving him up against the wall. Johnnie took a reflexive defensive half-step toward Billy, but he stood rooted.

"In the cell area," she ordered crisply. "Where, Mr. Ramsey?"

Ramsey calmly wiped the spit from his face with a red bandanna. "I think four and five would be real nice for 'em, Miz Sheriff."

Tim Riley still looked wild with crazy anger, but Epperly had his billy club out now, and there was no arguing with that. Johnnie moved in beside her deputy, and they herded the brothers through the back doorway into the dismal cell block. Except for a city arrest, a drunk, there was no one at all back here.

"Put us in jail," Tim Riley fumed, "and let the little Indian cheater go free."

"He's hardly free, Tim. You put him in the hospital."

"Let damn Indians kill people with arrows."

"In you go," Johnnie said, nudging him into the cell next to his brother's.

Ramsey clanged the doors shut. Tim gripped the bars with hands that looked like rubber baseball gloves. "When do you start applying the law to that trash down in Big Gully?"

Butt Peabody appeared in the cell block doorway, a sawed-off shotgun in his hands. "Everything under control back here? I heard—"

"No problem, Butt," Johnnie replied, and led him back out of the jail area to the front office.

"Tim got rambunctious," she explained once they were out by the counter again.

"Lot of hate in that boy."

"He's talking racist talk."

"Some people are. That arrow murder stirred up a lot of old stuff."

"Butt, I'm worried."

Peabody paused long enough to find loose tobacco and cigarette papers in his shirt pocket. He started rolling a smoke. "Call from the ER. The Burlingame kid is all right, but they're keeping him overnight just to be on the safe side. Some of the Utes are going to be mighty hacked off about this incident, too."

"He caused it."

"Maybe. But he's seventeen, and weighs maybe a hundred thirty pounds, and the Riley boys are grown-ups, and what would you say they weigh? Two hundred twenty? Two-thirty? And they ganged up on him."

"We've got to keep peace around here."

Peabody yawned. "Well, no problem. All we've got to do is solve that murder and show an Indian didn't do it."

"We've agreed that arrow must have been a plant."

"Sure. Only now all we got to do is prove it."

The back doors opened, and Dean Epperly strolled in.

"I'm going home," Johnnie decided wearily.

After giving her deputy some instructions he probably wouldn't follow anyway, she waited while Peabody got his hat on and his hand-rolled cigarette smoking. Then she walked outside with him into the back parking lot. The sliver moon and a universe of stars beamed down feebly onto the blackened skeleton of the burned-out courthouse annex building next door. The night had gotten downright cold. Johnnie climbed into her Jeep again, and it started this time. Peabody limped to his truck and waited while she backed out and left the lot first.

Heading out of town into the countryside, she tried to relax. But it was important not to relax too well, because she was so tired she knew she could fall asleep at the drop of an eyelid, even with her insides churning from all the recent disasters.

Ute curse indeed.

The lion incident, after all, had had a normal enough explanation. The driver worked regularly, transporting large animals from zoo to zoo, theme park to theme park. In this case he had been hired to transport the aged lion from the winter quarters of a circus down in Arkansas up to Wyoming, where a small zoo would take any lion at all, even one so old and lazy he could no longer be counted on to mount the circus stool or snarl convincingly when the trainer cracked the whip.

The driver said he had been sleepy and had pulled over earlier at a truck stop south of town in order to get coffee for a wake-me-up. A half hour later, when he returned to his van, he found the back doors agape and his lion among the missing. He had immediately started searching, but locating Brutus had taken a while—long enough for the old cat to throw a scare into some townspeople, Johnnie among them.

Johnnie had checked up on his story, and as far as she could determine it was 100 percent true. She had also checked out the truck, and the latches and locks were solid; someone had evidently thought they could find something valuable inside, had pried open the locks, and had found—instead of loot—a lion. The picture would have been funny if it hadn't been so potentially dangerous: she didn't care *how* old or lazy Brutus might have become; he was still a wild animal, and he still had his teeth. She could remember those teeth.

So, although she felt sure Brutus had not been a sign of a curse, as Wakinokiman had so solemnly suggested, she couldn't forget how close they might have come to another disaster, either. She almost felt cursed, after the reports of earth tremors to the south, the bizarre murder, and the conflagration that razed the courthouse annex, all in less than a week.

She did feel lonely, driving home alone and thinking about the enormity of the cases facing her office. She wished she had someone to go home to. But then—she gruffly reminded herself—sometimes she tended to wish a lot of things.

JOHNNIE HAD RETURNED to Tenoclock after her divorce intent on trying to start a new life and reorder her priorities. The same old story, she had thought with profound discouragement: the cliché—girl thinks she has talent, goes to New York and fails, goes to the West Coast and can't get more than a few meaningless bit parts, watches her marriage crumble, goes back to her roots to try to start again. Cliché or not, however, she had been desperate and couldn't think of any other course of action, any more than she could change the dismal details of what had happened in her life.

Her parents were gone by then, but the old home place remained, boarded up and surrounded by acres of sagebrush. They had been sheep people once. Johnnie took her remaining money and invested in bringing the house up to minimal living standards before buying a small flock on a bank loan, intending to eke out a living for a while through hard work outdoors. It had been a crazy but possibly workable scheme . . . until the blizzard that first winter killed most of the sheep and left her staring at foreclosure.

That had been when Sheriff Jim Way—lazy, easygoing, former professional football player Jim Way—had decided she might be just the neat public relations gimmick his underfunded office needed: a tall, leggy, ash-blond former actress, still youthful, to work behind the desk at the courthouse and sometimes put in a cameo appearance at a safe and routine investigation scene where the tourists might see her and murmur about how colorful and cute Tenoclock County was, etc.

Johnnie had needed the job, badly. But instead of being merely decorative she had dug in and started learning. The commissioners, amused when she sought permission to attend some short-term seminars in law enforcement, had indulged her. And issued precious press releases about "the showgirl sheriff."

It might have gone on that way a lot longer if Jim Way had not died under mysterious circumstances last summer. The commissioners tried to mute the image-damaging news by appointing Johnnie as his temporary replacement. She had hung in there since that time. The commissioners wanted her to be cute. She wanted to do the job right. There had been continual friction. She served at their pleasure. She could be replaced; they kept reminding her of that. But so far, after coaxing former lawman Butt Peabody out of embittered retirement to be her chief deputy, she had gotten the job done. Even the county commissioners of Tenoclock County couldn't fire her without cause.

But—and this was what tugged blackly at her mind as she drove through the deep of night alone toward her house—the last week had created more problems than she had encountered in the previous six months. The county did not like serious crime problems. The commissioners, ever-focused on their public relations image, could not abide serious unsolved crimes.

Her job was on the line here. The murder had to be solved. If the fire at the courthouse annex had been arson, as it appeared, that had to be solved, too. Maybe the lion incident could be overlooked, and no one was paying much attention to the reports of midnight earth tremors in the southern end. But murder and arson were something else. And now, possibly—probably—the beating out at the Eastside tonight was going to cause more problems between the Ute community and the white majority. She was beginning to feel trapped and overwhelmed.

Up ahead on the highway, the familiar side dirt road came into the glow of her headlights. She slowed, shifted, and turned between sagging fence posts. The corrugated dirt surface made everything inside the old Jeep hammer and bang and clatter. A possum, caught in the headlights, wiggled off into the deep weeds choking the ditch on the right. Up ahead, a rural mailbox marked the long driveway back to the old family place. She turned again, proceeding along a rutted path with tall weeds that brushed loudly against the underside of the vehicle.

A lone security light cast a pale white pool around the front yard of the old two-story log house. She pulled up near the light pole and cut her engine and lights. Climbing out, she walked to the front porch under a deep, clear night sky filled with so many stars that all the tiny pinpoints nearly blended into a single faint silver glow. An owl yammered somewhere. She got her key into the lock and went inside, turning on lights. It was all very still and familiar, the old-fashioned furniture and golden log walls faintly dusty. The great stone fireplace gaped like the black mouth of a cavern, and on the big oak mantel her extra walkie-talkie sat on its charger, a single small green diode showing full charge.

There were no messages on the answering machine.

Pulling off her blouse as she went, she climbed the stairs

toward her bedroom. It was past four o'clock. Feeling the crushing fatigue, she decided she would cheat a little and sleep until seven.

Someone had other ideas, however.

THE BEDSIDE TELEPHONE shattered her deep sleep with a noisy clamor that brought her to a startled sitting position in the bed. For a few seconds she felt dizzy and disoriented. Beyond the windows stood the full blackness of night.

The telephone rang again.

Fumbling the light on, she glanced at the little digital clock as she reached for the phone. The red numerals showed 5:45. She got the telephone to her ear and cleared sleep out of her throat. "Sheriff Baker."

"Johnnie?" The high-pitched nasal voice was all too familiar. "Commissioner Rieger here. Listen. You'd better get yourself down to the courthouse pronto. You've got some explaining to do, young lady."

Johnnie closed her eyes and prayed for patience. Carl Rieger, chairman of the Tenoclock Board of County Commissioners, had been a thorn ever since her appointment. It wasn't that he was against her, exactly; it was more that she had several times found herself standing between him and the path of least resistance.

She cleared her throat again. "What is it, Carl?"

"I've got Mayor Copley on hold," Rieger brayed nervously. "He says he's got several mad Utes on his front porch, demanding some action on some kind of violence involving an innocent teenager last night. I suppose you know something about that?"

"I worked it, yes. But—"

"Well, you know old J. Max, he gets upset easy. He says the Indians are yelling bloody murder. He says he checked with Chief Mayfield, and it's a county deal. Is that right?"

"That's right, Carl. The boy—"

"Boy?" Rieger's voice shrilled. "*Boy?* Oh, no. It's true, then. Listen, Johnnie. Mayor Copley is going to send this delegation down to the courthouse. He says they're our problem, not his. I need you down there chop-chop, savvy?"

Stifling a groan, Johnnie hauled aching bare legs out of the bed. "I'll be there in about an hour, Carl."

"Make it faster if you can, Johnnie, all right? I hate having irate citizens banging around the courthouse. You know how I hate that. You better be thinking on the way how we're going to pacify these people, too. With the tourist season almost upon us, the last thing we need is any more bad publicity, especially after all the stuff you've already let happen this spring."

Thirty minutes later, with cold morning wind gushing in on her shower-wet hair, she drove toward town, pondering Rieger's exact, accusatory wording just before he had hung up on her. She wondered how he thought she could have prevented the murder of the stranger west of town five nights ago.

Driving into the pearlescent brilliance of dawn over the mountains to the east, she felt another headache coming on. To try to stop thinking about it, she turned on the standard-issue AM radio rattling around in her dash. The voice of Charles Ducharme, top disk jockey and alleged newsman at the local station: "Hey, boys and girls, that was 'Mood Indigo,' by the incomparable Duke Ellington, on the voice of the Tenoclock Valley, KTCK, all the latest news and all the greatest golden oldies, all the time. It's forty-one degrees here in God's country, Tenoclock, Colorado, and it looks like another perfect spring day dawning all around us, so get up and get shakin'! Enjoy what we have here in the greatest of all places!

"A further note about that news bulletin we brought you a few minutes ago, this just in to the KTCK newsroom: the youthful victim of a fight out at the Eastside Saloon on Highway 127 last night is to be released from the hospital sometime today, according to hospital authorities. His name is being withheld because he is a juvenile. Meanwhile, as we told you earlier, law enforcement officers continue to scour the countryside at this hour in search of a mystery man—or woman—who broke up the altercation at the Eastside, according to reliable witnesses. The peacemaker, all agree, was wearing what appeared to be a diver's wet suit when he intervened."

Ducharme paused dramatically, imitating Paul Harvey.

He resumed, "Yes, friends, that's what the man said: a wet suit."

Another long pause, then:

"Amazing world we live in, isn't it? I wonder if the sheriff will be able to spot a man in a diver's outfit. My goodness, the man ought to just blend right into the crowd on Silver Street, right, boys and girls?

"All right! Here's our next memory-bringer-backer, and this one dates back to the old Bluebird label in the forties—"

Johnnie angrily twisted the knob back to off. Ducharme, twenty-two, was beginning to make a local reputation as a wit. He was also beginning to get on her nerves. Now, if she didn't find last night's skin diver, she was going to look more like a fool. She didn't need this.

She drove on into Tenoclock, entering on the northwest road, old 16, and passing by the line of garish motels strung along the pavement nearest the point where it forked, sending one arm up to the Interstate. After Holiday Inn, Quality Inn, Raddison, Marriott, Ramada, Motel 6, and three locally owned and more quaintly named places, the row of service stations, convenience stores, and fast-food restaurants began. She drove by them without registering many names, half-noticing the golden arches, the big Burger King sign, and the crowd already in the lot at the twenty-four-hour-a-day Kettle. After this stretch she cut off the old highway and took side streets downtown, turning finally onto Court Street and entering the Courthouse back lot just as her $39 digital watch showed 7:00.

She didn't have to look for Commissioner Carl Rieger and the delegation of angry Utes. They were standing there on the pavement in front of the back door that led to her offices.

Rieger, rumpled and red-faced, his bald head glistening wet in the morning sun shafting between buildings, waved gratefully at her. He had pulled on his usual checkered sports coat over a white sports shirt and lemon-colored golf slacks, but he hadn't shaved or gotten all of his shirttail tucked in; a lot of it hung over his western brass belt buckle along with a considerable expanse of tummy.

"Sheriff! Hurry over here, please!"

Johnnie strode toward the group. She saw that the Indian delegation totaled five. Three of them, young men in jeans and flannel shirts, she did not recognize. The other two, she did. One was old Ab Wakinokiman, the traditional old man who might have been considered a medicine man in the old days. The other was George Bonfire, about thirty, a sullen and influential member of the Ute clan who operated a local trucking and hauling company out of the tiny community of Big Gully, down southwest.

She walked up to face them. "Gents—?"

"Sheriff," Carl Rieger huffed, "Mr. Bonfire and these other gentlemen have come to inquire about action your office intends to take in connection with an alleged attack on a youth from their community—"

"Henry Burlingame," Bonfire cut in, glowering. Six feet tall, muscular, with dark brown skin and eyes and jet hair tied in a bun at the back of his head, he was as handsome a man as Johnnie had ever laid eyes on. He was also perpetually one of the angriest. "Aren't there laws against serving alcohol to minors?" he demanded. "Or are they only enforced in taverns owned by Native Americans? If a seventeen-year-old *white* lad had entered a saloon where he wasn't supposed to be, would the owners and John Law have allowed him to stay there, where he could be roughed up by thugs? Do you intend to bring any

charges against the tavern owner, sheriff, or against the perpetrators of this attack? Do you only enforce the law when it pro-
tects white people?"

Johnnie felt her own stubborn anger bubble, but she controlled it. "I share your concerns, Mr. Bonfire."

"I'm sure you don't, Madame Sheriff."

She ignored the shot and went on steadily. "If the boy was
served a drink, and we can establish that as a fact, my office
will investigate the possibility of filing a charge. As to the two
men who beat him up, they're in jail downstairs right now, and
they'll be charged in county court later this morning."

Bonfire's lip curled. "With something horrendous such as
'disturbing the peace'? Handed a twenty-five-dollar fine and a
lecture by the judge?"

She felt her face begin to burn. "I can't predict—"

"Right," Bonfire interrupted again, the single word dripping
sarcasm. "Equal justice for all. As long as they're white."

"Dammit, George," she exploded, "you and I went to high
school together. You know I'm not a damn racist. I've got Choctaw blood. I'm an official member of the nation. We—"

"Don't talk apple Indian talk to me, Johnnie: red on the
outside, white on the inside." He pointed a finger at her. "We
won't tolerate white thugs picking on our innocent kids. This
isn't the first incident since that killing. If you don't do something about it, maybe some of us will."

Carl Rieger, who had been standing to one side with eyes
that bulged apprehensively, raised a chubby hand. "Now, now!
No need to get worked up, here! I'm sure the sheriff is doing the
best that she can do!"

Old Wakinokiman took a half-step forward. His eyes under
the brim of his battered straw hat appeared to be more closed
than open, almost as if he spoke from his sleep: "I counsel
patience . . . and peace. But justice must be done. Do not mistake
us on that count, Sheriff."

The others grumbled agreement on that point. Wakinoki-man stepped back. Johnnie took a deep breath. "Charges will be brought, and more investigation will be made."

Bonfire's mouth twisted again into that bitterly knowing sneer. "We plan to watch. Remember what we have said."

He started to turn away.

Johnnie could not resist.

"George? You might remember to get that kid back into school where he's supposed to be, too."

Bonfire glanced back with a look of vicious anger. But he did not reply. He turned and walked on with the others, his stiff posture showing how close he was to blowing up.

Carl Rieger slipped closer to her, whispering. "We've got to consult on this, Johnnie. We don't need any more trouble. I want to go over this entire matter with you right away, now."

Johnnie took another deep breath, still fighting for patience. "Later, Carl." She turned, pulled out a big key to unlock the back security door, and went inside. Rieger huffed and puffed right after her, then turned away. She pushed the doors open and entered the headquarters area.

Hesther Gretsch, the office secretary, had not come on yet. But Deputy Dean Epperly was not alone. As Johnnie entered with the commissioner right behind her, a bulky, middle-aged man in a wrinkled winter suit got up from a desk where he had been perusing a magazine.

She hadn't been expecting to find Leonard Simonson, the field agent from the state fire marshal's office, waiting for her at this hour.

She hadn't expected him at all today. He had told her his investigation of the fire that leveled the courthouse annex would take several more days. But the somber expression on his beefy face told her he was not here for a coffee break.

4

JOHNNIE STRODE UP the aisle between the unoccupied olive-drab desks. "Leonard, I didn't expect you."

Simonson's perpetually mournful and pessimistic expression seemed deeper than usual. Johnnie saw that he had soot on his long, bony hands and some similar dark gray stains on his pantslegs. He had a 1930s briefcase in one hand, a small white plastic bag of the kind used for kitchen trash in the other, and a clipboard under his arm. He reeked of the strong, nasty smell of a dead fire.

"Have some news," he said in a sepulchral tone.

"So soon?" Johnnie blurted.

She was surprised. At her request, the state fire marshal's office had been poking around the burned-out wreckage of the old courthouse annex building practically since the ashes had begun to cool, but that had been only a week ago now. She had thought a probe would take longer.

The midnight conflagration had seemed to start from no identifiable cause. Old Amos Pinkstaff, seventy-four, the janitor–night watchman, was not a smoker. No one else was supposed to be in the building in the middle of the night. But the fire had seemed to start all over the place at the same time, and the flames had spread with a swiftness that rivaled the devastation of the Branch Davidian compound down in Texas.

Johnnie and Butt Peabody had found no obvious signs of arson—and maybe there weren't any. But old Amos was dead—his charred corpse dug out of the basement where he had been trapped by the flames—and the fire had taken virtually all the county's older land and legal records; there was no way to dismiss the tragedy as blind accident; there had to be a thorough investigation.

Of course the county commissioners, always bird-dog vigilant to avoid any publicity that might harm the area's pristine reputation, had been ready to issue a proclamation of sadness about Pinkstaff's death, bulldoze the annex site, and forget the whole thing. This time Johnnie had won out, however, thanks to state law, and the somber Simonson, with two helpers, had come promptly to begin his slow poking and digging in the blackened ruins.

"Is the investigation complete, then?" she added when Simonson did not answer her at once.

His eyes sagged glumly. "Not quite. Can't work miracles, you know. But have some evidence. Bad news." Simonson always seemed to talk in sentence fragments, which somehow added to his sour impression. "Go in your office room? Better have privacy."

With a sigh that combined resignation and dread, Johnnie turned to lead the lank inspector through the sea of vacant desks toward the grungy glass door that enclosed the corner private office she never used if she could avoid it. The printing on the glass still read JIM WAY—SHERIFF.

Now, since Inspector Simonson wanted it, she opened the glass door and reached inside to find the seldom-used light switch. A fly-specked fluorescent fixture buzzed to life in the yellowed acoustic-tile ceiling, illuminating water-stained gray concrete walls, an old legal bookcase crammed with out-of date maps and folders containing God knows what, another of the olive-drab metal desks the county seemed to have an inexhaustible supply of, a steel filing cabinet with two broken drawers hanging out, and three straight metal chairs. A picture on the wall showed a young boy in knickers and a sweater standing with a bat in his hand, as if awaiting a pitch in a sandlot game. Looking down out of the clouds, rooting for him, was the ghost of Babe Ruth. The picture looked as current as anything else in the office.

Johnnie walked around to the business side of the desk, crunching two dead crickets underfoot in the process. She sat down. Simonson took a chair facing her across the vastly dusty desktop, putting his clipboard, white trash bag, and briefcase on the dirt. He looked up at her with dull, oleo-colored eyes. "Not good news, I'm afraid."

"Tell me."

He leaned forward and unwrapped a rubber band from the neck of the small white plastic bag, which didn't appear to have much in it. Reaching inside, he brought out and placed on the desk in a neat row two scorched, wadded pieces of what looked like terry-cloth towel; three sealed sandwich-size plastic bags that appeared to contain charred pieces of newspaper or magazine; and two small crushed, incinerated tin containers of the type that usually had a pop-up squeeze cap.

There was just enough blue-and-white lettering remaining on one of the cans that Johnnie could make out the symbol unquestionably identifying a popular charcoal starter.

"Oh, shit," she murmured before she could stop herself.

Simonson sourly held up one of the charred, wadded rags. "Bath towel or something similar. Dug down deep, found this one in the southeast corner of the basement, this one opposite side, northwest, under rubble that fell down into the basement from up above. First floor, most likely. Records room." He raised the filthy rag halfway to his nose. "Charcoal starter. Saturated. Debris fell, choked it out before it all got devoured." He thrust the cloth across at Johnnie. "Want a smell?"

She recoiled. "I'll take your word for it, Leonard."

With a little puffy cloud of ash, he replaced the rag in the bag. "No matter. Another piece to the lab in Denver. But no doubt. Soaked with lighter fluid. Ignited." He picked up one of the small plastic containers with ash in them. "Paper. Wadded. Same way. Want a—?"

"No! I said—I'll take your word for it, Leonard."

Simonson looked hurt, but turned to pop the zipper on his old briefcase. "Not much question, Johnnie. Arson. Plain and simple. And not very clever, neither. A man can make it awful hard for someone to detect it if he's halfway smart. You take jelly like in napalm. Can. Deep down. Debris buries her real good. Add some paint cans and stuff. Chemicals mixed up. Accident, looks like. Or jimmy your gas valve coming in. Put you a little candle twenty feet away, get clean away, pretty soon—boom—"

"Leonard, you're sure the courthouse annex was burned down intentionally, then?"

"Oh, yes. Oh my, yes."

"Damn."

"Not the worst of it."

She braced herself. He reached into the briefcase, withdrew something, and held it out for her to see.

This time, with a sinking sensation, she reached out to take it. It was an object about eight inches long and quite thin at one end, swollen at the other. The thin end was flint or hard, black stone, finely chipped many times to form a cutting edge. Despite the ashen filth still coating it, she could see how its thicker end had been fitted into the remains of a piece of carved staghorn or bone to form a handle. Enough burned shreds of leather thong remained to tie blade to handle.

"Dug around in the junk near the back," Simonson said, his voice mournful and hollow. "Know what it is?"

"It's a primitive knife," Johnnie said, wishing she didn't have to.

"Don't know a lot about such stuff," the inspector told her. "Knives like this have been used since prehistoric times."

"Maybe. Only this ain't old."

She looked up, surprised. "What makes you think that?"

"Leather thong. Not hand-formed. Machine-cut. Bootlacing, most likely."

She reexamined the thong, saw he was right, and began to think she might have underestimated him.

He added, "Seen these in gift shops around. Indian-made."

"Anybody could make one, Leonard!"

He shrugged, took the knife back from her, and carefully put it back into his briefcase. "Going to be arson in the report. No question. Look around more, but this is enough. Knife wasn't where it might've been in an exhibit. Report will say might have been left by the perpetrator. Chip out of the point. Might even match scratches on the top of the starter can, where the lid was pried off, make 'er pour faster."

Johnnie felt like she had been kicked in the stomach. She stared at Simonson and didn't know what to say. She certainly was not going to say the one other thing she might have added to his cache of information.

The lank inspector heaved a sigh, as if infinitely weary, and got to his feet. "Call HQ. Get a couple more men in here. Dig around more. But this information will go in today, preliminary report. Copy to the commissioners, state office. Thought you ought to be informed first. More later."

Feeling sick, Johnnie walked him to the door. "Thanks, Leonard. You've done a terrific job. I mean that."

"Day's work. See you, Johnnie." He walked out like a man with a thousand pounds on his aching back.

Johnnie went back to the front counter, where her deputy, Dean Epperly, gave her a friendly, vacuous grin. "That poor old guy! I think he could root around out there a year and not find anything, huh, Johnnie?"

"Oh, you might be surprised, Dean," Johnnie told him. "Has Butt called in on the radio yet?"

"Yep, just down the street. Ought to be pulling in—" Epperly stopped, cocking an ear to the sound of truck tires in the gravel lot outside. "Speak of the devil, huh?"

It was the devil's work they were up to around here, Johnnie thought, and turned to wait for Butt Peabody to show his face.

BACK IN THE private office, Peabody's face, always as lined and rutted as ten miles of bad road, took on a few new furrows as Johnnie filled him in.

"You're sure it's an Indian-type knife?" he asked.

"Worse than that," Johnnie replied. "Simonson either didn't notice or doesn't understand the significance of it, but the bone handle had one of those little flute player symbols carved on it."

"The crippled flute player? The Anasazi symbol?"

"Yes."

"Shit! They still make those knives like that—the old traditionalists do—down there in Big Gully. Wakinokiman wears one all the time. A couple of the others—"

"Just because they make them down there doesn't mean this one came from down there," Johnnie cut in, face heating.

"I know that, babe, I know that. But you say the charcoal starter can was Gulf? They sell that brand down there at the crossroads store in Big Gully. I've bought some myself down there on the way to—"

"They sell it everywhere else, too, Butt!"

"I know that, too. Will you calm *down?* What are you so het up about?"

"We've already got George Bonfire and some of the other traditionalists down there all stirred up about that kid of theirs getting beat up by the Riley brothers. Now we've got this. The Utes have bellyached forever about old tribal documents they say were stolen and stashed in the courthouse. Now some white people are sure to get wind of this knife deal and jump to the conclusion that Utes felt the earth shake down there, took it for an omen, came in here on the warpath, and just burned down the annex."

Peabody dragged out tobacco and papers and began rolling a cigarette, doing it the expert cowboy way with one hand. "That's crazy talk."

"You know it and I know it, but this is going to cause more trouble, Butt. We've *got* to get to the bottom of some of this stuff."

His chest heaved. "Well, I better go down there to Big Gully again and have another talk with those old boys."

DRIVING OUT THE dirt road south of Tenoclock toward distant Big Gully, Butt Peabody could not help but feel just a little depressed and anxious.

The country he drove through was typical lower-elevation Colorado, especially in the southern half of the state: slightly rolling, arid country, bare yellow dirt pocked by ugly little gullies torn open by the infrequent gully-washer deluges, studded by clumps of half-dead sagebrush and an occasional tumbleweed or chunk of dried-up cactus. Off in the distance were the indistinct blue lines of the mountains, so close yet so far away, making everything closer seem so much more barren and lifeless. But here and there it wasn't lifeless; Peabody could see a single-strand power line out in the brush now and again, carrying electricity to some small trailer house or broken-down adobe, where local Utes clung to a hardscrabble existence on the basis of a cow or two and a garden watered by the bucket on the days the old well sucked up enough brackish moisture to allow it.

No wonder the younger ones were so bitter. Once they had had everything. Then they had trusted the Great White Father.

Some whites, of course, figured the local native Americans deserved no better than they had, and couldn't have been trusted if they had any more. The Riley boys' attack on the Burlingame kid—even if the kid had provoked it by being a smart-ass—was one indication of this sort of racist attitude. And when the stranger had been found dead a few days ago, with that ancient Indian arrow through his neck, there had been plenty of rednecks ready at once to say it just proved the Utes weren't worth a damn, and couldn't be trusted farther than you could throw a buffalo.

Peabody knew better than that. But Johnnie was right: this new twist about the knife in the gutted ruin of the courthouse annex made things potentially more incendiary, no pun intended.

Things just seemed to keep getting worse.

Not that they hadn't been bad enough before. The courthouse annex fire had done more than destroy enough records to break the heart of anyone with the slightest interest in history around here. It had also killed a good old guy.

Peabody had known Amos Pinkstaff for what seemed like a hundred years: a gentle old fart, always smiling and showing his ill-fitting false teeth, a schoolteacher here once and then a farmer, the father of one boy killed in Vietnam, an old man who went to the Presbyterian church every Sunday with his wife of fifty years, and not just because she made him do it.

Everybody had liked old Amos. If—when—the knife evidence leaked out, more people were going to be mad.

Peabody turned onto the narrow gravel road that led down through a scrub thicket in the direction of Big Gully. After the fire, he mused, the reports of rumbling noises and an earth tremor down this way hadn't seemed like much, although—unlike a majority of whites in the valley—he did not discount the stories as just so much make-believe. All the Colorado Rockies were still seismically active. There could have been a very small earthquake or slide, even though the sensors at Boulder hadn't picked anything up. Whatever it had been, it hadn't seemed to do any damage. So it was a curiosity, but one they could all forget about. Like the lion.

The murder of the Alamosa junkman had been a different matter.

Of course, they hadn't known he was an Alamosa salvage yard operator then. All they had known was that one of the Tenoclock valley's lifetime residents, a fifty-year-old sheep man named Roger Swank, had been driving back to his spread west of town after a late-night poker game with some pals in town when the headlights of his pickup spotted a man's body on the gravel shoulder beside the road. Like everyone else in the world these days, Swank had a cellular phone, presumably so he could stay in constant communication with his sheep, and he had used it to call the sheriff's office at once.

Peabody had been the first on the scene. Johnnie, deputy Dean Epperly, and two city cops pulled out of their legal jurisdiction by curiosity had all arrived within ten minutes.

What they found was the body of a skinny, unkempt white man, probably in his late thirties, wearing dirty bib overalls, a dirtier white sweatshirt, work boots, an old wood-shafted arrow through his throat, and an expression of great surprise. Despite gathering night chill, the body was not entirely cold yet, and local doctor Gene Aamon, arriving as ad hoc medical inspector, found no signs yet of rigor mortis. These facts put the time of death at no earlier than 11:30 P.M. and no later than 12:05, the time Swank had called 911.

A driver's license in the dead man's billfold identified him as Tomlinson, Richard T.; height 5' 10", weight 165; hair brown, eyes green; date of birth 9/3/1957; home address 310 Plover, Alamosa County. Other papers showed he owned the JimDandy Salvage Co. in Alamosa, specializing in automotive salvage and construction equipment repair and supplies. The standard billfold ID card said to contact Naomi Tomlinson, wife, at an Alamosa telephone number.

Except for the arrow through his neck, Tomlinson appeared to be untouched. His body was taken away. A search of his Ford pickup, found nearby, turned up nothing except some hand tools and a couple of shovels.

Contacted by telephone, Mrs. Tomlinson had gone all to pieces. She said Dickie had departed for Tenoclock on business early in the day, but she didn't know the specific nature of the business he had planned to conduct there. She wasn't much help.

The official coroner's report would not come for a day or two yet, as the body had to be taken to far-off Gunnison to get the job done. In the meantime, Peabody worried that this might be one of those that never did get solved.

Old Amos Pinkstaff dead, he thought.

The Alamosa junkman dead.

The damned lion, and things going bump in the night.

Then the Burlingame kid getting his tail whipped by the Riley boys—and finally *this* damned thing with the Ute knife in the courthouse annex ashes.

Peabody slowed his truck and fished in his shirt pocket for the makings. If he drove slowly enough, he would just have time for a smoke before driving into Big Gully proper. He needed one. Some days he wished he had stayed out on his land, "retired" by the good voters of Tenoclock County in that rigged election seven years ago. Only Johnnie Baker could have talked him behind a badge again. Sometimes he wished she hadn't.

Fifteen minutes later he wished it even more when he pulled up at Underwood's Ute Texaco, smack in the middle of Big Gully's one-block "downtown," and looked out his truck window into the 12-gauge eyes of a double-barrel shotgun.

5

"GEORGE," PEABODY SAID wearily, "stop being an asshole."

George Bonfire's shotgun didn't waver. His dark eyes ablaze with resentment, he shook his head slowly from side to side, making a single silver earring glint in the sunlight. "Nobody here had anything to do with it."

"Had anything to do with *what?*"

"The courthouse fire. I know what you bastards are thinking, finding that old knife and all. But there are a dozen knives like that around these parts. Out in the ceremonial groves, one washed out of the side of a burial mound just last winter. Do you think somebody around here would be stupid enough to go burn down the courthouse and wear an ancient knife like that so he could lose it and show we did it? I don't know where that knife came from. It didn't come from anybody who lives down here. We've had damned shard-hunters out there, sneaking around all over our sacred ground. We've chased a dozen away already this spring. Any of them might have found a knife and taken it away. If you've got any ideas about coming in here and asking a lot of questions aimed at implicating any of us in the fire, you can forget it. Now get out of here. You're trespassing. I've got a right to defend my property here."

"It always amazes me," Peabody sighed, "how fast news can travel in this county. How did you hear about that knife being found? We only heard about it ourselves an hour or two ago. Have you got some kind of satellite system the rest of us don't know about? Damn! The people at CNN ought to hear about your—"

"Get going!"

"This is a public gas station, George, and it don't belong to you anyhow. It belongs to Henry Coyote. How can I be trespassing? And I'm not here to accuse anybody of anything, I'm just trying to get ideas of where that knife might really have come from, and that arrow in the Alamosa man's neck, too. I'm on your side. Now will you *cool it?*"

Bonfire's mahogany face began to go slack. The barrels of the shotgun slowly lowered below the level of the window. The muscular man moved half a step backward. "You need regular unleaded or premium?"

"Beg pardon?"

Bonfire pointed the shotgun at a red-on-white sign hanging from the pedestal beside the trio of pumps Peabody had stopped alongside. "You pulled up to FulServ. You want Self, you've got to back up and pump it yourself on the other side."

IN THE STUFFY little office of the gas station, Peabody palavered with Bonfire, owner Coyote, and a third man named Mockingbird. Nobody was pretending to be especially friendly, but it was cordial enough, and the comforting masculine odors of oil, gasoline, sweat, and tobacco made everything seem almost pleasant.

"Simonson told Mabel, down at the Pick & Shovel Cafe, about finding the old knife," Peabody repeated for verification.

Bonfire nodded. "Naturally Mabel called us."

" 'Us'?"

"Me."

"Why?"

"She's a friend."

"And she figured you'd need to be warned?"

"Wasn't she right? You're here."

Peabody dragged deeply on his hand-rolled cigarette and watched the smoke curl around in the sunlight from the big glass front window. "Look," he said finally. "Old Amos Pinkstaff was a much-loved old man, and that fire took out a century of historical records to boot. Everybody this side of Kansas City knows how your people have bitched and moaned about old tribal documents being taken by white settlers and stashed in county records. You haven't made any secret of threats to destroy old land-transfer documents you say were signed under duress in the first place. Now just a minute, just a minute. I'm not saying anybody from out here had anything to do with that courthouse fire, *or* with that man from Alamosa being killed with an old arrow. What I am saying, though, is that you've got as much of a stake in clearing these cases as we do, almost. Because until we get them cleared, there are going to be people saying folks from Big Gully *did* do it, and maybe stirring up new trouble. We don't need that kind of crap. I don't, and you don't. Hell. That mess-up with the Burlingame kid last night might have been a sign of just the kind of thing I'm worried about."

Peabody paused and inhaled again. "So if you do know anything, or hear about anything, I hope you'll let us in on it, guys. This time, for sure, we're on the same side."

The man named Mockingbird, about forty, wearing a frayed leather vest over his sun-bleached blue shirt, made a sharp clicking sound with his teeth. "And maybe that speech of yours is just so much BS to put us off guard because you really suspect us anyhow."

Peabody grinned at him. "Sure. Might be. Only it ain't."

Bonfire said, "The arrow was stolen."

Peabody made it a point not to show surprise. This was new. "That right?"

Bonfire nodded. "Just found out. Jerome David, down the road from the blacksmith shop, been down in Albuquerque visiting kids. Got back not long ago. Somebody had busted in the back door of his place while he was gone. He's kind of a collector. Quite a lot of shards, arrowheads, some painted rocks, stone corn pan, various things—parts of two bows, several arrows."

"And somebody stole an arrow?"

"Yes."

"How about a knife?"

"No."

"When did you say this happened?"

"Week or two ago."

"And you just heard about it?"

Bonfire's face darkened. "He just noticed the arrow missing, since word spread about that murder with an arrow."

"It strikes me a little strange, him not noticing before."

Bonfire gave him a hostile stare. "Jerome was preoccupied with what else the thieves took, I guess. Big silver tea serving set he brought back with him from a visit to London five years ago. Two Nikons, a six-hundred-dollar Winchester, and a 486 computer with a four-hundred-megabyte hard drive, CD ROM, and full multimedia capability."

Peabody was incredulous. "He didn't report any of it stolen?"

"What good would that do? You wouldn't look for it, and the publicity would only advertise that he had other stuff worth stealing."

"Wait a minute, wait a minute," Peabody groaned. "Is this the same Jerome David—"

"Retired from the NFL last year," Bonfire said. "Yes."

"I didn't even know he had moved back here."

Bonfire shrugged, but his tone betrayed satisfaction. "None of your business—a man might say."

Peabody thought about it. "So the arrow maybe came from there."

"Maybe."

Peabody changed tack. "Why would somebody stick an arrow through another man's neck, except to make it look like a Ute deal?"

"Can't think of a reason."

"So you don't know anything about the knife?"

"Only what I already said."

"And the arrow—maybe—is one stolen from Mr. David?"

"Probably."

"You say he lives down thataway?"

"Why?"

"I'm going to go see him. I'll want him to come to town and see if he can identify the arrow."

Bonfire nodded at that. "What about the Rileys?"

"The ones in jail for whipping up on the Burlingame kid? Johnnie—Sheriff Baker—ought to be seeing the county attorney about now. She's wanting assault charges, and maybe a couple of other things."

Bonfire's face darkened again. "We want justice."

"I know."

"The Riley family is prominent."

"Johnnie will do her best, George. You know that."

"We're sick of people blaming us for everything. Then vandals come down here and try to dig in our old burial mounds, too. We intend to see it stopped. If your department can't put someone out here to stop it, we'll stop it ourselves . . . our own way."

"We've got our hands full, George. But I'll talk to the sheriff again about trying to give you more help. We'll do all we can."

"Nice talk. No action."

Peabody slapped his knee. "I better be rolling."

He walked to his pickup alone, aware of all three men's eyes on his back. He climbed in, started the engine, and pulled back onto the gravel road, proceeding slowly. He did not immediately reach for the microphone to check in with headquarters as he usually did. He needed a minute or two to digest the sudden, disconcerting idea that George Bonfire's last comments had exploded inside his brain.

The ancient burial mounds, verified as having been built by prehistoric precursors of the Anasazi, were sacred to Ute traditionalists like Bonfire. There had been near-violent confrontations in other years between the area's Utes and treasure-hunting whites trying to slip in unobserved to dig for pottery shards, ancient weapons, or other implements that might fetch a fortune from collectors in the outside world.

Peabody had been leaning to the theory that salvage yard operator Richard Tomlinson must have been in Tenoclock to see somebody else's wife, but the cuckolded husband had found out about it and taken the surest way of making sure his wife didn't mess around with *that* gentleman anymore. Now, however, it occurred to Peabody that Tomlinson might have been here for an entirely different kind of errand.

Maybe the use of an arrow as a murder weapon and the apparent loss of a traditional knife in the annex fire had not been crude attempts to frame the Ute community after all.

Maybe Tomlinson had been looking for something other than his usual variety of junk. It was within the realm of possibility that he had been digging around for Anasazi treasure this time, and someone like George Bonfire had caught him at it and supplied him with a piece of just what he was looking for—right through the neck.

6

"NOW LOOK, JOHNNIE, let's be *reasonable* about this,"
Max Shoemaker, the county's prosecutor, whined. A youngish
man with curly black hair, a perpetual dark stubble on his
cheeks, and the eyes of a wounded squirrel, he looked up from
under a shelf of shaggy eyebrows with the look he believed was
his most sincere. "Nobody wants trouble . . . do they?"

"Dammit," Johnnie snapped, "they beat the crap out of
that kid. They might have killed him. Then you file nothing
but a *mischief* charge and let Fred set bail at fifty dollars
apiece?"

County Judge Fred Otterman, trying his best to look patri-
cian behind the huge expanse of his old walnut desk, twiddled
a thin index finger back and forth across his pale lips. "Now,
now, Sheriff. We all know it would have cost the county a fortune
to try these boys, and Max could hardly have expected to win a
conviction anyhow. The Riley family has influence."

"So you let the two bullies go free with a symbolic charge."
Johnnie was steamed and didn't care who knew it.

"They'll plead guilty in a day or two," Shoemaker told her,
"and that will be that. Justice will have been served—"

"Justice! *Justice!* What the hell do I tell that boy's friends and family?"

Judge Otterman's forehead wrinkled. "Better to handle it quietly this way. The Indian folk have no clout, to speak bluntly. And we all agree that Tenoclock certainly needs no more controversy or unfavorable publicity at this time."

Johnnie stared first at one man, then the other. "Damn!" she gasped, and walked out of Otterman's palatial old office, by far the grandest in the aged courthouse.

It was going to infuriate the Indian people, she thought, heading downstairs toward her own offices. They might not say anything at once—they too often suffered in silence, just as Fred Otterman had hinted—but in the long run this decision would mean possible worse trouble. And even if it hadn't meant that, it infuriated her to see justice so miscarried.

Not that it was the first time. Since the start of its phenomenal growth, Tenoclock had been protected from bad publicity every way the local power structure could contrive. This was just another case, no big deal.

Except that it really burned Johnnie up.

It was past time, she realized, to see if the Burlingame boy was still in the hospital. She hoped to see him before he got out, on the off chance he might be able to help identify the mystery man who had perhaps saved his life. She decided to walk because she needed a breath of fresh air anyhow, and time to cool down.

Bypassing the doors that led to the basement and her own offices, she veered into the courthouse's main lobby, passing ornate mahogany doorways and paneling, and hurried down the wear-cupped marble stairs to the outside doors opening onto Court Street. She turned north, toward the busiest part of town.

Forcing herself to slow down and take deep breaths of the cool morning mountain air, she began to feel a little better almost at once. A pair of small, silvery clouds far to the west, over the snow-gauzy peak of Red Mountain, were the only punctuation in an otherwise flawless cobalt sky. To the south she could make out the blue-misty jaggedness of the Emeralds, with the sun bright on the white peak of Killdeer Mountain, the tallest, one of the Colorado "fourteeners" so dear to climbers. Low business buildings blocked her view toward Anvil Mountain to the east, but she spotted a hawk or perhaps even an eagle far off in that direction, wheeling with wings motionless in a thermal, hunting. The scent of ponderosas and firs in the small park across the street from the courthouse reached her, and she felt a small burst of gladness just to be allowed to be in this place she had always called home.

The first two blocks she walked were lined by "old-town" buildings, two stories tall, most with the kind of false plastic fronts that had been fashionable for business remodeling forty years ago. Quite a number were closed, vacantly black windows staring out onto dusty pavement. But a number of other long-established little businesses clung to life here in the part of Tenoclock the boom had passed by. She passed a small carpet store, a dry cleaner's, a shoe shop, a carpenter's, a plumber's, an old-fashioned hardware store with dusty hand tools in the window, a florist, a drugstore, and a lunchroom. On the next corner stood an abandoned gas station, a peeling wood flying red horse still in place on a tall pole. Across the street, bright blue do-it-yourself pumps dominated the tarmac surrounding a modern convenience store.

Johnnie had always wondered why they were called convenience stores. For a motorist with car trouble or a flat tire they were anything but convenient. Service-station mechanics were about as scarce these days as an honest lug wrench or a car you could tune yourself.

Reaching the corner of Gunnison and Court, she turned west, heading up toward the major tourist area of town. Several blocks ahead, up at the intersection of Frontier Street near the

Mountain Man Theater, the hollow bark of gunshots echoed, and a flock of startled pigeons bolted out of the park's trees up there and wheeled across the sky. Johnnie glanced at her watch: 10:00. The Chamber of Commerce's fake cowboys had staged the day's first street gunfight for the tourists right on time.

By the time she reached the middle of the block, there were plenty of pickups and cars angle-parked near one of her favorite hangouts, the Pick & Shovel Cafe. Owner Mabel Murnan was doing her usual brisk local business in kitchen sink omelets and flapjacks the size of a Frisbee. Johnnie resisted the temptation to join the mob inside and kept walking.

As she moved up the block, the character of the two-story buildings began to change, all the remodeled prosperous ones sporting the rustic wood shingle roofs and phony weathered redwood exteriors that the city council had decreed several years earlier, lumping such zoning requirements in with a batch of ordinances that ordered wood plank sidewalks, old-fashioned streetlight posts, and no advertising sign of any kind made out of anything but rough-cut timber "hand-painted to denote the look of the Old West." All the parking spots were filled here, nearer the heart of town, and vans and RVs trundled along the street one behind the other, anxious tourist faces gawking out of windows in search of a place to park. The board sidewalk started to get crowded, bony-kneed retirees toddling along under their funny baseball caps, wives clutching fat purses to their chests, camera-slung young couples dragging small kids along to the next Really Neat Thing to See.

Johnnie sighed. It was *still* a nice area, dammit.

And part of her job was to try to keep it that way.

But Max's cowardice about filing meaningful charges against the Riley brothers was not going to make that job any easier. Fred's setting of a meaninglessly low bail made it worse. Every minority group member in the county—not just the Utes but the Hispanics and the handful of blacks, too—was going to be pissed. They had every right to be. Tenoclock's carefully orchestrated boom had passed every one of them up, unless you wanted to consider it a great gain to have available more minimum-wage jobs at McDonald's and Hardee's or an average of three bucks an hour to be a domestic cleaning rich people's toilets.

She had to figure out a way to convince the have-nots that she intended to continue enforcing the law with an impartial hand, Johnnie thought. She also had to get through to the Rileys and others like them that they might not be as lucky if they got involved in such trouble again. She also had to make sure the Burlingame boy was all right—and would be sent back to school instead of the pool hall—without making it look like she was picking on him or his family. She also had to figure some way of putting more county law enforcement down there around Big Gully to keep some of the damned thieves and shard-hunters out of the sacred burial mound areas. She also had to get the commissioners to loosen the purse strings just a little to pay for the extra deputy she would have to have in order to make the showing at Big Gully. She also had to try to figure out who torched the courthouse annex, who killed the Alamosa junkman, and—

There were too damned many *also*s. Her head began to hurt.

AT THE NEXT corner, a half-block from famed Packer's Alley, where all the expensive places clustered, one of Tenoclock's finest was out in the intersection trying to manage some of the gridlocked traffic. As ordered by city fathers, the poor cop was wearing tight blue cowboy pants and high-heeled boots, a cream-colored western-style shirt, a big white Stetson, and a nickle-plated six-shooter that would have made any self-respecting thug with a Street Sweeper fall down laughing. The cop's black aviator-style shades were his own addition, but probably were okay because they added a Lone Ranger look.

Part of the congestion, Johnnie saw, stemmed from some sort of commotion up in the next block. People had spilled out into the street up there, and others were rushing in the same direction.

"It's Harrison Ford!" a plump matron nearby cried with excitement.

"No!" a leggy girl in short shorts and red cowgirl boots shrilled in reply. "It's John Travolta!"

Whatever. Both women hustled toward the scene. Johnnie turned away, heading over toward Silver Street, which might or might not be quieter.

She did not have a clue—not a trustworthy one, anyway—on either major crime facing her department. No witnesses at the annex fire, and so far nothing she could go on in terms of hard evidence.

Nothing she had turned up about the Alamosa man had helped, either, and the state crime lab had come up empty on a background investigation as well as a thorough checkout of the dead man's truck. It seemed that the late Richard T. Tomlinson had come to Tenoclock either to scout out promising salvage stuff for his yard back home, or possibly—although this was sheer speculation—to have a tryst with an unknown lady not likely to come forward and admit it. Which could identify the perpetrator as some very angry husband in the area.

Butt Peabody leaned toward the husband explanation in the Tomlinson case. Johnnie had no reason to believe or disbelieve it. One thing was clear: Roger Swank, who had found Tomlinson's body, hadn't done it. A close check on the interval of time between his departure from the poker game and 911 call, and comparison with estimates of time of death, made it impossible that Swank could have been at the right place at the right time. And he had lived a blameless life, making him an unlikely candidate, anyhow.

That left nobody.

So far, Johnnie was discounting the Indian-related evidence

found at both crime scenes. She thought the primitive knife found by Leonard Simonson reeked of a plant. As to the arrow-murder, she thought nobody in their right mind would have used such an object unless it was their clear intention to point the finger of suspicion south, down toward the residents of Big Gully.

Which meant both crimes involved attempted frame-up.

Which was all well and good as a theory. But it didn't help her solve anything.

Turning onto Silver Street, she headed directly toward the hospital another block away. Then she would have to get back to the office, she thought, because Butt Peabody might have returned by now.

She had gotten only a few strides farther on, however, when she encountered a plump, red-faced, western-suited cherub of indeterminate middle age waddling right at her, his yellow lizard cowboy boots clomping on the board sidewalk.

Police Chief Chubby Mayfield's considerable number of shining white teeth seemed to ignite in the sun as he spied her. "Sheriff Baker! A cheerful good morning to you!" Removing a big black cigar from the middle of his face, he doffed his tan Stetson and hurried closer. "My, you look quite glamorous to-day, my dear! Of course, you always do, eh? Even in old jeans and a plain blouse, like you're wearing today! Have you given any more thought to that proposal I sent you *in re* outfitting yourself and your force in uniforms similar to those of the city department?"

"No, chief, I haven't," Johnnie replied sweetly. "My two younger deputies already have uniforms they bought and paid for themselves. But about my suggestion that possibly the city could provide the county with some help in the jail in order to free up one of my people to help better patrol the south end of the county—"

"Oh, Johnnie my girl, I wish I could find a way to do that for you! I really do! But good lord, girl, you *know* how strapped the city is these days, what with funding for the new municipal golf course and all the extra security my small force is required to provide for some of our celebrities like Faye Dunaway last week, and then there was Rob Morrow. My goodness, what a mess that was! I'll tell you what, with only twenty-seven men to call on, there are days when I am driven almost to the brink of despair! I would help if I possibly could, however, Johnnie. You know that."

Johnnie hadn't held out much hope, but she felt a small twinge of disappointment anyway. "I appreciate your thinking about it, chief."

"Think nothing of it! Think nothing of it! Tell me: have you cracked that murder case yet? Any leads on the annex fire? What disposition do you anticipate on that tavern ruckus out east I heard about on the scanner?"

"We're working on all that."

Mayfield shook his head sadly from side to side, making his jowly cheeks wobble. "Crime is on the upswing, Johnnie. No doubt about it. Oh, we'll soft-pedal things, of course—keep the image of Tenoclock pristine, eh? But just last night we had another burglary, this time at the ski shop, and teenage hoodlums egged five tourist cars in the Holiday Inn parking lot. Terrible! My men are working night and day, and we still can't keep up!"

"Chubby," Johnnie murmured, "I feel for you. I really do."

Mayfield frowned. "Were you aware also that I did some valuable PR work for you and your department only an hour or so ago?"

"No, I was not." She braced herself. Mayfield loved to pull surprises like this, and they were invariably unpleasant.

"Dr. Riley was in the department," Mayfield told her. "Don't see him very often . . . very busy man. But he was angry. Oh my, yes. Very, very angry. He didn't appreciate how you arrested his boys last night."

"I didn't appreciate how his boys almost killed a kid."

"Hmm. Well, you know the Riley boys. Ornery. But they come out of good stock. Anyway, I calmed the doctor down. Told him you might have saved his boys worse trouble by taking them in, and they're out on bail today anyway, so no harm done, eh? But I did want to warn you, Johnnie. I think he went on back to the hospital, but he was still steaming. You never know. He might lodge a formal complaint of some kind yet."

"I'll keep it in mind," Johnnie said grimly, and turned away. She wanted to say how sincerely she appreciated the police chief apologizing for her enforcement of the law but couldn't quite come up with the right words.

Lengthening her strides, she pushed through the swarms of tourists to reach the next corner and the long, low white stucco hospital building across the way. She crossed over into the chill dimness, which smelled of antiseptics and other unspeakable things, and got the room number of the Burlingame boy from the gray-haired volunteer lady at the information desk.

A quick ride to the second floor in the elevator put her at the door of the Burlingame room. Two thickset native Americans, a middle-aged man and woman, stood just inside, looking worried. Sitting up in the bed, skinny legs sticking out of his striped hospital gown, was the teenager who had to be Henry Burlingame. He had a bandage on his forehead, an arm in a sling, and dark bruises all over his face.

Johnnie stepped tentatively inside. "Hi. I'm Sheriff Baker. I wanted to check on our young man, here."

The dark-faced man, wearing a worn flannel shirt and Levi's, solemnly extended a thick hand. "Jarvis Burlingame. Henry's father. And this is my wife, Naomi."

"Hello, Naomi." Johnnie shook hands with both of them and turned to the boy. "Henry, how are you feeling? My, you had a—"

"Suck my dick," the boy said.

His mother gasped. "John Henry," his father growled threateningly.

"It's all right," Johnnie said, face heating. "I heard your son was going to be discharged. I just wanted to make sure he's okay, and—"

"A rat's ass you care," young Burlingame said, his face twisted with resentment.

"John Henry!" the older man repeated.

"—and," Johnnie went on as if nothing had been said, "to see if you possibly could give us any help identifying the man who broke up the fight, Henry."

"Some fight! Fucking bastards kicking my guts out—"

"Did you see the man in the diver's outfit?"

"I didn't see shit except my own blood flying."

"You were unconscious, then, when he intervened?"

"I guess I was, since I don't know what the shit you're talking about."

"We're trying to identify him," Johnnie explained to the parents.

It was the father's turn to turn stony-faced with hostility. "It will not be a big deal, whether you find this mystery man or not."

Johnnie didn't get it. She leaned closer. "Say again?"

"We have already heard the laughable charge filed against the Rileys. We are not stupid. We know they will never come to trial. They are white and their family has money, according to everyone. They will plead guilty and pay a little fine and go free again, to attack other innocent Native Americans."

Johnnie's face was burning now. "I wanted stronger charges. We'll do the best we can. In the meantime, sir, your boy might get in less trouble if he went to school, as the law says he should, and if he didn't go around white men's saloons in the middle of the night, playing pool hustler."

The mother made a choking sound. "He never do that!"

Johnnie glanced at the glowering boy. "I'm glad you're going to be okay. Good day." More angry than she should have been, partly because some of the family's accusations had stung, she turned and hurried out of the room and back down the corridor.

Out on the street again, she practiced more deep breathing, but this time it didn't seem to help.

Damn . . . *damn!* Trouble everywhere, and she couldn't even find a man gallivanting around in a rubber diving suit. What kind of an incompetent did that make her?

She could remember all too vividly the jokes and snickers when the commissioners named her interim sheriff last year after the murder of "Big Jim" Way. "Maybe she would be more effective if we could get her to wear tighter pants," she had heard one of them say soon after her appointment.

A public relations gimmick, that was all she had been at the start. A joke. A gambit to convince the outside world that all was well in Tenoclock County, and look at the cute girl they put in as sheriff, ha ha.

It had stung. But she had stayed in there. After the initial ghastly events that took place as she finally solved Jim Way's murder, it had been relatively peaceful, too. Until the Anasazi curse struck.

As the last thought went through her mind, she stopped dead in her tracks there on the sidewalk in front of the hospital. *Anasazi curse?* Had she actually thought that thought? Was she losing her grip?

Oh, boy. She hurried back to the courthouse, saw that Butt Peabody's truck was still not back, and entered the sheriff's department.

Up at the front, a wiry little man, blondish hair mostly silver now, wearing battered jeans, a flannel shirt, and brand-new Minnetonka moccasins, hopped up off the waiting bench as if he had been jolted with electricity. "Is this she?" he demanded of clerk Hesther Gretsch, filling in behind the counter. "She's the sheriff? Oh, good!"

He hurried toward Johnnie, his small hand extended. "Sheriff? Hi there! I hear you've been looking for me. I'm the wet suit guy."

7

JOHNNIE STARED, TAKING in details while the surprise sank in. The man was probably in his early fifties, with more weathered lines in his cherubic face than should have been there. He had bright green eyes and an infectious, gap-toothed grin, and his left shoulder seemed to slope an inch or two lower than his right. A pair of reading glasses hung around his neck on a shoestring, and he had a pack of Marlboros sticking half out of his left breast pocket.

"The wet suit guy," Johnnie repeated, still getting her balance.

"Right! I'm the one who hit those guys with the stun gun last night. I was listening on my pickup radio a while ago, and I heard somebody say you were wanting to question me. Hey." His grin spread radiantly, with more than a little touch of healthy irony. "I'm not in trouble, am I?"

"Maybe we'd better start at the beginning," Johnnie said. "I'm Sheriff Baker."

He pumped her hand again. "Great! I'm Webster. Noah Webster. True story. My parents had a sick sense of humor. My brother is named Isaac. He gripes about *that*. I always remind him what they called me, and tell him he's lucky they didn't name him 'Unabridged.' What's the deal, Sheriff? Am I going in the can?"

"Let's talk back there," Johnnie suggested, pointing.

"Great!"

Still a bit dazed, she led Webster back to the rear office, which she seemed to be using a lot lately. He bounded along beside her like a teenager. "I sure am sorry about not coming in sooner. I didn't realize you would want to talk to me. I felt like I just broke up a fight, you know, no biggie."

Johnnie sat behind the desk and gestured him to the chair facing it. "How did you happen to be out there, Mr. Webster?"

"Oh, that." His fingers dived into his shirt pocket after the cigarettes. "Mind if I smoke?"

"Actually, yes. This office is kind of small."

Webster sighed and replaced the pack. "Too bad. Well. I had been out south there doing some diving out at that little lake—what's it called?—Chambers Pond. No, no, not after dark. I was camping out there, and after I finished diving I had some Beanie Weenies and stuff and then came in for gas. I'm a historian. Well, actually, my Ph.D. is in serum hematology. Gave it up. My newest degree is history. Well, sort of archaeology and anthropology, actually. It's all very complicated. I teach down there at Oklahoma in the history department, but I kind of cross over into Native American studies and some other stuff."

He paused and barked a laugh. "They don't know what to do with me, to tell you the truth. I'm on sabbatical. Research into the Anasazi. I heard there might be some old Anasazi stuff under that lake, so I drove up here to check it out. No, I didn't find anything, but I'll probably go back later and look a little more. Don't worry. I'm a responsible person. If I did locate anything, I wouldn't disturb it without notifying the proper authorities and getting careful supervision.

"Anyway, I swam around down there and struck out, and it

was getting dark, so after the Beanie Weenies I put my wet suit back on because I'd got some mud all over it and I thought I could drive into that gas station and use their water wand dealie-whopper to wash myself off instead of the truck, you see? So I had it on and washed off pretty good and gassed up, but then I saw this fracas across the road, and I went over and tried to be reasonable and stop them from practically killing that kid, but they were drunk and got belligerent, so I just knocked them on their ass with my stunner and tied them up with some extra tubing I had in the truck. I didn't realize I would be needed as a witness or something. Anyway, here I am now. What I am, see, is a scholar. Specifically I'm here to research the Anasazi curse and burial mounds. But the lake story took precedence. I'm from Norman, Oklahoma. I used to teach at Rice, but—"

"Wait a minute, wait a minute," Johnnie groaned.

His face went blank. "Am I going too fast?"

"Among other things, Mr. Webster, yes."

He looked contrite. "Sorry. Ask away."

"How long have you been in the Tenoclock Valley?"

"Two days. Well, actually three, counting today, but I got in kind of late because I drove in all the way from Dumas, Texas. You remember that old song, 'I'm a Dingdong Daddy from—' Oops, there I go again. Sorry."

"Are you here alone, Mr. Webster?"

"Yes. And therein lies a story. But I'll keep my mouth shut."

"How long do you intend to stay?"

"I don't know. A couple of weeks, probably. You see, there's still a tremendous amount we don't know about the Anasazi. It's never been firmly established beyond doubt that these burial mounds and artifacts found around here really do prove an Anasazi connection. We know they were at Mesa Verde and some other places, and that they'd evidently moved there from farther north. Then when they had pretty well trashed their local agricultural environment there, or maybe because of prolonged bad luck with the weather, possibly combined with raids by other hostiles, they moved farther south, down the Rio Grande. If we could definitely establish that the relics here are Anasazi, it would be a big deal—move their history back maybe centuries. I hope my work around the burial mounds might accomplish that."

"I guess you know those mounds are on Ute land, and they hold them sacred."

"Oh, sure. I don't intend to do anything to antagonize anyone."

"The mounds were plundered long ago by some of the earliest pioneers. The present-day Utes protect them vigilantly."

Webster nodded. "Down in Oklahoma we've got the Spiro mounds, which people just tore the shit out of—pardon me, really desecrated—back in the thirties. Ruined them for scientific research. In southern Ohio you've got the mound-builder culture around Chillicothe, and those mounds were all wrecked, too—even flattened by the army to make space on an old training field down there. Of course, the Ohio mounds and the Oklahoma mounds were built centuries apart by different cultures. These around here were, too. But all I'm saying is, I fully appreciate the importance of not just messing into something; I know my history of how other sites were ruined."

"You'll have trouble with the Utes."

His radiant grin returned. "I can handle them. I'm a very winning kind of guy."

"I wouldn't count on it."

He shrugged. "Well, then, I'll just have to cozy up to my kinfolks and convince them to let me investigate the mounds that are on their land."

Johnnie was lost again. "Kinfolks?"

"Yeah. Their name is Herman. Old-time family, I guess. Pioneer stock. They're my third cousins twice removed, or something like that. I've written them a couple letters saying I'm coming. There's a little mystery about the family that my uncle Jack—he's a big-time genealogist—would like me to get cleared up. Also, they've got an old burial mound on their property. I want to take a look at it."

Johnnie leaned back in her chair, aware of an ache behind her eyes. "Mr. Webster, I don't think you'll get to first base with the Hermans."

"How come?"

"They really are hostile folks."

"I'll work it out, don't worry about it." He frowned and started to reach for his cigarettes again. "Is there anything else, Sheriff? Do I need to sign a statement or something?"

Johnnie sighed. "Not at the moment. Where are you staying?"

"I'll keep on camping down by the lake for right now."

"And your immediate plans?"

"Dive some more today. Tomorrow, I guess I'll try to contact both these Herman folks and some of the Utes down south and talk to them about what I want to do out at the mound sites."

"Mr. Webster," Johnnie said sternly, "I want to advise you to be most careful in your contacts with the Herman family *and* with the Utes. The Hermans used to be rich. They may still be. They're very odd people. They don't like strangers." She reconsidered that. "They don't like anybody."

Webster grinned widely and hopped to his feet. "I'll be careful, Sheriff, no kidding. Now am I free to go?"

Her warning had gone right past him. He was hopeless. "You can go," Johnnie said glumly, leaving the desk.

"Hey, thanks again!" Then he was gone before she could offer to shake hands or lead him out.

WHEN SHE WALKED into the main office seconds later, Johnnie found Webster already gone through the outside door, leaving behind a small cloud of cigarette smoke. Butt Peabody stood beside the front counter, an expression of wrinkled perplexity all over his face.

"Who was that?" he asked.

"That was our man with the stun gun."

Peabody reared back in disbelief. "*That* little guy? The one that knocked the Riley boys out?"

"The same."

"I find that hard to believe."

"Butt, there's a lot about that man you might find hard to believe."

"What's he doing in Tenoclock?"

Johnnie told him. As she did so, Peabody's scowl deepened.

"Johnnie, he could stir up more trouble, messing with those mounds."

"I know. I warned him."

"Did he pay you any mind?"

"Not really."

The older man made a snorting sound through his nose. "This is all we need. Another source of friction."

"Butt, what did you find out down there in the gully?"

"A bunch of people that are pissed off."

"I don't believe anyone down there set this annex fire. I don't believe they would be stupid enough to do such a thing, then leave such an obvious clue that points right at them."

Peabody solemnly shook his head. "Maybe."

"And I don't believe anyone in his right mind would use an ancient arrow as a murder weapon, except to point suspicion in the wrong direction."

"Maybe," Peabody repeated.

Johnnie's teeth grated. "But we've got arson and poor old Amos Pinkstaff dead in the fire, which makes his death a murder. And we have a salvage yard operator from Alamosa dead on the highway, clearly murdered. And we've got the Indian things as our only leads in both cases."

"I met a man named Jerome David down there," Peabody told her. "Ever hear of him?"

"Sure. NFL, all-pro three times, retired early because of injuries, moved back here, bought the old Anderson place down there in Big Gully. Why?"

Peabody's chest heaved. "Why didn't *I* know about it?"

Johnnie felt a lurking pleasure to realize she had known something that her veteran deputy didn't. Usually it seemed he knew everything locally, and she was the humble acolyte. "I guess I just paid more attention on this one, Butt," she said sweetly.

He gave her a glare. "I went to see him."

"Today? Why?"

"Seems he's an amateur collector of Indian stuff. He was in Albuquerque a couple of weeks ago, and his place here was broken into while he was gone. Thieves took quite a few relics and such."

Johnnie groaned, seeing it coming a mile off. "And among the stolen items were an old knife and a ceremonial arrow or two?"

"Yep."

"Dammit! We never had a report of any burglary down there! Why—"

"I asked him that." Peabody morosely rummaged into his shirt pocket, came out with a small bag of tobacco and some papers, and began rolling a cigarette, tapping the finely ground tobacco leaves onto the thin little paper, then adroitly forming the paper into a tube with only the fingers of his right hand. "Mr. David is a very bitter man. The injury cut his NFL career off short. He had just gone through a divorce, and his ex-wife took him for something over two million cash settlement, which he had figured he could recoup by playing another few years. Now he's pretty close to broke. He came back here, tried to get a loan for a new house, and got told by all our good white businessmen locally to shove it up his, uh, in his ear. He's not a happy camper down there. He's listened to the talk, and he remembers from when he grew up here." Peabody paused, ran the tip of his tongue along the rolled cigarette paper, and sealed it. "He figured making a report to us would just result in the local paper running a neat story about the poor injun down on his luck, and here's a list of the kind of stuff he's got left in his house in case some of you other thieves want a shopping list."

"Do you believe him, Butt?"

"Yes."

"So do I. But dammit—"

"The way I tend to figure it now, somebody broke in down there because they had wind of the fact he had old Indian stuff. They were already planning the annex fire, and maybe the Tomlinson killing too. They wanted to leave clues pointing the wrong direction—"

It was Johnnie's turn to interrupt. "You're now thinking the fire and the Tomlinson murder are related?"

His eyebrows raised. "Why, hell yes. I always did; didn't you?"

"Not for sure," she admitted lamely.

He sighed again and cracked a wood match on the seat of his pants to light his cigarette, puffing smoke furiously.

"There's no visible link between the fire and—" Johnnie began.

"When things happen close together in time," he told her, "look for a cause-and-effect relationship."

"But—"

"It don't always work, but most of the time it does, when the events are highly unusual, like the fire and the murder."

She rubbed her eyes. "So you think the fire and the murder connect."

"Yep."

"And you don't think anyone down in Big Gully—"

"Probably not. Who's to say for sure?"

She began pacing the floor behind the counter. "That man Tomlinson has to be the link. He *has* to be. But how?"

Peabody's forehead resembled a washboard. "Dunno. Are the crime lab people completely through down there in Alamosa?"

"The background check, his house, interviews—yes. They're still sifting through some of his records at his junkyard office, but they told me he wasn't much of a believer in paperwork. So we don't have much hope."

"Well, maybe they'll turn something up yet." Peabody did not sound convinced.

"I'm going to go down to the Pick & Shovel for lunch. Then I plan to get with the guys still combing through the fire mess next door—see if they've listed any findings that might give us some additional help."

Peabody nodded. "Good idea." He looked around, seeing only the dour Hesther Gretsch at a desk far down the room, hammering at the keyboard of an ancient Intertec Superbrain computer. "Guess I better mind the store. Where's Billy? Ain't it his time on the desk?"

"Yes, but we've got that crafts fair west of town. He was needed out there to watch traffic."

"Damn city could watch that traffic."

"Out of the city limits, Butt."

"Goddam Chubby Mayfield anyway."

Johnnie left the courthouse and headed uptown again, on foot as before. The day had warmed, and more tourists were on the street. Looking at some of the old, familiar buildings nearby, and at the ageless mountains blue through heat-haze on all sides, she felt a gust of gladness that she could be here in a place she knew and loved so well. That feeling, however, lasted only seconds.

The thought that replaced it, as her mind automatically reverted to the problems facing her office, was considerably less pleasant.

I could fail at this.

8

WHEN COUNTY COMMISSIONER Carl Rieger returned from lunch to find a visitor waiting for him in the darkly paneled outer office, he recognized the face instantly.

And almost wet his pants.

"Mr. Rieger? Good afternoon, sir!" He was in his mid-thirties, handsome, six feet tall, lean and tan, with dark, curly hair, piercing eyes, and a granitic jaw softened just now by a smile. His dark blue suit was in the $900 class, and the jeweled watch on his hairy left wrist had surely cost more than the first six or eight automobiles Rieger had purchased years earlier.

He clasped Rieger's hand in a grip that almost broke bones. "I'm Jack Wakefield, sir. Denver Channel—"

"I know who you are," Rieger croaked.

Wakefield's brilliant smile, the same one he had used while skewering the governor in an exclusive interview only a week ago, now beamed directly into the stricken Rieger's eyes, rendering him cold with fear and mute with shock. "I'm in Teno-clock, sir, to do a piece on your crime spree."

"Crime spree? Crime spree?" Rieger's voice became a shrill gargle. "We don't have any crime spree!"

"This is for the network," Wakefield intoned in that big, dark, jar-of-Vaseline voice of his. "They read something somewhere. Thought it would be a good piece. Little Tenoclock, now booming, begins to face the urban realities of crime and violence. Now, I'll be talking to the city also, Mr. Rieger, and my cameraman will be down later in the day to shoot some tape. But I wanted to have a preliminary visit with you now, if you have the time, in order for us to set the guidelines for later on-tape discussions of your growing problems."

"But we don't have any problems," Rieger moaned.

Wakefield's laugh was as big and oily as his famed speaking voice. "A lion on the loose, Mr. Rieger? Reports of an unidentified explosion of some kind rocking the ground? Arson at the courthouse, with a body found in the ashes? A murder on the road, with an arrow through the victim's neck? And you have no crime problems? You have a sense of humor, I see. That's good. That's very good. Now where can we have our talk, Mr. Rieger? In your office? Through here? You lead the way, sir. I'll follow. Good man."

"HE WAS RIGHT *here*," *Carl Rieger squeaked, pointing around the room. "Right here*! Right here in my goddam office! Jack Wakefield, from Denver! For a story to put on the CBS Evening News, he said! Jesus, Mary, and Joseph! This is *terrible!* Tenoclock is going to come out looking like the South Bronx or something. Everything we've all worked for will be ruined!"

"Now, now, Carl," fellow commissioner Madison Blithe said gently, and then a funereal silence descended over the office.

They had assembled hastily for an emergency confab behind locked doors just as soon as Denver television newsman Jack Wakefield had departed and Rieger could contact the other two via their pagers. Now they sat around the old oval coffee table at the far end of Rieger's office and assessed the potential damage.

Rieger, as chairman of the board and the target of Wakefield's casual, murderous questions, was the most upset at the moment. Five-foot-six in his elevated cowboy boots, the bald political veteran had removed his red sports coat and loosened the string tie around the neck of his western-cut shirt. His considerable tummy bulged over the silver buckle of his belt, almost concealing it. What he could not conceal was the stark panic making his close-set little eyes sag in sallow cheeks. He was looking for someone to produce a miracle and get him—and the county—off the public relations hook.

In one of the battered cloth easy chairs facing him, Madison Blithe, thirty-seven, looked far cooler, although people generally agreed that it was impossible to know what Tenoclock's youngest millionaire real estate developer was really thinking or feeling at any given time. Tall, thin, blondly handsome, impeccable as usual in his expensive suit and Gucci loafers, Blithe had eyes the color and temperature of ice cubes and the coldly calculating heart to match. As usual, he was being cautious and waiting to see what developed.

The third commissioner, Earle Fisch, sat silent, looking like a pile of bones inside the aged suit that had fit him once, before the years began stripping weight off his body with inexorable efficiency. At seventy-seven, Fisch had already announced that he intended to retire after his present term. He had served the county long enough, he liked to say. Anyway all his farmland had by now been favorably zoned and provided with new county road access for his maximum financial benefit, so there was little motivation for further selfless public service on his part. All this meant Fisch was no longer politically vulnerable, which might have been why his cadaverous face appeared sleepy, and his wrinkled eyelids drooped.

"He'll be back in here in the morning with this camera crew,

I tell you," Rieger resumed nervously. "What am I supposed to do?"

When Blithe did not respond, Fisch slowly opened his eyes. "Tell him we ain't got no crime."

"I can't tell him that! He knows better!"

Blithe said, "Talk about how we intend to raise new taxes to improve law enforcement."

"Are you *insane?* This is an election year!"

Again no one spoke. Blithe looked worriedly around the office, examining some of Rieger's familiar mementos: the rows of framed photos on the back wall, each depicting the commissioner with a notable, each fondly autographed by such luminaries as John Elway, Faye Dunaway, John Madden, and Dinah Shore; on shelving along another wall, the collection of trophies Rieger had won over the years as a tournament bridge player, and on his old oak desk the row of miniature American flags, each from a different era, each embedded in the cork atop an empty vintage beer bottle. None of this might be very much in itself, Blithe reflected, but here it represented not only home base but power.

Something like the pending Wakefield report could swing that power, and they all knew it. This was not a matter for panic such as Rieger was displaying, but it was damned serious. Blithe focused his mind on the problem.

"As I see it," he told the others, "if we have no credible way to deny the whole question, then we have three possible courses of action."

Carl Rieger leaned forward, his expression pitiful with hope. "What? What?"

"First, we could insist that our crime rate is very low—as it actually is—for a city with our kind of burgeoning growth."

"But that will just sound like weaseling."

"Second, we could refuse to cooperate in any way, including interviews. Chubby would go along with that, and we can convince the mayor. In the face of our dignified silence—"

"The network will imply we're all rubes! Incompetents who have something to hide!"

"Third," Blithe went on as if he had not been interrupted, "we could insist that Tenoclock County is doing everything possible to prevent crime—spending as much as we possibly can, being every way vigilant."

Rieger made a whining sound. "All they have to do is look in the basement to know *that's* a lie!"

"Then we have only one other possibility," Blithe said, "if we are to swing the spotlight of blame away from the county commissioners. And I believe we are in agreement, gentlemen, that the morale of county employees, as well as the image of Tenoclock County far and wide, depends on our maintaining a spotless reputation as the county's governing board."

"Yes, yes," Rieger said, and old Fisch nodded. "What do we do, Madison?"

Blithe sighed. "We take the only course of action left to us, Carl, as sad as that might be. We shift the spotlight, as it were. We alter the center of attention. Or, in a word, we find someone other than ourselves to blame for whatever problem may exist."

There was a moment's silence, and in a corner of the old office a grandfather clocked chimed half past the hour.

"But how?" Rieger demanded at last. "More to the point, *who?*"

Blithe looked back at him. Rieger looked at Fisch, who looked at Blithe.

"Oh, of course," Rieger said at last. "Why didn't I think of that myself?"

Old Fisch stirred bony legs and arms. "It's a cruel, cruel thing, boys. A mighty mean and cruel and nasty thing."

"But necessary," Rieger said briskly, leaning forward and rubbing his chubby hands together over the coffee table. "Now, how do we do it?"

AS OFTEN HAPPENED in the Tenoclock Valley at this time of year, clouds had begun to scud in from the southwest, ringing Killdeer and Red mountains, late in the afternoon. By five o'clock the sky overhead had become completely overcast, and by five-fifteen the chilly rain began to mist down.

The collar of her windbreaker pulled up against the cold, Johnnie trudged around in the ashen wreckage of the old courthouse annex, mutely watching inspector Leonard Simonson direct his four assistants in their work. Simonson had called the crime bureau agents back in, and two of them were on the far side of the razed building, carefully removing several small panes of glass from window frames that had survived the fire in the building's only remaining standing brick wall. The theory was that the panes might contain useful fingerprints. Johnnie doubted it.

She had known custodian Amos Pinkstaff a long time, if not well, and still felt the distant shock and sadness of his death. The coroner's report indicated that the old man might have been sleeping in his basement office and been overcome by smoke or carbon monoxide fumes without ever awakening to realize his entrapment. Johnnie hoped it had gone that way. The alternative—a futile, panicked struggle to get through dense smoke and flames to the safety of the outdoors—was harder to contemplate.

She did not consider the old man's death anything but an accident. The fire had been set—it was arson. Pinkstaff had never done anything in his life to motivate anyone to want to kill him; she felt sure of that. The motive for setting the fire—if it had not been simply blind malice—had lain elsewhere.

If she could come up with any theory as to what that motive might have been, she thought, she might be far closer to developing a theory that might lead her on to some profitable angle of attack. But she could not come up with a thing, even on the most abstract theoretical basis.

The annex had been used for many, many years as the repository for old records: court cases, land transaction ledger books, records of the county and court clerks ranging from marriage licenses to divorce decrees. Except for some old office furniture and such things as the courthouse Christmas decorations, nothing else had been stored in the decrepit, decaying brick structure. The old files and books had contained information priceless to a historian and possibly a few genealogists, but nothing of known money value. Only a maniac would have burned records that reflected a century's life in the Tenoclock Valley. There was nothing to be gained by anyone through this kind of vandalism.

It might have been left at that—a tragedy for historians—if it had not been for old Amos. His death put the disaster also in the category of murder to be solved.

Johnnie was walking back and forth, waiting to visit again with Tomlinson and blindly staring at burned timbers and wallboard, when she saw Carl Rieger approaching. The portly little commissioner picked his way almost daintily—with every sign of disgust—through the burned rubbish that had once been annex roofing material. He saw her glance and waved to her, signaling for her to come over. She went that way.

"Nasty," Rieger said with distaste, wiping small fat hands on a handkerchief. "Found anything new?"

"Not yet," Johnnie told him.

Rieger shook his head. "It's a sad thing, Johnnie. This, along with the vicious murder of that innocent man from Alamosa, has given the county a very bad name throughout the state. We—my fellow commissioners and I—had devoutly hoped your department could bring the culprits to justice by this time."

"They're still going through the salvage operator's office

down there," Johnnie told him. "Also, we found out something interesting today. The murder weapon in that case was stolen from a man in Big Gully a week or two ago."

"Does that give us a murderer?" Rieger's voice cracked with tension.

"No, but—"

"And then there is that sad case last night—a young boy beaten half to death, and two sons of a pioneer family taken into custody without the filing of formal charges—"

"Plus," Johnnie cut in acerbically, "the sad fact that my guys are running themselves into the ground night and day, and we can't get a supplemental appropriation—"

"Now, now," Rieger snapped. "This is not the time or the place to discuss that."

"Dammit, Carl, I've got to have some help!"

The small man's round face became pale and nervous. "Johnnie, the county commissioners had every confidence in you when we appointed you last year in the aftermath of the tragic death of Jim Way."

She stiffened, catching the strange inflection in his voice as he made what seemed like an even stranger transition. "So?"

He heaved a theatrical sigh. "The present deteriorating situation, Johnnie, is a great burden and worry to the board. We have just concluded a lengthy—and I might add most painful—discussion in which we have been forced to reevaluate the situation vis-à-vis law enforcement in Tenoclock County."

"What does that mean?"

"Now, now, nothing has been decided as yet—"

"What are you saying, Carl?"

His chest heaved again. "The board has reluctantly decided to hold a special meeting to consider calling a special election for your office. It's not that we don't think you've *tried*, Johnnie. It's just that ... well ... the way things are right now, something simply may have to be done."

Johnnie studied his dishonest expression. She felt tumult in her chest, and possibly a little sick at her stomach.

Rieger reached out to pat her arm. "I hope you understand, Johnnie. It may just be that the job has simply gotten too big for you. You can see that, can't you?"

"What I can see, Carl, is what an asshole you are." She turned and strode out through the broken wall, half-running for the back parking lot.

So angry and frustrated she did not know exactly where she was going, she climbed into her Jeep and started the engine. Her two-way Motorola radio came on with the ignition, a green panel light glowing. As she backed out, wheels chirping angrily on the broken asphalt, the radio blatted at her:

"Sheriff's unit two to base." Butt Peabody.

From inside the courthouse, Jason Ramsey replied: "Unit two, this is headquarters, go ahead."

"Jason, get the sheriff on, ten-four?"

Johnnie pulled her microphone off its dashboard clip. "Unit two, this is one. I'm just getting mobile at the courthouse. Ten-twenty?"

"One, this is two returning. I'm on the south road headed for Big Gully. Advise you follow, meet the gas station. Ten-four?"

Johnnie keyed her mike again. "What is it, Butt?"

There was a long moment of silence on the radio, then Peabody's voice again, now straining to be heard over the roar of his truck engine winding up to high speed: "Advise number six, over."

Shit. Cranking the wheel of the Jeep with one hand, Johnnie used the other to grab her notebook out of her jacket pocket. Getting the notebook open with the one hand, she fumbled to extract the small notecard inserted inside the back-cover leaf.

When it had begun to be apparent that an ungodly number of valley residents had their radio scanners turned on twenty-

four hours a day, and knew the usual law enforcement codes as
well as the officers did, she and Peabody had devised a crude
code system of their own to identify major incidents over the air.
She had written the code numbers and corresponding crimes on
a three-by-five card and put it into the back of her notebook but
hadn't memorized everything yet.

She looked at her card, went slightly numb, and thumbed
her mike again. "Unit two, this is one. Did you say number six,
over?"

"Affirmative, one. Advise number six."

Number six was their private code for murder. Somebody
else had just died, this time in Big Gully.

9

IN THE WEEDS not far off the dirt road just south of Big Gully, the dead man's egg-white eyes stared upward, unblinking, into the steady cold rain.

Quite a crowd had gathered before Johnnie's arrival, including Butt Peabody, old Abner Wakinokiman, George Bonfire, and a half-dozen other male residents of Big Gully she didn't know by name. Some other people stood back a few yards away, huddled close and whispering among themselves. Four or five small kids were running in this direction, but one of the female onlookers hurried to head them off and send them back the way they had come.

Everyone was standing well back except Peabody, who stood over the body, scowling as he wrote into his notebook with the stub of a yellow pencil.

"Name of Billy Kickingbird," he told Johnnie. "Age thirty-two. Lives here in Big Gully, down the road a half mile. Has a bunch of junker cars in his yard, salvages parts. Been gone to Denver a few days. Showed up at the gas station last night, saying he'd just got back. He did steel construction work sometimes, had a temporary job up there."

Johnnie leaned over the body. The rain had soaked the dead man's clothing, but it hadn't removed much of the blood or disturbed the obvious cause of death: a heavy Buck hunting knife, its single blade buried in the middle of his chest.

"How long, do you think?" she asked.

"Early this morning, I'd say."

"No witnesses, of course?"

"No."

"Who found him?"

"Kids going fishing."

"Where are they?"

"Sent home. I've got names."

Johnnie looked down into the dead man's eyes again, suppressing a shudder. His dark face had already tightened into the kind of grimace that so often followed violent death. He looked far older than thirty-two. The rain matted his long black hair and made glistening jewels in the graying stubble beard on his chin and cheeks. His clothes were of the cheap work variety, Levi's, a faded Denver Broncos sweatshirt, badly worn lace-up boots.

She asked, "Has his family been notified?"

Peabody shook his head. "No family. He was divorced. Ex-wife moved away someplace."

"I heard you radio for the ambulance. Have you got your camera?"

The older man shook his head in disgust. "No. But I'm sure Niles had his scanner on down at the *Frontiersman*. He'll be hauling ass out here as fast as possible, camera in hand."

Johnnie nodded with irritation. Niles Pennington would never publish a picture in the local weekly that might make Tenoclock look bad. But that didn't stop him from popping shots of every crime he could find in hopes of bootlegging an anonymous shot to one of the national scandal sheets. He would provide crime-scene photos for her investigation files, as usual. She wished she didn't have to depend on him, but it was just another reality of her anemic budget.

She turned to the bystanders. "Does anyone know anything about this?"

Several of the men shuffled their feet and looked uncomfortably in other directions. Old Wakinokiman stared, his sunken eyes dark beneath the rain-dripping brim of his battered felt hat, but he said nothing. Only George Bonfire responded. "What's to know, Sheriff? It's just another little Indian deal, right?"

Johnnie held her temper. "No one has any idea how or why this happened?"

"We already told Butt everything we know. Billy got back last night from a job in Denver. Usually when he does that, he buys a bottle and takes it out to his junkyard with him, and nobody sees him for a day or two. Only this time I guess he didn't go alone. Or somebody followed him."

She nodded and turned back to Peabody. "I'm going to call Billy Higginbotham out here for backup. I'll also notify the assistant DA's office in case he wants to come out and look over the scene. Let's not let the EMS guys remove the body before I get those calls through. Can you handle it here? I think I want to get right out to the victim's house, check for signs of a break-in, anything like that."

Peabody shoved his notebook into his pocket. "I'll keep up with you on the radio."

She took a step away, then wheeled back to the onlookers. "Can someone show me where this man lived?"

No one volunteered.

"George?"

Bonfire's voice dripped sarcasm: "Is that an order, Sheriff?"

"I can't order you, George. I'm asking you."

Bonfire nodded with ill grace. "I'll go with you."

She walked to her Jeep. He followed. Once inside, she

started down the road in the direction he mutely pointed, then used the radio to get some arrangements made. Behind them on the road came the sound of a siren, and the distant flashing lights of the EMS truck coming at high speed.

"George," she tried, "you don't have any idea why anyone might have done this?"

"No," Bonfire said, stony face looking straight ahead. "I didn't like Billy much. Nobody did. But nobody particularly hated him, either, that I know about. He was a nobody." He paused, then added, "Like most of us down here."

They rode the rest of the short trip in silence.

THE KICKINGBIRD PLACE was an acre or two of weeds and scrubby pine off the south side of the dirt road, a double-wide mobile home up on cinder blocks, the paint faded to grayish brown, litter everywhere. Scattered around under the trees in no apparent order were the rusting hulks of perhaps two dozen derelict automobiles. Parts of others, from hoods to doors to a couple of oily black engines, were strewn in the brush. A sign, its paint almost gone, proclaimed KICKINGBIRD ENTER-PRISES. "Enterprises" indeed: Johnnie wondered sadly what kind of dreams had died since that brave little sign had been painted.

She pulled through the broken wire fence posts and trundled slowly up the dirt driveway to the mobile home pulling up beside a well-rusted old Chevrolet pickup truck parked near the two-by-six porch. Before she got out of the Jeep, she saw that things were not right here. The front door of the trailer hung half-open on ruptured hinges.

Getting out, she went to the door and peered into the trailer. The smell of stale cigar smoke and decay wafted out into the drizzling rain. She reached inside the door, found a light switch, and flicked it on.

Everything inside was a mess. Kickingbird had not been a good housekeeper. The rotting remains of TV dinners and fast-food carryouts covered the sink and cabinets. Empty beer bottles and milk containers spilled out of a plastic garbage bag near the refrigerator. Clothing, old newspapers, and even some small salvaged auto parts littered the tiny living area floor.

None of that, however, made the worst mess. Some bookshelves and cabinets along one wall had had their contents pulled out and thrown all over the room. A battered rolltop desk stood buried under papers. Its drawers had been pulled out, and more paperwork of all kinds strewn across the floor. Pages had been torn out of an address book.

Going down the narrow hall to the bedrooms, Johnnie found more of the same. Every drawer, cabinet, or shelf in the trailer had been pulled out and rifled. Someone had been in a hurry. But they had tried to be very thorough.

She walked back to the wrecked living room, Bonfire following silently.

"What do you think?"

"You're the law officer, Sheriff."

"I *asked,* what do you think?"

Bonfire looked around with bleak eyes. "Burglary. Either they broke in while he was here, or he came home from his trip and found them inside, most likely."

"So he caught them, and there was a fight, and they stabbed him?"

"Might be."

"Then why was his body found up the road?"

"Don't know. You're the—"

"I know, I know, George," she cut in impatiently.

He stared around the room again, then surprised her: "My speculation would be that he caught the thief and tried to chase him on foot. You noticed his pickup parked outside there. He almost caught the thief. Or the thief turned around and caught him, up there on the road where we found him."

"What would somebody be looking for in here?"

This time Bonfire's tone was neutral, and quiet with puzzlement. "I have no idea."

She took another look around. "Shit. I'd better call in the state crime boys. They'll need to check all of this, dust for prints, that sort of thing."

Bonfire walked back outside with her. The rain had let up, and it had become a gray, depressing evening. "Do you think looking for prints and all will prove anything?" he asked her.

She turned to study his expression. "I don't know. I can hope."

"Can you?" he flung back with quiet hostility.

"What does that mean?"

His face worked now. "He was just a drunk, a junkman. An Indian down in Big Gully. Does his death mean a goddam to you or anyone else?"

"It does to me."

"Then why don't we have any law enforcement down here?" he demanded, anger visibly growing. "We have break-ins every night of the week. Our kids have dope in the school. Drunks ramrod around, driving off roads and breaking their own bones. Who gives a shit up there at Tenoclock? Why pretend?"

He stopped, chest heaving, slightly out of breath, very, very angry. Johnnie studied him, and her own frustration and disgust suddenly coalesced into an idea that she might have had earlier but had never until this moment really considered.

"I don't have any money for more deputies," she said.

Bonfire's lip began to curl in a sneer.

"But I've got an extra badge," she told him.

His eyebrows knit. "What?"

"You want more law down here? Fine. I've got a badge for

you. I have the power to deputize. I can pay mileage. Twenty-nine cents. Nothing else. You furnish everything else. There will be paperwork to fill out. Some people will give you a bad time. You're asking for nothing but hassle, but if you want it, you've got it, baby."

Bonfire's mouth dropped open. "Me? Are you saying you would appoint *me* a deputy?"

"Yes."

"My God! They'd—they'd laugh you out of the county! They'd have your job!"

"They may be fixing to try to get that anyhow. Will you help?"

His eyes bulged. "I can't believe this."

"Yes or no, dammit. Fish or cut bait. I don't have all night."

He recovered. His jaw set. "Yes. Damn you, yes!"

She grinned at him. "I don't have the badge here. You'll have to come into the courthouse. It's in my desk drawer."

"I can't *believe*—"

"You said that. Now. You're on the job effective immediately. I want you to stay here until I get either another deputy or the crime lab guys down here. That might be tomorrow morning. I can't help that. I need this place secured in the meantime. Understood?"

Bonfire glowered at her. "This is some kind of trick."

"The trick," Johnnie told him, "is that I just got some help in this part of the county, at last." She stuck out her hand. "Welcome aboard, Deputy."

When she backed out and drove away minutes later, George Bonfire was standing in the trashy front yard near the trailer, hands jammed deep into his pockets, with the expression of a man who has just been poleaxed. She smiled to herself and felt good for a moment.

Then reality began to come back. Now she had another murder on her hands. And when they heard about this deputizing at the courthouse, they were going to have cats.

Well, to hell with them. She was in danger of getting buried here. She had to get some things done, and right away. Maybe she had been carrying out her duties too cautiously. If so, it was not a mistake she intended to repeat.

Nightfall caught her on the road. She was exhausted. It had been a very, very long day.

10

HIS TUNELESS WHISTLING almost drowned out by the rattling and banging of his camper-backed pickup, Noah Webster drove slowly along the back dirt road west of the town of Tenoclock, following gas station instructions on how to get to the Herman property. Light rain in the night had passed, and he had had a glorious early Tuesday morning diving in the pond and mucking around in some oddly shaped gravel mounds near the shoreline. Now a warming sun beamed down out of a flawless blue mountain sky.

Noah Webster was feeling optimistic and cheerful. He nearly always did.

He had made what he considered a really neat find at midmorning. After noticing the odd shape of some of the small gravel-covered mounds near the shoreline of the pond, he had gotten out his narrow spade and rake to dig around in a couple of them. Not much bigger than a bale of hay, the little earthen humps didn't require much excavation. He had scarcely stuck his spade into the second one before the edge hit something that sounded funny, and as he continued digging with careful fingertips, he had unearthed several small pottery shards of unmistakable antiquity.

Highly excited, he had dug around a little more and uncovered another four broken pieces, the largest no bigger than an
Oreo cookie, but each bearing the familiar geometric decorative
patterning so often found on Anasazi urns and bottles.

At that point the temptation had been strong to fling himself
onto the other small hillocks nearby, convinced as he was now
that they represented the remnants of ancient trash heaps that
no one else had ever noticed, and which might contain God-
only-knew-what of enormous anthropological significance. But
he was not a savage or a criminal, he had reminded himself, and
so, after placing the found shards in carefully labeled small
plastic sandwich bags, he had photographed the scene from all
angles, made careful notes, and did his best to scatter gravel
back just the way it had been, so no one else would see evidence
of digging and mess anything up.

He would—after completing the rest of his planned inves-
tigations—hightail it back to Oklahoma, further examine and
catalog his precious clay fragments, get some carbon dating on
some chunks of wood ash he had also dug up, and figure out how
to (a) announce his findings and (b) secure sole permission to
widen his dig.

It was neat, neat, neat, and he was almost giddy with excitement about it.

It wouldn't do, however, to just ram in there and devastate
the pond bank right now. It could wait; it had waited undetected
for centuries. Far more important at the moment was his original
plan to check out the major ceremonial burial mounds to try to
come up with additional evidence.

That was where his distant kinfolks, the Hermans, came in.
He was not clear how the remote blood relationship should be
described, but someone on his mother's side had married a
Herman long ago. He had it all written down just as he had gotten
it from his uncle Jack.

Webster might never have gone to any trouble to track down

some genealogical stuff. But earlier in the year he had read a piece on the old burial mounds around Tenoclock, and the Herman name came up in the article. It seemed they had one of the mounds on their property. *That* had enormously increased Webster's interest in the family tree.

And now, piddling along the dirt road slowly winding its way upward along the wooded side of a mountain, Webster could hardly have been happier or more optimistic. Everybody said these present-day Hermans were antisocial, maybe crazy . . . some of them . . . and in general a decidedly bad lot. But blood was, after all, thicker than water, wasn't it? And he had a delightful personality that everyone loved, didn't he? No problem.

Turning a sharp curve in the one-lane dirt roadway near the top of the tree-shrouded mountain, he saw that the aspens and pines had fallen away on his left, allowing him a long view across a mile or more of rolling meadow ablaze with spring flowers. Beyond the scattering of beautiful colors, a hazy drop-off on the far side hinted at an invisible valley far below. Beyond the haze, miles off, stood the snowy sides of massive Red Mountain, with its smaller sister, Jumbo, to the north. It was a day of days, Webster thought happily, and if the Hermans lived up here in this kind of wonderful, rugged country, they couldn't be all bad . . . could they?

Just ahead, however, he encountered a pipe-rail bridge forming a cattle guard across a narrow, steep rivulet of creek, and beside it a wood sign with the letters fresh and black on a white background.

PRIVATE
KEEP OUT!
TRESPASSERS SHOT

About eighteen head of prime-looking dairy cattle stood in the knee-high grass on the far side, staring at Webster as if curious to see if he was smart enough to get the message.

He read it twice and then chuckled. Ah, the good old western knack for hyperbole! He drove slowly over the cattle guard, heavy pipes rattling under his tires.

After cutting diagonally across the small pasture beyond the guard, the dirt road narrowed, its raised center sprouting high yellow weeds that rustled against the underbelly of the pickup. The path—it could no longer be called a road—entered a dense stand of ponderosa pines. Instantly sunlight was cut off and it felt dark and dank in there. Webster poked on, and a minute or two later emerged partly from the woods into a weedy clearing, at the far end of which stood a gigantic black stone house that might have been built as backdrop for one of the old Frankenstein movies.

"Transylvania West," Webster muttered, awed. "Neat!"

The house, its granite walls stained by ages of rain and snow, stood four stories tall and sat astraddle the crest of a hillock more than two hundred feet wide. Blocky, with rows of prisonlike rectangular windows spaced perfectly evenly across all four of its floors, it had three chimneys, one at either end and one precisely in the middle. No porch adorned the facade; weeds just marched up to a slab, and atop the slab stood a door that looked strong enough to repel an army.

The hulk of a 1950s blue-and-white Chevrolet BelAir sat a few feet from the front entrance, thick red rust forming long stains down its sides. Nearby, an age-blackened tractor sat low on long-since-flat tires. Elsewhere, the thin steel ribs of a derelict combine device protruded from the high brush. Wadded bits of paper, remnants of crates and cartons, and discarded tin cans and barrels were strewn here and there at random. All the weeds looked strangely brown, as if struck by some alien blight.

Farther back across the trashy lawn stood two old barns, planks blackened and holed by age, tin roofs falling in. Around what must once have been corrals and holding pens, fences had rotted and fallen down in geometric chaos. Nearby stood an ugly concrete-block garage of much more recent vintage. All six overhead doors gaped open. The rear ends of dirty pickup trucks showed through five of them. In the sixth hole gleamed the dark red backside of a new Cadillac DeVille.

His distant kinfolks, Webster thought cheerfully, might be messy, but they still seemed to have some bucks.

He drove up the path toward the front of the massive house. Four large black dogs larruped out from somewhere and started raising a ravenous racket, leaping up on the sides of the pickup as he parked it. They were either Labs or rottweilers, Webster thought, looking into all the snarling fangs and flying saliva.

He opened the door and stepped down. "Oh, shut up, you guys," he said loudly over all the barking. "Good grief! Can't you tell a good guy from a bad one? *Hush!*"

The dogs went down onto all fours again and milled around and stared at him, sort of confused. Then they fell into step with him on all sides as he strode to the front slab, climbed up on it, and banged his fist on the giant oaken door.

There was no response right away. He waited, whistling and looking around and patting the head of the biggest, meanest-looking dog.

Still no answer after a minute or two. He banged again, harder.

A scant sound of movement came inside. Then a gruff male voice called out, "Go away!"

"No!" Webster called back, startled. "Wait a minute! I'm your cousin from Oklahoma. I wrote you two letters."

Silence.

Webster hammered again with his fist.

A louder and more violent sound came from inside, something heavy hitting a wall. The door opened about four inches.

"Hi, there!" Webster said brightly. "I'm—"

Something stuck out of the crack in the doorway. It was the business end of a double-barrel shotgun. The muzzles looked extremely large from Webster's vantage point.

A gravelly man's voice came from inside. "Git! Last warning!"

Signaled by the hostility in the voice, the dogs started growling and snarling again. One of them sank his teeth into the material of Webster's Levi's, missing flesh but starting to tug back and forth. Something ripped. Webster took a half step back, almost falling off the porch slab.

"Elmo?" a woman's faint voice sounded inside. "Elmo! Put that down! Land sake, how many times do I have to ask you?"

"Shut up, woman! This is man's business."

The shotgun barrel retracted out of sight. The door swung half open. A large, gray-haired woman of about sixty stared out. She looked as if she had spent far too many days outdoors in bad weather. Her eyes had an odd, wary alertness in them, like those of a wild animal hunted often and now frightened of the slightest movement. She was wearing a shapeless cotton dress and high-top work shoes with no laces, and the odor that wafted out from her combined garlic, tobacco, possibly oregano, and some other things Webster did not want to identify.

"Yes?" she said.

Webster tried again. "Hi! I'm your long-lost cousin from Oklahoma!"

She swung the door a few inches wider, revealing a small, wizened man in a wheelchair beside her. His bloodshot little eyes glowed with animosity. He shifted the double-barrel shotgun across the thin blanket covering his withered legs. "Get out! We don't want any!"

"Elmo," the woman protested weakly, "this is our cousin. Don't you remember the letters?"

Elmo Herman's bony face twisted with pure malevolence. "Shut your face, Aggie."

Webster decided to turn on the charm. He barked a laugh. "Golly! I don't blame you for being irritated, sir! If I had a beautiful spread like you have up here, and some dang stranger came gallivanting up to the front door without a proper invite—"

"Can the phony western dialect, mister. What do you want?"

Before Webster could reply, something else moved in the dimness of the hallway behind the two oldsters. The hulking figure of a much younger man hove into view. Wearing bib overalls and a torn flannel shirt and a ratty St. Louis Cardinals baseball cap, he looked big enough to rupture the doorway if he tried to step through it. Beneath a low forehead and shelf of bushy eyebrows, he looked about as friendly as a grizzly.

"Hi, there! I'm Noah Webster, your cousin from Oklahoma!"

The man moved nearer the door and stuck out a paw half the size of a loaf of bread. "I'm Joseph. We don't want you here."

"Yeah, but hey, I wrote you two letters!"

"Go away."

"Listen, Cuz, I didn't come all this way to get turned away. Can't you give me a few minutes?" Webster produced his most winning chuckle. "I'm a stubborn cuss. I might keep bugging you forever."

Joseph Herman bit his lip. "You can come in, I guess. Get back out of the way, Poppa."

The dogs swarmed eagerly through the doorway with Webster into an entry hall almost too dim to allow identification of detail. Once it must have been ornate and impressive: a great staircase curved upward to an open second-floor railing. On the black, paneled walls hung what might have been valuable oils under their thick coating of grease and cobwebs. Torn oriental carpets were shoved against the walls. Doors led off to other rooms—a huge living room to the right, a sitting room of some kind left, the brightness of another and even bigger room straight ahead.

Joseph Herman led the way to the brighter doorway. Webster followed, the old woman and man behind him. This room had a high, raftered ceiling and many tall casement windows looking out on three sides toward weeds and tumbled rocks from the mountainside behind, and scattered aspen. The battered furniture appeared to be something like Sears Modern Oak Ranch. Newspapers and old magazines were strewn all over the bare wood floor. In one corner a TV screen big enough for a theater shone with bright color: a Western, lots of horses running and gunshots.

Joseph Herman went over and dropped into one of several massive blond oak easy chairs, hiking a booted foot onto a hassock. He pointed brusquely at the chair nearest. "Put it there."

Webster gladly obeyed. The dogs started trying to lick his face and swarm all over him. He laughed and fended them off while the parents moved around beside a couch facing him and their son across a six-foot coffee table.

"It's awfully kind of you to have me in," Webster began. "As I started to tell your mom and dad, here—"

"She's not my mom. My mom died."

"Oh. Well. Still, it's kind—"

"No kindness in it," Joseph grunted. "The sooner we see you, the sooner we'll be rid of you once and for all. Now get said what you want to say. Then I want you outta here. We want no part of you."

Webster barked his short laugh and kept his grin pasted on, but a thin film of cold sweat had begun to form on his back. Joseph was *mean*—not merely hostile, but something worse. There was a clever, chilly watchfulness about him. A quickness in his eyes bespoke far more intelligence than his clothes or slouching posture indicated.

The two older folks simply stared, animals in a cage, watching without a trace of identifiable human emotion. The house felt—dank—spooky. Webster didn't like the feel of any of it.

"I'm here to research some possibly Anasazi stuff, like I said in my letters," he told the three of them. "I would like very much to have you take me out and let me have a look-see at the burial mounds I understand you have on your property, here. At the same time, gosh! After all, we're sort of kinfolks, right? I've got an uncle down in Texas who's really into genealogy. I've spoken with him, and he gave me this list of questions to ask you guys so he can bring his records up to date on your branch of the family. We haven't been in touch for a long time. You're sort of our mysterious branch, as it were."

Joseph's right hand formed a fist on the arm of his chair. "No."

"No on the genealogy," Webster asked manfully, "or no on the mounds?"

"No on any of it. Look, mister. We tend to our own business up here. We don't like people. We don't like you. You got an uncle that wants information? Tough. You want to visit the mounds? Tough. Your letters made it pretty clear you wouldn't take no for an answer by mail. So now you've seen us. You've gawked around. You've had your thrill. Now it's finished. Understand?"

Webster forced another smile and persisted. "Gee, I sure understand your desire for privacy. I really do. Maybe just a *couple* of questions? I mean, it's like I said in my first letter, I thought then I could get any info I wanted out of the courthouse records—births, deaths, dates, all that kind of stuff—but then I heard the darned annex that contained all that stuff had burned down. So you're just about my only hope, you see? As to the Anasazi—"

Somebody else entered the room. Webster turned to see who. Another man about Joseph's age came ponderously in from the hallway. He had a slack expression and dull eyes.

He looked down at Webster. "Hullo."

"This is my brother Luther," Joseph said, his lip curling with distaste.

Webster jumped up and extended his hand. Possibly this brother could be an ally. "Why, hello, Luther! It's very nice to meet you!"

"Luther is not all there," the older woman murmured.

Luther's face twisted. "That's not so, Aggie. I have these spells, but that's all. I'm as good as anybody."

"Sure you are," Joseph said, rising. "All right, mister. You've had your say. Now leave."

"I sure would like to have a better visit," Webster protested, but the larger man was already moving toward him, propelling him toward the hallway.

Luther, the evidently slower brother, followed him. "Ain't nobody needs to know any of our business," he said without intonation. "Anything any of us ever did, we had good reason. Ain't nobody else's—"

"Shut up, Luther," Joseph said pleasantly.

Webster let them escort him to the door, the dogs swarming all around as before. He said something friendly and inane on the porch, and hurried to his car. As he neared it, the dogs seemed to get the idea they were repelling him. One of them snapped at his hand. He got inside the truck and started the engine, backing around. The old man and woman and two bulky sons stood clustered at the doorway, watching without sign of feeling of any kind.

Webster shuddered. These people were extremely, extremely weird.

Driving back down through the woods and across the pasture and the pipe cattle guard, however, he began to feel calmer. Maybe, he thought, they were just going to be assholes and not tell him the old family stuff Uncle Jack so badly wanted. Well and good. But as to checking out the burial mounds on their property . . . well, if the Utes down south gave him a hard time, these were the only other mounds available. And he did not intend to go home without checking some of them.

There was more than one way to skin a cat, as Dad used to say.

Whatever that meant.

11

JOHNNIE BAKER SPENT Tuesday morning, the day after the body of Billy Kickingbird had been found, back in Big
Gully. She interviewed residents who had known him, but she
didn't get very far.

Even though the locals' notorious reticence made most of
the interviews dismayingly short, it took until past the noon hour
to touch base with everyone. To her surprise, George Bonfire
pitched in energetically, locating some of the victim's friends
out in the countryside, but he reported nothing helpful either.

Two state crime investigators went through the ransacked
house trailer but didn't uncover anything of obvious usefulness.
Running the office back at the courthouse, Butt Peabody told
her on the telephone that he had confirmed Kickingbird's temporary job in Denver, which had ended three days earlier; the
work, helping repair a TV station's tower, had been entirely
legitimate.

"He operated this car salvage and junk business here,"
Johnnie told the dour Bonfire when they met at the Kickingbird
place after the lunch hour.

"So?"

"The man from Alamosa we found with the arrow in his neck was a junk dealer down there."

"So?" he repeated.

"Their deaths have to be related in some way."

"How?"

She studied Bonfire's dark, expressionless face. "I thought you might have an idea. Is there *anything* that this man might have been involved in that you can think of—"

"No." Bonfire paused and spat. "But then, I'm just a dumb Indian."

"You can just cut that shit out," she snapped.

He looked down at his muddy boots. "You're right. That was not a good thing to say."

"I'm going back to town. Keep an eye on this place as best you can. We don't want anyone scavenging around. If anything comes up, call. If I need you for something, you have the beeper I brought this morning. Please keep it with you all the time."

Bonfire nodded in silence. He seemed bemused, unsure whether to say something positive or show his usual cynicism.

Heading up the winding dirt road out of Big Gully, Johnnie checked in with the courthouse by radio. Jason Ramsey returned her call. Butt Peabody had gone out to join the highway patrol working an auto accident on Anvil Mountain Road. He seemed to be out of the car at the moment, because she could not raise him directly.

The death of Kickingbird had given her another restless, headachy night. The damned annex fire—certainly arson—and the resulting death of old Amos Pinkstaff. Then the Alamosa guy, Tomlinson. Now Kickingbird. *What was going on?* Bizarre scenarios spun through her mind, but nothing added up. There was a pattern here. She felt it with increasing certainty. If she was just smart enough, she thought, she ought to be able to see it—make an instinctive leap of some kind, come up with a great Perry Mason web of guesswork that could make it all make sense. But all she felt was confusion and mounting desperation.

Driving north, she came to the road that led east toward Chambers Pond, where the crazy galoot from Oklahoma, Noah Webster, had said he was camping. She wondered if he was still out there. It would be just like him, she thought, to go look up the Herman family despite her warnings. And maybe—the thought lanced into her mind without warning—it might just be possible that he was not the eccentric innocent he pretended to be; he was here, and bad things were happening, and what if he was involved in a more sinister way than his eccentric behavior had suggested?

She had time. She decided to take a quick detour to see what he might be up to.

The drive east did not take long. Following the back road, she approached Chambers Pond, an isolated little lake in the piney woods that few people frequented because the fishing there was no good, and the earth was too rocky and barren for comfortable camping.

Driving through scattered litter—paper bags, fast-food wrappers, and beer cans—scattered by kids out for joyrides, she neared the lake. It looked as desolate, rocky, and unattractive as she remembered it. Scrubby pine, mostly blighted lodgepoles, rimmed the colorless water. Irregular rock mounds on the far side from the dirt road looked like cancerous eruptions.

She found Webster's campsite not far off the dirt road, under a canopy of browning trees: a small dome tent, along with other things he had foolishly left out for the taking of any thieves: a Coleman stove, an ice chest, and a carton of canned goods. But there was no sign of him or his camper.

Turning around, she drove back up the rutted dirt road to the paved highway. There, remembering that Butt Peabody had been working an accident farther out, she waited at the stop sign and reached for her mike. "Unit two, this is unit one, over."

After a slight delay, his gravel voice came back: "One, this is two, go ahead."

"Ten-twenty?"

"Alameda and Crocker, headed in."

"Ten-four." She started to hang up the microphone, but another voice—Jason Ramsey, in the courthouse basement—came back: "Unit one, headquarters."

"Base, this is one, go ahead."

"Ten-twenty?"

"Chambers Pond Road and Seventy-four, over."

"One, be advised, um, you are wanted urgently at headquarters."

She frowned. "Advise nature of call, over?"

There followed what seemed like a long pause, then Ramsey's voice again: "Negative, one."

Ramsey was not going to say anything over the radio, where all the scanners could pick it up.

"Ten-four," she said, and put the microphone on the hook. Pulling out onto the pavement, she pressed heavily on the accelerator, headed for town.

PERHAPS NO ONE had ever seen County Commissioner Carl Rieger quite this enraged. His face had no color whatsoever, and the pudgy fists he clenched on the walnut table trembled. Beside him in the commissioner's meeting room, fellow commissioner Madison Blithe stared at Johnnie with icy, unmasked hostility.

"You don't deny it, then?" Rieger demanded, his voice shaky with anger.

Johnnie, still out of breath from arriving at the courthouse and being ushered up to the meeting room by the two livid commissioners, tried to look and sound calm. "No, because it's true."

"You deputized that malcontent, Bonfire?"

"We're desperate for additional help. He's to serve without pay—"

Rieger's little fist hammered on the tabletop. "Goddammit, woman! You can't do something like that without consultation with the board of county commissioners!"

Johnnie knew he was wrong about that. As long as expenditure of county funds was not directly involved, the law allowed her to name as many special deputies as she wished. But she had never done it before. As far as she was aware, except for a few meaningless public relations deputizings of local businessmen in years past, no one had ever done it.

She had expected hostility. But their reaction was far more violent than that.

She said carefully, "Big Gully has been asking for law enforcement assistance for some time. George Bonfire is respected—"

"George Bonfire is known to the entire white community as a radical! He led the demonstrations for better school bus service just last year. When they had the Native American rally at Red Mountain two years ago, he was the main speaker, the one who called for cancellation of the old treaties and return of ten thousand acres to the Utes. He was involved in that big class-action lawsuit against the Herman family—the one that brought us so much bad publicity before the family settled a few years back. He and that old man, Wakinokiman, spread nothing but discontent and disrespect for proper authority."

Madison Blithe, splotches of pink on his normally bland cheeks, put in, "Publicity of this kind does nothing but encourage the growing perception that crime is out of control in the Tenoclock Valley."

"We've been trying for over a year to get approval for development of a new condominium village and golf facility in the south end," Rieger went on, drumming fingertips. "Bonfire and his ilk are the very ones rallying the malcontents, organizing opposition behind the scenes, convincing some of those local landowners to refuse to sell their land—at fine prices, I might add—holding up everything! And then you *reward* that kind of obstructionism with an honorary deputy sheriff's badge!"

Ah, so. "I wasn't aware that Mr. Bonfire was obstructing a county project—"

"It isn't a county project, and you know it! Don't get smart with us, Johnnie. You're in enough trouble already."

Blithe added, "We won't have it. We can't allow it. It's out of the question."

"What are you asking me to do, then?"

"Take it back," Rieger snapped. "Immediately."

"Take it back? I can't—"

"Take it back? Take it back. You deputized him, you can *un*deputize him. At once!"

She felt sweat rill down between her shoulder blades. "I can't do that."

"Why?"

"For one thing, we need him down there. We've just had a murder. They've had a rash of home break-ins. They deserve some help! Deputizing Bonfire is the only way I have of providing it. And for another thing, if I take back his badge now, it only makes matters far worse down there—makes a lot more people mad, makes us look stupid."

Rieger leaned forward, and there was an ugly hostility in his eyes that she had never seen before. "You will revoke the appointment. Now."

Dismayed, Johnnie spread her hands. "Carl—I can't! I told you that."

Blithe said, "We appointed you. You can be recalled."

She felt cold in her belly. Only stubbornness kept her from caving in. "You have to have cause."

"Incompetence," Rieger said, tight-lipped. "The annex fire,

unsolved. The murders, unsolved. Naming Butt Peabody a deputy last year was bad enough. But *this*—this proves total ineptitude on your part."

Johnnie was shaking inside now. She fought to hang on. "If you recall me now, it will result in the one thing the two of you can't abide: bad publicity for the county—the kind that could stop tourist and celebrity housing development for months, if not years."

Rieger's round face went rigid with surprise. The large, empty meeting room became so silent that the sounds of distant voices—clerks or customers on the floor below—penetrated the thick building partitions. Johnnie realized that she had struck at their greatest fear, the only thing that might stop them from taking extreme action against her right away.

"The new Vail," *Time* magazine had called Tenoclock not so long ago. The carefully orchestrated and only marginally legal development projects of the county and town had resulted in a growing influx of celebrities seeking winter play-homes and a tidal growth of simpler tourists eager to share a bit of the glitter as best they might. From the wording of tax-supported road and airport projects to control of Niles Pennington and his *Frontiersman*, nothing had been allowed to blight the meticulously crafted image of Tenoclock as a little paradise—clean, honest, beautiful, without the stain of serious crime. Johnnie's appointment had been part of the general PR effort, although she had not realized it at the time—the appointment of a pretty former actress and model, a hometown girl come back, as proof positive that Tenoclock was just as colorful and sweet as its image-makers portrayed it. And crime-free, as proved by the fact that it could appoint such a chief law enforcement officer.

Seeing that she had stumbled onto her own best defense tactic, Johnnie pressed: "Is that what you want? A blot on our image? Your little lady sheriff fired because Tenoclock is having a crime wave?"

"We're having no such thing," Blithe said in a choked tone.

"But isn't that the basis on which you'll recall me?"

"Now, now," Rieger muttered, his hands shaking. "All you have to do is take back the Bonfire appointment. We can wait awhile on everything else, if we must."

"I can't take it back," Johnnie told him.

The little man's face stiffened, and the rage narrowed his eyes again. "If the sheriff's department fails to cooperate, the commissioners will call a special election for the post, in conjunction with the July bond election, as we had been contemplating anyway."

Quiet and chill, Blithe put in nastily, "No suggestion of discontent with your work, Johnnie. A special election to verify our appointment procedures of last year and give you a full four-year term."

Suddenly Rieger broke out in a smile. "But you will never be elected, missy. We can see to that."

Johnnie felt hot tears of frustration just behind her eyes. She fought them—damned if she would give these people *that* satisfaction. "I won't give in on George Bonfire. I need him down there."

"We'll meet without delay to consider this matter in public hearing."

Johnnie clung to a straw. "Earle Fisch isn't here. He's a fair old man."

Blithe's lip curled. "That senile bastard? He'll do whatever we tell him to."

"If you do this, I'll run hard. I'll get elected on my own. I swear I will."

Rieger got to his feet and hooked his thumbs into the western-style leather belt stretched across his ample belly. "Solve the annex fire, Johnnie. Get a conviction on that, and clear Pinkstaff's death. Find out who killed that man from Alamosa, too, and why. Oh, and solve this latest killing down there in Big Gully, also, while you're at it. If you do that, maybe you'll have a chance."

Madison Blithe's lips quirked with undisguised contempt. He had mostly hidden his dislike for her ever since she had parried his not-so-subtle passes six months ago. But it was all in the open now, and virulent. "I think Carl is right, little girl. Unless you do all that, maybe you'd better plan to go back to your Hollywood tap dancing, or whatever you did out there, because your little ass is going to be grapes in the Tenoclock Valley after we get done with you in that July election."

BUTT PEABODY'S BIG hands formed thick fists. "I'll just go up there and beat the shit out of them."

"Yeah, that will do a lot of good, Butt," Johnnie said wearily. "Son of a bitch bastards."

It was late in the afternoon, but they had just sat down in a booth at the Pick & Shovel for a long-deferred lunch. Peabody had looked sharply at her and asked what had gone wrong now, and she had blurted it out to him. At this hour only a few patrons were scattered around the old-fashioned lunchroom, and Peabody's voice had been raised enough in anger to draw curious glances from all of them.

"Cool it, Butt," Johnnie urged quietly now. "There's nothing we can do about it. All we can do is just keep on with our work, and try to get something accomplished for a change."

Peabody's face had turned the color of tomato soup. "The sonsabitches. It's like the campaign they engineered against me way back, after I enforced some county zoning regulations they wanted ignored. They'll eat your lunch, Johnnie." He stared at her, and the pain on his weather-beaten face made him look a decade older. "They'll kill you. You don't know how shitty they can be. You really don't. There'll be anonymous leaflets making you out to be a whore. There'll be ads listing every penny-ante little unsolved crime in this county for the last ten years. Remember how nasty it got when you caught Dave Dickensen, and half the businessmen in town wanted it hushed up so the town wouldn't look bad? There'll be racist crap. They'll drag out those old pictures of you when you posed in swimsuits for that movie you was in. They'll make it impossible for you to ever live around here again. They *will*. Believe me. I know."

Johnnie's insides fluttered again, but she clung to her self-control. "Butt, there's nothing we can do, I tell you!"

He glowered. "You could beat them to it."

"How?"

"Quit."

"No!"

Across the room, the wall telephone behind the counter rang. Mabel Murnan hustled out of the kitchen and answered it. She listened, then turned to look across the room. "Johnnie? Your office."

Johnnie got up and went across to the counter. Mabel Murnan stretched the cord to hand her the telephone. "This is Johnnie."

"Johnnie, Jason here," the voice drawled. "There's a man here from the sheriff's department in Alamosa. He says he needs to talk to you."

The corpse of Tomlinson, the Alamosa junkman, on the highway with the antique arrow protruding from his throat. "My God, does this guy know something?"

Jason Ramsey lapsed into his bogus shufflin' Mose accent. "Dunno, ma'am, I sho don't. He woul'n't say nothin' to the likes of me."

"Jason," she snapped affectionately, "you're being an asshole again. Tell him I'll be right there."

12

WITH BUTT PEABODY at her side, Johnnie pulled open the rusty security door leading into the courthouse from the back parking area, hurried down the filthy metal stairs to the basement, and pushed open the damp-warped double doors leading into her department.

The near end of the long, concrete-floored room was vacant. At the far end, her office was as heavily manned as it ever was: lean, gray-haired Jason Ramsey behind the counter facing the side door, his chocolate face sober as he worried a pencil over one of his jail records spread before him; secretary Hesther Gretsch scowling as her bony fingers stabbed at the keyboard of the department's only computer, an early-1980s-vintage Intertec Superbrain (64K of RAM, two floppy disks); Deputy Billy Higginbotham sitting in front of a dark gray Underwood manual typewriter at another desk, his florid middle-aged face a mass of puzzled wrinkles as he searched for and then found the key he was looking for, punching it with his index finger to send a single letter key on its way up toward the report form sticking out from behind the platen; Deputy Dean Epperly standing at the mirror on the front wall, handsome as a young Robert Red-ford in his gray uniform, carefully recombing his hair. Hail, hail, the gang was all here. But no sign of the man from Alamosa.

Turning to see their approach, Ramsey left the counter and walked back to meet them. He walked with a slight limp, courtesy of a war injury eons earlier, but since no strangers were in sight he did not put on any part of his dumb darkie act. It would have been wasted; all the regulars were quite aware of his multiple college degrees and current hobby of translating classic Greek manuscripts.

Johnnie didn't waste time on preamble. "Where is he?"

"He asked to read our incident reports on Mr. Tomlinson," Ramsey said in his real voice, chill with precision. "As they're public record, I had no choice and saw no problem with it anyway. I put him back in my jail area office with them in order to prevent interruption during his perusal."

Peabody muttered, "Sounds like he might be onto something, if he wants to see the originals."

Johnnie turned toward the back of the room again. "Let's go find out."

She led the way back to the rear area again, this time turning into a narrow concrete bunker of a vestibule that led to another metal door, this one with the simple word Jail painted on it. Peabody trailing her, she opened the door and went in.

The jail office was a windowless room, all concrete and barren, about twelve feet square. Another of the army-surplus metal desks, a couple of straight chairs, and a battered brown file cabinet comprised the furniture. Sitting at the chair behind Ramsey's desk, the deputy from Alamosa looked up from the manila folder of report forms he had been studying, a pencil and notebook beside him. He was a thin man, thirtyish, with red hair that tumbled in curls onto the shoulders of his western-cut shirt. A handlebar mustache, string tie, and large turquoise ring on his right hand completed the cowboy getup. His close-set eyes matched his ring.

"Sheriff Baker?" he asked, getting to his feet and extending a hand. "Purser Welles. Undersheriff, Alamosa County." He was well over six feet tall.

Johnnie shook hands with him and introduced Peabody. "I see you're looking over our incident reports and follow-up investigation file on the Tomlinson case."

Welles's long mustache twitched. "Yes." He gestured at the other chairs as if he owned the place. "Please be seated."

She exchanged looks with Peabody. "Thanks," she said with heavy irony, seating herself. "So what's going on? You have new information of some kind that might help us?"

Welles spread immaculate, capably large hands on the opened file folder. "Explosives."

"I beg your pardon?"

His red eyebrows tightened. "Further search of subject Tomlinson's business records and personal accounts indicate in-shipment and subsequent out-shipment or delivery of an undetermined amount of explosive material, i.e., dynamite."

"How does that relate to us?"

Welles's curly locks moved on his shoulders as he turned briskly to flip over pages in his notebook. "Gasoline credit card purchase records indicate subject Tomlinson purchased fourteen-point-eight gallons of unleaded gasoline at the Highline Conoco on State Sixteen on four-seven of this year."

"Just this month," Johnnie said.

"Roger." Welles traced a long fingertip down a page of his notes. "However, subject was back in Alamosa, as reflected by eyewitness testimony as well as a bank deposit slip and other business records, on four-ten."

Johnnie waited again, irked that she seemed to be drawing blanks. Beside her, Butt Peabody stirred. "Meaning," he growled, "that Tomlinson came up here on or around the seventh, was back in Alamosa three days later, and then had to have made a second trip up in order to be around to be murdered on the fifteenth."

Welles's large teeth clicked together. "Precisely."

"Which means what?" Johnnie demanded.

Welles seemed to ignore her, turning pages of his notebook. "Subject purchased one split box of highway construction dynamite, with caps and necessary detonation device material, from a construction supervisor's assistant, working on the Wolf Creek Pass project, on or about four-four. This illegal transaction has been verified by apprehension and interrogation of subject supervisor, with subsequent confession."

The Alamosa man paused and looked up from his notes, his eyes snapping. "My department believes subject Tomlinson procured said explosive materials for a person or persons unknown in Tenoclock County, delivering same on or about the date of his first-verified visit, that being on four-seven of this year."

"Proof?" Butt Peabody grunted.

"Subject's bank deposit, made on four-ten after return from this area, was for cash, in the sum of one thousand dollars. No record exists of any other major transaction made by subject Tomlinson in that period of time . . . no other likely source of such an amount in cash. Immediately following this deposit, subject gave a car dealer in Alamosa a deposit check for the same amount, along with a signed promise to pay an additional two thousand within seven days as deposit on a 1993 half-ton pickup."

Welles paused, then went on. "We believe one or more persons in the Tenoclock Valley procured said illegal explosives from Tomlinson on four-seven or four-eight. We believe Tomlinson then returned to this area on or about the fifteenth, at which time he was murdered because—*a*—he failed to deliver additional explosives or—*b*—he fell into a dispute about further payments or—*c*—persons unknown decided he posed a danger of revealing their part in the transaction or—*d*—he returned for reasons unknown and was killed for another motive not yet identified."

Johnnie sighed. "I'm glad it's all so clear."

Welles blinked. "Beg pardon?"

"Nothing. Okay. Let's assume you're right. Tomlinson came up here to sell somebody some dynamite illegally. He went back to Alamosa and banked the cash payment. Then he came back up here a few days later and was murdered for *some* reason having to do with the earlier transaction. Where does that leave us? What can we do at this end to carry forward on the basis of this new information?"

"I've examined your reports," Welles replied, frowning. "We had hoped there might be something in your files indicating that subject Tomlinson had on his person some clue as to who he was dealing with here."

"There wasn't anything like that. Any local contact would have been followed up on long before this."

"Unfortunately, yes. All right, Sheriff Baker. We intend to continue going over all Tomlinson's records and files again at our end. I suggest you continue your investigation locally in search of any person or persons who might have use for explosives, almost certainly for an illicit purpose. Knowing the subject made an earlier visit to Tenoclock than previously suspected, you may wish to question employees at the service station we have identified, et cetera. Further, with your permission, I will canvass construction sites in the area and attempt to glean information about possible talk of some usage of explosives not obtained through normal channels."

Johnnie stood. The new information was interesting and troubling at the same time. She couldn't see how it really helped. "We'll discuss all this and of course cooperate in every way possible."

Welles closed his notebook and the investigation folder, handing it across the table as he got to his feet again. "Thank you. I'll maintain close liaison." He shook hands and walked briskly out of the room.

Left standing there beside Butt Peabody, Johnnie looked at the thick folder in her hands. "Well," she said finally.

Peabody awkwardly patted her shoulder. "That was good," he said gruffly.

"What was?"

"Not saying anything more."

She stared, trying to read his weathered face. "Anything more about *what?*"

"You mean you didn't pick up on the dates?"

"Of what, exactly?"

Peabody's eyes narrowed. "This Tomlinson feller first came up here on the sixth or seventh."

"Right . . ."

"Do you remember everything that happened, when all this shit started hitting the fan?"

She was totally at a loss. "The lion?"

"Yeah. And then?"

"The fire."

"Yeah. And then?"

"Tomlinson."

"No."

"What?"

"You forgot one."

"What? —Oh! When we had those calls from people saying they felt an earthquake?"

Peabody's eyelids drooped as if too heavy. "Yeah. We figured that was what it was, a little tremor they didn't pick up in Denver. Which was weird at the time, but we didn't have time to worry about it."

"But maybe it wasn't a natural tremor," Johnnie said, seeing it now.

Peabody nodded. "I think it must have been an explosion. Tomlinson's dynamite."

————

JOHNNIE STOOD VERY still a moment, and she was aware of the pulse in her own ears. She felt a small tingling along her spine, the kind she sometimes got when she sensed someone was watching her . . . or she might be very, very close to an insight that was important.

"But you drove all around that end of the county, Butt," she protested finally. "You didn't find a damned thing."

"Right," he said heavily. "I drove the back roads and asked a lot of people. Some felt it, some slept through it and didn't feel a thing. But I didn't find any damage of any kind—no big slides, no bridges out, no roads damaged. No reports of houses hurt or anything, either. So we blew it off."

"Blew it off," Johnnie said, smiling humorlessly. "That's a funny way to put it, if what some people felt was Tomlinson's dynamite being shot off somewhere."

Peabody grunted again but said nothing.

"Maybe we need to do a lot more looking out west and south," Johnnie said, thinking out loud.

"There's thousands of square miles out there, Johnnie. Some of it in the higher elevations, nobody has been over it for decades—maybe never. You remember the air force plane?"

She nodded silently, seeing his point. Only four years earlier, mountain hikers had stumbled upon the wreckage of a small air force fighter that had nosed in vertically into a heavily wooded crevice well above the fourteen-thousand-foot level. Military experts had been called in, and identified the wreckage as the remains of a plane lost in June of 1964.

"We could search forever," she said.

"All right. What *can* we do, then?"

His forehead furrowed even more deeply. "Talk to the guys out at that gas station. Take our pictures of Tomlinson and his truck. See if they might remember something. Go back around where I went before and see if we can jar anything else out of people who felt the earth shake that night."

"Go back and search all of the records and personal things belonging to Billy Kickingbird, down there in Big Gully," Johnnie added.

Peabody nodded, and they looked at each other. Neither of them had to point out the obvious. Tomlinson had been a junkman, and he was dead; Kickingbird had been a junkman, and he was dead too. It could be a mistake during any investigation to attribute cause-and-effect relationships to facts that might be related only by coincidence. But Tomlinson and Kickingbird might have known each other. Sometimes junk dealers exchanged salvage items or sold materials to one another. Their murders might link. The possibility might open the way to new theories about things happening here . . . if one were just smart enough to come up with the theories.

13

NOAH WEBSTER WOKE up at dawn Wednesday to the
sound of something light but persistent sifting against the thin
plastic walls of his tent. Rolling over in his sleeping bag, he
realized it was a lot colder. He stretched out to unzip the front
tent flap a few inches, raised it, and peered outside, getting a
gust of chill air in his face.

First silver light of day made trees and brush nearby indistinct. A light, steady shower of fine white snowflakes obscured
all view of the lake. The ground was covered with about an inch
of the powder.

"Neat!" Webster muttered, sitting up. Then he reconsidered. "Shit!" Then he reconsidered again. "Okay, no prob."

He wrestled around inside the sleeping bag, pulling on his
jeans and a heavy flannel shirt retrieved from the duffel sand-
wiched in between himself and the bulging tent wall. He had
known the weather could change drastically in the Colorado
mountains, especially at this time of year. Still, the contrast
between yesterday's clear, mild weather and this sudden snow
perturbed him. He had been planning to go out and check out
some of the burial mounds down southwest today. The snow

would make it uncomfortable. Well, too bad. He would go any-how. He had to be back in Oklahoma late next week to get ready for the trip to Dallas and the archaeology conference; he couldn't mess around waiting, just because of an inch or two of snow.

After lacing up his boots and pulling an OU Sooners stock-ing cap down over his ears, Webster crawled out, getting his knees covered with the dry powder snow in the process. As usual he saw no one else around. He had sort of hoped for some deer, or maybe even a bear, if he got lucky. But Chambers Pond seemed to be such a blighted and neglected area that all it grew were periodic outbreaks of fresh beer cans tossed by high school boys with too much money and too much use of Dad's pickup.

Well, fine on that, too. This was it for Chambers Pond on this trip, as far as he was concerned. He intended to camp somewhere else from now on—not stay out here any longer and raise suspicions that maybe he had stumbled onto something when in fact maybe he had. The highway map showed a public campground west of here several miles, much nearer the moun-tains and possibly in the foothills, quite close to where his notes said some of the big burial mounds were located. A lot more convenient all around.

Humming "Winter Wonderland," he pumped up the Cole-man stove and got it going, then poured water out of the big thermos into a small aluminum pan. Instant coffee went into one cup, a package of oatmeal into the other. Some sugar into both. While waiting for the water to boil, he rolled up his sleeping bag and pad, knocked the tent down, and stowed it all in the back of his pickup. Dragging out his heavy canvas coat, he returned to his stove and poured the coffee and oatmeal water, carried the two cups over to the ice chest, and sat down to enjoy break-fast. The snow sifted down against his face, and some got down the neck of his coat and shirt. He shivered.

Signs that the small mounds around the lake might contain

valuable native American artifacts—an almost sure sign of burial rituals—tempted Webster mightily to forget the big burial mounds that had been his primary motivation for coming here. But he felt confident the small mounds could wait; they had waited a hell of a long time already. And he still wanted badly to see the big mounds . . . look for any possible sign that they might actually betoken Anasazi forebears.

He knew the mounds had been superficially checked out in times past, and that researchers then had proclaimed them historically interesting but not especially significant. But he had done a lot of computer analysis of Anasazi art and crafts in the last three years, and his data modeling provided analytical clues to the Anasazi that nobody else had ever had.

Webster could have published these, he believed, and made something of a name for himself on that basis alone. But if he could find even a single significantly marked pottery shard in these big mounds—and his computer models confirmed early Anasazi influence—he would make a hell of a lot more than a couple of obscure scholarly journals. Man, he could make *Smithsonian*. He could make *Newsweek*—maybe even that TV show with Jane Pauley or Stone Phillips or somebody like that.

Then what would pissant Gertrude think, after throwing him out of the house and divorcing his butt because she said his research was stupid and made her a "lab widow" instead of an appreciated wife?

Oh boy, oh boy. Locals might not like him poking around the mounds some, and the snowy day might make things a little uncomfortable, but look at all he had to gain, and sweet exoneration too.

The oatmeal and coffee gone, he finished breaking camp and packing the pickup. Before closing the back of the camper shell, he dug into the ice chest one more time and got out a nice cold Coors and a plastic bag with three Snickers bars remaining in it. He got into the truck cab, adjusted his seat belt, started the engine, and sipped the beer and ate one of the Snickers while waiting for the defroster to get going and help the wipers clear the light snow off the windshield. After a few minutes, with the snow melting nicely on the glass, he shoved his remaining two candy bars into his coat pocket, perched the beer can on the edge of the dash, and put the truck in gear, easing away from the campsite.

About forty minutes later, after a stop at a convenience store to reprovision the ice chest with a few staples such as bologna and cheese, he trundled slowly into the service station that formed the center of the community of Big Gully. The lights were on inside the station, but the front door was shut. He parked at the side, hurried to the front, and pushed into the station office.

It was nice and warm inside, a small wood stove aglow in one corner. Behind an old-fashioned oak-and-glass display cabinet, two young men sat smoking cigarettes and drinking coffee. Both were dark-skinned, obviously Native Americans, and neither looked particularly friendly. Actually, they didn't look anything at all; they just stared silently at Webster with no expression whatsoever.

"Hi, there!" he said. "My name's Webster. I'm a scientist on a research project. I wonder if you gentlemen can help me?"

They looked at him and then at each other and then back at him again. Silence.

Webster chuckled, being real cool and friendly and nice, he thought. "Here's the deal. There are some ancient burial mounds out west of here a ways. I have them located on this map, see, and I figure this road goes right out that way, and from what I can tell, some of them at least are on state land, along the river where it runs under the cliffs. What I would like to do is just drive out there and take a few pictures—nothing disturbing, nothing disrespectful, I assure you. You see, as you know—I mean, Native American culture has been treated disrespectfully far too often in the past, right? So I can assure anyone that my intentions are strictly scholarly, and I would be the last person in the world to disturb anything. So am I right? Is this the road that will take me out there?"

The slightly taller Indian reached forward to put out his cigarette in a shallow aluminum ashtray. The other one sipped his coffee.

Webster giggled. He was starting to get a bit unnerved by their silence. "I have credentials, of course, and if there's some local authority—a tribal councilman or somebody—I ought to visit with before going out, I would be glad to do that. I don't want to step on anybody's toes—"

"No mounds," the shorter man said.

"What?"

"Them mounds are miles and miles from here, man. There ain't no mounds around this area."

"You been sold a bill of shit," the other one said.

"I was pretty convinced—"

"No."

"Um. I see." Webster did not see at all. "The mounds are miles away, you say?"

"Thataway. Down beyond Archer."

"Archer?"

The taller man spoke again. "Any Indian cultural things near here are closed to the public. All on private land. No trespassing."

"I see," Webster said, dazed. "There isn't anything nearby. But if there is, it's no trespassing."

Both of them stared at him in silence again.

"Well. I guess I came out this way for nothing."

Silent appraisal.

"I sure got the wrong information, eh?"

Silence.

"I see. Well. Thanks, guys. I really appreciate it."

Nothing.

Back in his truck, Webster got the windshield wipers going again and backed out of the parking place beside the station building. He pulled up past the pumps and out to the snowy ramp leading to the narrow road. He could *feel* them watching from inside. Waiting for him to turn left and head back the way he had come.

He felt irked and stubborn and confused. But mostly he felt determined. If these people thought they could intimidate a legitimate scientist and prevent qualified site inspection through some kind of stupid silent act, they were mightily mistaken. Hell, he had been through faculty meetings scarier than their little performance; lots of them, in fact.

He turned right, heading out the way he had intended to go in the first place, toward where the mounds were supposed to be.

TWENTY MINUTES LATER, after winding down through a willowy creek bottom and becoming a narrow, sandy single-lane path through weeds and trees, the road simply stopped altogether at the foot of a sheer rock cliff overlooking scattered fires and pines. A narrow brook, water black as carbon paper against the pure white snow, burbled along just in front of Webster's front wheels.

Sighing with irritation, he cut the ignition, set the emergency brake, slung his Canon around his neck, and popped the truck door, stepping down into almost two inches of fresh snow.

The road, long since a pasture path at best, had descended a few hundred feet in the last mile to reach this level. The rock cliffs, perhaps eighty feet tall, formed a solid, meandering wall blocking further progress beyond the little brook. On Webster's other three sides the terrain under its light snow cover resembled river-bottom grassland, this area open at least a hundred yards right and left, to humpy ground near the water over there

. . . and over there . . . where stands of lodgepole and young firs competed with snow-shrouded young aspen in an attempt to reforest the openness. It was still, eerily so, the only sound being the murmur of icy water over rocks nearby. The sky seemed lower here and looked like old smoke.

Webster was considerably discouraged. He had been on the wrong road all the time, he thought, and the damned guys at the gas station had let him ramble on out here, knowing he would come up nowhere, with nothing. Now he would have to turn around and go halfway back to town and take the side road south that he had passed.

As he stood beside his truck thinking this, the sky suddenly lightened a bit, and the clouds changed color to a sort of pale lemon. The snow eased off and almost stopped. The lemon color came from the sun trying to break through, of course, Webster realized, and that signaled a possible great improvement in the weather. Neat! He dug out a Marlboro and allowed himself his first smoke of the day.

While he was standing there, enjoying the tobacco, the sky got even brighter. The light became more golden, bathing the snowfield in the most beautiful hue. With the blackness of pines in the background and snowy aspens drooping, and the meandering ribbon of the creek, the scene around him struck him as singularly beautiful. Suddenly fired up again, he removed the lens cap from his Canon and carefully composed a half-dozen pictures. Then, seeing how his pickup sitting here might make an interesting shot from the far end of the clearing, he hiked along the creek bank to the south, hurrying along and kicking up little clouds of snow with his boots, moving slightly uphill toward the tree line.

Nearing the first and youngest aspen, he skirted a clump of them and climbed up on the front edge of a long, irregular earthen embankment only about thirty feet from the creek's flowing water. Turning, he moved around and squatted down to put some of the snowy aspen in the foreground of his viewfinder, with a long look back downhill toward the open field and the snow in its golden light, and his pickup sitting out there, looking abandoned and forlorn.

It made a neat shot.

Replacing his lens cap and feeling somewhat better because he had at least gotten some pix, Webster turned to retrace his steps. He saw that he had climbed a steeper embankment than he had realized in order to get here. As a matter of fact, he was standing on the side of a hillock perhaps forty feet long and almost as wide, judging by the way it rose further behind him, here, covered with snowy brush, and the sides formed smooth curvatures—

Jesus Christ.

Suddenly out of breath with excitement, he took a new look around. Through a rent in the pines he saw a gentle declivity on the far side of this rise, a weed-choked bottom, and then the unmistakable curvature of still another hill.

Or mound.

Turning to his right, or south, to look along the creek where it meandered farther away, he saw another one—a bigger one—down there, more in the open. And beyond it, two—no, *three!*—smaller ones back nearer the trees.

He might have missed all of them if he had not walked up here. He might have missed them even from here if the curious lemon-colored sky light did not invest the world at this moment with a strange contrast and clarity, almost like that provided by polarized goggles.

He was standing right on the edge of a whole goddam cluster of burial mounds.

WHEN HE REACHED the pickup again, he was badly out of breath from haste and excitement. By the time he got back to his previous vantage point, he was huffing like a wounded bear. This time he had with him his lightweight two-hundred-foot measuring reel, a couple of thin metal tent stakes, pencils and graph paper on a clipboard, and his other camera. Bunched up over the bottom edge of his coat and sticking out of his belt like a pirate's sword, he also had his prober—a four-foot length of flexible stainless steel CB antenna with electrician's tape wrapped thickly around one end to form a makeshift handle.

Softly whistling "Happy Days Are Here Again," he hurried around in all directions, popping pictures from various angles. Hunching down in the snow with a young ponderosa pine as a backrest, he roughly sketched in the lay of the land—the creek, the tree lines, and the location and relative size of the mounds. Then he hiked on downstream and took a good look around to make sure there were not more mounds down there.

Returning to a point near his original discovery, he forced himself to sit down and rest. He had gotten shaky from all the dashing around. But this was so neat he could hardly sit still, even allowing himself another Marlboro as incentive.

There were nine burial mounds in this complex. The largest, about one hundred feet long—he hadn't measured it yet—and shaped roughly like a crescent moon, stood farthest to the east, in the trees. Another large one humped up out of the forest floor nearby. Then came the smaller ones—egg-shaped, one as big as a half-buried Quonset hut, the smallest not much larger than a doghouse—strewn in no apparent pattern down very near the water's edge. The complex strongly reminded Webster of the reconstructed moundworks at Chillicothe, Ohio, although he knew their building had been done centuries apart, and by vastly different Indian cultures.

But no one had ever established with absolute certainty precisely where this mound-building culture fit into the general historical picture. With any luck he would soon change that.

Finished smoking, he gathered up his gear and hurried off to his east, heading for one of the smaller mounds at the edge of the reestablishing forest. He put his camera and other things down against a pine trunk and pulled his probe out of his belt, wielding it like an epee while walking quickly around the small mound and examining it from all sides.

It stood possibly four feet tall at its domed center, and five feet in diameter. Standard practice—if such a thing could be said to exist—would have put ceremonial objects nearer the edge of the mound, with the body or bodies closer to its center.

Holding his homemade probe by the taped end, Webster carefully inserted the point into the soft, snowy soil and started to drive it deeper down.

Something made a sharp, nasty whistling noise inches from the side of his head. Then, even as he jerked back in surprise, he registered the loud *thunk!* against the tree behind him. He turned to see what had happened. An arrow vibrated wildly from impact into the pine tree trunk, its steely tip buried a good two inches in the wood.

It was not a traditional Indian arrow, Webster saw. It was the finely tuned product of modern archery hunting technology—black composite shaft, steel jacketing, stiff aerodynamic directional vanes. You could shoot an arrow like this a long distance with great accuracy. You could kill a deer with it. Or an elk. Or a man.

The arrow stopped its impact-trembling in the tree. Webster began trembling about the same time. The thing had missed him no more than six inches.

Baloney, one part of him thought. Just a corny warning.

He looked all around, staring hard out through the scant tree cover in the direction the shot must have come from. Nothing moved. Everything was silent.

He chilled more deeply. I don't care if it was a warning or what it was, he thought. I'm outta here.

He gathered up his gear and staggered back through the snow.

Maybe the arrow had been shot to miss, and only scare him away. Even so, a warning shot—if that was what it had been—could go amiss. Let a puff of wind change the trajectory only slightly, and the arrow would have gone through his skull, no matter what the intention might have been.

In his truck, motor roaring, Webster backed around and headed back the way he had driven in, but at a considerably higher speed. I'm not going to be scared off that easily, he thought bravely.

But possibly it was time to try Plan B.

14

LATE WEDNESDAY MORNING, Butt Peabody drove slowly up Silver Street, returning to the courthouse. The light snowfall had abated by now and the sun was trying to break through. Tenoclock's ordinance-mandated plank sidewalks still glistened wetly, and near Packer's Alley the early-season tourists were out in heavy numbers despite the cold.

In a few more weeks, Peabody thought dismally, the streets would be crowded from one end of town to the other, and they would stay that way into early winter. Then the celebrity flights would get more frequent, bringing in Hollywood's pretty people for the ski season, and things would be still just as messy in the valley, only in a different way.

Peabody hated what "development" had done to the area he had always called home. He did not consider hordes of people, traffic jams, air pollution, increased crime, maddening traffic, and cheap glitz as real progress, no matter how merrily the cash registers rang in the Alley's shops or how many millions were being banked by early-bird real estate developers like Carl Rieger and the town's illustrious mayor.

He recognized that he was in a bad mood because he had

had a particularly frustrating morning. A trip to the gas station and interviews with everybody who worked there had elicited no memory of the murdered Tomlinson on either of his apparent visits up from Alamosa. A three-hour drive out south and west, and repeat calls on landowners who had reported the early-month ground tremor, had gotten him nothing new. Nobody had heard or felt anything further, and no one knew anything about any landslides, building demolitions, or anything else that might be identified as cause of the original commotion.

To make matters even worse, he had talked to Johnnie on the radio, twice. She was down in Big Gully, going through some of the slain Billy Kickingbird's possessions and records yet another time. So far she reported nothing helpful. They were getting nowhere fast. This kind of dogged, slogging investigation irked him at the best of times. When they seemed to be gaining no ground whatsoever, it was even worse.

Pulling into the back parking lot of the courthouse, Peabody saw that a county crew was completing work on raising and reinforcing the stout wooden barricades built all around the ruins of the burned annex next door. Signs had been put up, warning people to stay away. A white panel truck parked nearby identified Swift Demolition Co. of Denver. Peabody wondered if the name was a promise or the name of the company's owner. No matter: the truck signaled that the old walls would be torn down soon, and before long the site would be cleared, all remains of the venerable old building vanished forever, along with the ashes of the priceless records once contained inside.

And they were no closer to finding out who had committed that crime either, he reminded himself.

Parking his truck, he started across the back of the courthouse sidewalk, heading for the basement entry. Before he could reach it, however, it opened, and an unwelcome person—*Frontiersman* owner and editor Niles Pennington—hustled out and headed his way.

"Butt! Just the man I was looking for!"

Peabody stopped in his tracks and reached for the cigarette makings. He kept his face as neutral as possible. There were a few people around whom he disliked more than Pennington; it was just that he usually couldn't bring any of them to mind.

The tall, slender newspaperman was wearing one of his ice-cream-colored western suits, along with a broad white Stetson. A Leica was slung around his neck, and a reporter's notebook stuck out of his side coat pocket. His deep, tanning-booth tan made his teeth blinding white as he treated Peabody to his best grin. "Hello, Butt! Long time no see. You've had a busy time of it, haven't you?"

Peabody started rolling a smoke. "What do you want?"

"I wonder if you have any comment on the special election."

"What special election?"

If there was one thing Pennington was expert at, it was insincerity. He outdid himself with the look of surprise he showed. "Why, the special election called an hour or so ago by the county commissioners. Actually, Butt, it might be a fine thing for Teno-clock County, don't you agree? A positive step. As the commissioners say in their formal resolution, Johnnie has served with distinction, and the county owes it to her to give her the chance to run for election as soon as possible. She's served by appointment, at the pleasure of the commissioners, long enough. She's *earned* the right to be elected on her own merit—"

"When?" Peabody cut in, shoving the cigarette between his lips.

"You mean when did they vote? Just a—"

"When is the goddam election?"

"July seventh. Now, Butt, as a former sheriff and current chief deputy for Sheriff Baker, what is your reaction to the commissioners' action this morning?" Pennington whipped out his notebook and a Cross ballpoint.

"I think it's a wonderful thing," Peabody said, "and it just goes to show what great and enlightened leadership our county commissioners provide for us every day of our lives. Believe you me: we should all fall down on our kneecaps and thank almighty God for men like Carl Rieger. When I pause to consider how great it is, that Sheriff Baker is being given this opportunity to run a reelection campaign during the height of the tourist season, I get tears in my eyes, I really do. It just demonstrates how great this country of ours is, too. My sense of humble pride—"

"All right, Butt," Pennington said sourly. He had started to scribble fast in his notebook, but now his pen had stopped and his eyes sagged with chilly antagonism. "Our town doesn't need that kind of cynicism."

"Oh, right, Niles. Absolutely, man. It wouldn't do for somebody to say or do anything cynical around here."

Splotches of pink appeared in Pennington's cheeks. "What's your problem, anyhow? Can't quite stand it, being a former sheriff yourself, who was defeated fair and square in that election seven years back? Or is it possible you think your little girl might be turned out of office?"

"Hey, asshole, I might answer that question if you'll promise to run the way you just asked the question, verbatim."

"You never did know how to go with the flow and get along here, did you?"

"I notice your fancy Cadillac over there is parked in a deputy's spot. I suggest you move it quick unless you want a ticket."

Pennington turned, face stony with anger. "I know how frightening it must be, facing the possibility that in another three months you'll be off the public tit."

"If she loses."

The thin journalist glanced back with a withering smile of superiority. "Oh, I believe it's safe to assume there will be ample opposition."

Peabody stiffened. "So that's set up already too?"

"Set up? Set up? I have no idea what you mean. However,

I have already heard rumors that Jake Wyse might be interested in filing."

Peabody snorted with surprise. Wyse, once a police chief in Tenoclock, had resigned years ago in the wake of a suppressed scandal involving departmental funds. He was well into his sixties now and ran a service station on Gunnison Avenue. "They'll have to do better than that if they hope to——"

"And Randall Simmons, too. Perhaps."

Peabody froze. The once-chief of the state's highway patrol had resigned in Denver two years ago, at the age of forty-seven, and moved to a home in the Tenoclock Valley for his retirement. His departure from public office had been regretted on all sides. There had never been a breath of scandal during his ten years of rebuilding the state organization into one of the country's finest. It was said he could run for governor if he wished. His popularity, locally as well as statewide, was enormous.

The prospect of Simmons running for Johnnie's job had never entered Peabody's mind. Now the very mention of the possibility made his blood run cold. If Simmons could be cajoled somehow into filing for the office, people like Rieger might not even have to bother with an anonymous smear campaign against Johnnie; she might not have a chance anyhow.

Pennington studied his expression, evidently taking great pleasure in it. "Well, as you pointed out, Butt, I'd better hustle and move my car. Good day to you!" He turned away again and strode confidently toward his red Seville.

Peabody took another drag on his cigarette, tossed it onto the pavement, and walked to the back basement door. Jerking it open, he descended the dank staircase and went into the office.

Dean Epperly, resplendent in his personally purchased uniform, was alone at the front desk. Seeing Peabody enter, he walked eagerly back toward him. "Butt! Have you heard the news? The commissioners——"

"I heard," Peabody snapped, and went over to slouch into his swivel chair behind one of the war-surplus desks.

"Man, isn't that a nice thing for them to do? Johnnie will be—"

"Don't you have a report to work on or something?"

Epperly's handsome face went slack with surprise at Peabody's openly hostile tone. "I've got that thing about the missing cows—"

"Then work on it and shut up."

Aggrieved, Epperly retreated. Peabody grabbed a stack of old reports out of his in basket and hunched over them, not seeing a word.

The bastards, he thought. The crummy bastards.

He was furious out of all proportion to the news, as bad as it was. Hell, he above all people should know what kind of men they were dealing with in the current board of county commissioners. His own job had gone down the tubes when he refused to look the other way from violations of zoning ordinances . . . wouldn't pretend the office was being adequately funded when he knew current staffing and equipment made the county dangerously vulnerable to serious crime. It was not like Niles Pennington had dropped his bombshell on a political virgin, for God's sake.

But this was what he had feared the most for Johnnie ever since she—foolishly, he thought—had taken the sheriff's appointment. Oh, he understood why she had done it. Jim Way was dead; she had been the only deputy who possibly might be able to handle the position of fill-in. She had been born in the Tenoclock Valley, and she loved the place, heaven help her. She had been touched and challenged by the commissioners' appointment offer and had impulsively said yes before realizing they were acting at their most cynical—naming her and publicizing her as a cute young former actress to illustrate to the world that Tenoclock was Fantasyland, harmless, rated G from Red Mountain on the west to Anvil on the east.

She had deserved all the help she could get back then. That—and his devotion to her—had been his reason for accepting the deputy's appointment when she offered it to him. He hadn't wanted it. He still felt the bitterness about what these people had done to him—how it had stung. And he had felt a deep, darkening worry about what the job would do to her idealism and dedication in the long run. But he had wanted to help—even protect her if he could.

Protect her! The thought made his insides cringe now. He had done everything he could, and it wasn't her fault this damned clot of violence and death had come down on the valley, but now he was helpless. Unless they somehow had an incredible stretch of good luck, and actually broke some of these cases—and fast—she was going to go right down the pipes, just as he had years ago. And it would break her heart.

As the prospect was already breaking his.

He had known her parents, loved the both of them. He had watched her as a little girl, and loved her then, as a child, like a fond godparent. He had watched her start to grow up, and loved her then, too, as a leggy, feisty, sometimes irritating little twit of a teenager. And he had watched her come back home for the death of her father, and then her mother, and felt his heart swell with loving her then, too, as a grief-stricken young woman.

Later, since she had come back to make the valley her home again, he had continued to watch, and listen, and make judgments about her. And now he loved her still, but in a way that quietly shocked him with the bittersweet impossibility of it, loving her as a man loved a woman.

She didn't know. He felt sure she didn't have a clue. That was good. It was the way things had to stay. He was old enough to be her father. Hell, he and her father had been high school classmates a hundred years ago. The last thing a beautiful young woman like her needed was complications posed by a lecherous old goat like him. She deserved a young man, a good one who wasn't all stove up physically and loaded up with old rubbishy bitterness, and had fifteen years yet to live, at the most. Nothing good could possibly come from his devotion. So she must never know.

It was the least he could do for her, to keep his yap shut and be careful not to show anything, and just help her all he could, like a grampaw. And it was okay. He could handle it because that was best for her.

But sometimes the feelings really ached, man, deep inside. Still, this was the way it was going to be. You played the hand you were dealt with. That was the way life was.

Peabody realized he was still staring at the pile of reports. He tossed them back into the desk tray and got to his feet.

Seeing him headed for the door, Dean Epperly called after him, "Where now, Butt?"

"See a man," Peabody muttered back over his shoulder, and kept going.

SITTING ON THE dirty floor of Billy Kickingbird's mobile home in the midst of scattered cartons containing old letters, bills, receipts, and miscellaneous papers ranging from grocery lists to ads for government-surplus sales, Johnnie wearily tossed another envelope onto the growing pile of materials she had gone through without result. Her back hurt, and she had missed lunch, and she didn't think she was ever going to get finished. She felt totally futile and inept.

A slight sound in the doorway behind her made her turn her head. George Bonfire was just stepping across the threshold, his face even darker than usual.

"Hey, I'm glad you're back," Johnnie told him. "I can use all the help I can get here. What did those guys want when they took you off a while ago? Trouble I ought to know about?"

Bonfire stood over her, hands on hips, like an avenging angel. "This man from Oklahoma. Webster. You know him?"

"Noah Webster? We've met."

"I'm warning you. You'd better stop him."

"From doing what?"

"He's going to get himself killed."

"What the heck do you mean by that? George, this is strictly between you and me. But he's the guy who rescued the Burlingame boy the other night out at the Eastside."

"No matter. He's been down here. Asking foolish questions. Meddling."

Puzzled, Johnnie bought a few seconds by climbing to her feet. Her back needed a rest anyway. "You mean here in Big Gully? Meddling about what?"

"He was at the gas station, early. Asking about the burial mounds."

"Oh, hell," she groaned. "He was warned not to bother the mounds!"

"The warning didn't take."

Her sense of concern increased sharply. "What did he do?"

"He went down to the mounds, down at the end of the road. On our tribal property."

"*Today* he did that?"

Bonfire nodded. "You know the mound area is sacred to my people. The Keepers of the Tradition maintain a watch almost constantly. You know when the fishermen went down there and the Keepers sent them away—"

"When the so-called Keepers scared hell out of those guys from Kansas, you mean, and it was all I could do to keep them from filing charges against your men."

Bonfire ignored that. "This fool Webster went down there without permission. One of the Keepers saw him go, and others were notified. Steps were taken."

"Steps?" she repeated in dismay. "Don't tell me—"

"He was not injured. He was warned. He vacated the premises. But he is a very big fool, not just a little one. The men who came here for me were members of the Keepers. They are very upset. They want me to arrest Webster for trespassing."

"You can't do that."

Bonfire's eyes flared dangerously. "Are you saying I am a deputy with my balls cut off? I can only do what a white woman orders?"

"No, George," she groaned. "I'm saying—dammit—your guys ran him off. I'll find him yet today and tell him in no uncertain terms that *I'll* arrest him personally if he comes down here on your tribal ground again."

"My honor demands that I make a response to the Keepers."

"Tell them what I just said."

"That will not satisfy them."

"It will have to satisfy them!"

His face working, Bonfire paused before replying. When he spoke, there was a tremor of tremendous emotion, barely controlled, in his voice: "The courthouse annex burned, and an old man was killed. He was a good old man. An Indian ceremonial knife was found in the ashes—planted there to point suspicion here. I know this. The man from Alamosa died with an arrow through his neck, one stolen from Jerome David's house. Someone is doing everything he can to bring hate and suspicion down on us. People like the Keepers are very strong young men. Some would call them radicals. They are already angry and scared. Somebody like this Webster fellow, trampling on our sacred rights, could set them off. This is not a warning, just a fact."

"I'll find him. He won't be down here again."

"Let me arrest him. Show my authority. It will calm some of the hotheads—show them not every member of the white community thinks we are nothing more than shit."

"George," Johnnie groaned, "I can't do that." Then she had second thoughts, possibly a faint hope. "What did he do down there? Did he break a fence or gate, maybe? Damage something around the—"

"He parked. Made sketches. Took photographs."

"George, the district attorney's office isn't going to file charges on the basis of that. No judge or jury in the country would sustain a conviction on the basis of that. You know it as well as I do!"

Bonfire paused again, and she could see the agitated motion of his chest. Finally he said more quietly, "I will try to explain to them."

"Now?"

His lips quirked. He really did seem calmer. "In a while."

"Can you," she asked hesitantly, "maybe give me a hand in the meantime?"

He squatted, touching one of the cartons of papers. "What are we looking for? The other investigators have been through everything."

"I'm just hoping they missed something. They didn't know to look specifically for evidence that might indicate a contact between Billy Kickingbird and Tomlinson, the Alamosa man."

He frowned at her. "How would that help?"

"I don't know if it would do much. But if Tomlinson sold dynamite to somebody around here, it might have been Kickingbird. If that's the case, then we can at least start backtracking every damned transaction Kickingbird had in recent weeks, hoping to turn up the end user."

"And the end user—?"

"I'm going on the theory that Kickingbird and Tomlinson both were killed to hide the fact that the dynamite transaction ever took place."

"So," Bonfire said slowly, "you establish a connection, and then you can assume that Billy bought the dynamite from this man Tomlinson, and then Billy resold it, and the final buyer killed them both."

"Yes."

His forehead wrinkled. "But how, if you get that far, do you learn who the final buyer was?"

"I don't know yet," she groaned. "I'm picking at straws. I'm trying to find anything. I'm groping around in the dark on the only line I can think of."

Bonfire nodded, put his hands on his hips again, and looked piercingly around the littered living room–office. He stared a long time at the battered rolltop desk against the far wall, with a broken leg, propped up on several old telephone books.

"I know what you're thinking," Johnnie told him. "The investigators took everything out of the drawers and pigeonholes. I took it all out again. That's what's in this couple of little stacks over here. I've already been through all of it another time. There are all kinds of bills and receipts and shipping orders and canceled checks and telephone numbers and I don't know what-all. But for the life of me I can't find anything that's helpful, or at least that I can identify as helpful."

Bonfire walked over to the old rolltop and bent over, keenly staring under the broken serpentine lid at the empty pigeonholes and narrow, ornately fluted little divider walls between them.

"What?" Johnnie asked, puzzled.

He reached under the sagging lid and started touching the vertical columns separating the compartments. As his fingers reached one of the two thicker dividers at the center of the row, he grunted with satisfaction.

"What?" Johnnie repeated, mystified now.

Bonfire's fingers gently grasped the paper-thin edges of the left partition divider and eased backward. The divider moved, coming out. A thin, deep, hidden drawer slid out into his hand.

"Hell!" Johnnie said. "I didn't know old desks had things like that!"

"Well," Bonfire murmured, peering down into the drawer, "you're young. You wouldn't."

"But the investigators missed it too."

Bonfire shrugged. "White men." A smile quirked his thin lips. "They can't jump. They don't think very good sometimes, either."

"Is there something in there?"

He snaked two fingers into the narrow opening and extracted a very old, partly rusted Prince Albert tobacco container. It had a piece of paper wrapped around it, secured with a rubber band. He removed the rubber band, put down the wrinkled sheet of paper, and pried open the lid with a thumbnail. "Huh!" It was a sound of total surprise.

As Johnnie watched, he poked a finger into the Prince Albert tin and extracted a thick wad of paper money, bound tightly by another rubber band.

Bonfire carefully put the wad of bills on the desktop and picked up the piece of paper that had been wrapped around the tin. He read it.

"What is it?" Johnnie demanded huskily.

He handed it to her. Block-printed in pencil was the name of Tomlinson Salvage Yard in Alamosa, and a street address. She read it twice, digesting the information.

Bonfire was examining the tightly rolled wad of bills. She saw for the first time that the one on the outside of the roll had "100" on it. If all of them were hundreds, this was a great deal of cash indeed.

15

NOAH WEBSTER DROVE slowly up the miserable mountain road again, going back to see the Herman family. His camping gear and tools rattled around loudly in the camper shell behind him. The early-day snowstorm was long gone, and a brilliant sun shone out of a flawless cobalt sky. Only lacy traces of snow lingered on the branches of some of the ponderosa pines. A gorgeous early afternoon.

Webster told himself to cheer up. Nobody had told him it would be easy, getting to check out the old mounds. And nobody had said these kinfolks would be easy, either.

He would just have to turn on all the charm, by golly, and get them to cooperate whether they wanted to or not.

Pulling into the trash-strewn field fronting the massive old mansion, he saw the black dogs come larruping and woofing out of the garages again. As he parked and cut his engine, they jumped up on the sides of the pickup, making muddy foot-slobbers all over the glass. They seemed considerably more hostile than they had on his earlier visit. He rummaged in his coat pocket, got out one of his remaining Snickers bars, carefully broke it into six pieces, and rolled the window down enough to drop out the gooey chunks as a bribe. It worked. The dogs started snapping at each other, fighting for a share, and when he opened the car door they wagged their tails and largely ignored him.

He walked up to the front porch of the old house and banged on the heavy door. The dogs milled around his legs, panting and tugging at his cuffs with wicked-looking teeth.

After what seemed like a long wait, the front door opened and one of the brothers stared out. "You again? We told you—"

"Hi!" Webster beamed, sticking out his right hand. "Joseph, right? Right! Listen, I don't want to be a nuisance, but I really would like just a few more minutes of your time, my friend. I need to see that burial mound that's back on your property somewhere, real bad. And like I told you in one of my letters, all this long-distance researching of courthouse birth and death records can only accomplish so much, and my uncle will be crushed, no kidding, if I don't get the answers to some of those genealogical questions I sent you."

His eyes black with menace, Joseph Herman started to swing the door closed. Webster shoved his arm into the narrowing crack. "Hey! No kidding! It won't take long, Cuz, and I intend to get this info one way or another. Why don't you just be friendly and fill me in on what I need to know? Otherwise I'm going to be down there at the courthouse forever and a day, digging it out piece by piece."

The door, which had begun to close painfully tight on his arm, stopped moving. For a few seconds there was no further movement. Then it swung wide open.

With a look that simmered with resentment and distrust, the hulking Joseph said, "Come in."

The dogs stampeded in ahead of Webster, as before. The sounds of their toenails clattering and scratching on the scarred hardwood floor was the only sound as Joseph Herman closed the door and pointed toward the bright doorway leading to the big living room where Webster had met the family before. Webster went in first, trying to ignore the crawly feeling of menace at his back.

No one else was in sight. The room smelled faintly of tobacco and wood smoke. Joseph lumbered over to the battered armchair he had used before, dropped into it, and glared silently at Webster.

Webster sat down facing him, worried his small notebook out of his inside shirt pocket, and found a pencil. "I appreciate this, Cuz, no kidding. I won't take long, just like I said."

Joseph's black, deep-socketed eyes stared unblinkingly from under the shelf of his eyebrows. "Ask."

"Okay. Well, here's the deal. Like I said in my second letter a month ago, I know that one old Indian burial mound is on your property west of here in a mountain valley because my uncle, in his tons of genealogy stuff, has this old, torn piece of paper he found somewhere back in Kentucky, rummaging through a bunch of old Sturdivant family junk years ago. It's about half a land area sketch that must have gone with the original deed. It showed the mound, among other stuff. When I told Unc I was coming up here to check the mounds, he dug it out for me. Like I said, he got excited.

"See—again, like I said in one of the letters to you—your dad's mom was a Sturdivant. Mary Alice Sturdivant. And *her* mother was a Webster. That's how my line links with yours. So my uncle Jack said I could use a copy of the piece of the old deed he found eons ago, but he cut a deal with me, the old fart, what he did was practically extort some genealogical help out of me in exchange for it."

Joseph clenched and unclenched his hands. Sweat gleamed on his face. He seemed ready to explode with anger. "You said all this in the letters. We don't know much. What you want to know—ask. Get it over with."

Webster began to feel more nervous. He hadn't counted on being alone in this gloomy old place with this man. He had never felt such a strong, primitive sense of raw violence. He was having trouble hanging on to his confidence.

So he hurried: "Look, Cuz. I know that burial mound that's out here someplace might be valuable. And I've been told how you guys in the family protect it, keep everybody away from it and all. That's good. It really is. I admire you for that. I just want to *assure* you that I'm not some crummy fortune-hunter. I want to examine the mound for scientific purposes. That's all. Otherwise, maybe you could give me some answers for Uncle Jack, and I can be on my way in short order. Okay?"

Joseph's big hands formed fists on the arms of the chair. "I said *ask*."

Webster tried to ignore the film of sweat he felt forming on his forehead. He pulled out the brief shorthand notes his uncle had given him. "Well, first, we know your line started in this part of the country with old Lincoln Herman, who was I guess one of the really earliest settlers, and he got all this land in one of the Ute Indian transactions in 1888, 1889. I guess that's actually the deal where this piece of the old deed map must have come from. Boy, it's too bad about that fire in town. I might have been able to check that out against the original records that got burned—" He saw Joseph's eyes narrow dangerously and cut himself off on that line of speculation.

"Well, too bad. Anyway! One of old Lincoln Herman's sons was Lincoln Jr. The date my uncle got for him from somewhere is 1896. Would that be right?"

"We don't keep no family records like that," Joseph growled.

Oh, great. "There was another son, Luther. The old man died around 1919, and the one son, Luther, died in a hunting accident the year after that. Right so far?"

"You know more than I do."

"Okay. I'm hurrying. This is where the Websters come in. Lincoln Junior married a lady named Mary Alice Sturdivant, who as I said comes down from the Websters through her mother. Your dad, the old guy I met here before—Elmo?—yes, Elmo—was born in 1934. He had a sister born later. But now is where we get all mixed up. Whatever happened to your grandma, Mary Alice? My uncle Jack would really like to clear that up. When did she die? Where is she buried? And your dad's sister, whatever happened to her? We're especially interested in Mary Alice, you see, because she's our line."

The fists clenched again. "She died. Back before World War II sometime."

"You don't know when exactly?"

"No."

"How about your grandpa, Lincoln Jr.? When did he die?"

"In 1969, I think. Listen. That's enough." Joseph started to rise out of his chair.

"Just another sec," Webster pleaded. "What about your dad's sister, this Lucy? When did she die? Your dad married a lady named Ernestine Hodges in 1970—my uncle got that by writing the county clerk here—but what happened to her?"

Joseph slumped back into the chair. "She died, too. 1978."

"Wow," Webster murmured sympathetically. "When you and Luther must have been little guys, huh? That must have been tough."

He paused and waited for a reaction. For a solid minute or two, Joseph did not budge or make a sound. The only noise in the entire vast house came from the dogs scuffling in the entry hallway.

Nervous, Webster gave his best winning grin. "Hello?"

"Are you through?"

"Where is your mom buried?"

Joseph shrugged. "Town."

"Town?"

"IOOF Cemetery, I think."

"Is that where all your family members are buried?"

"Far as I know." Joseph climbed to his feet. "I think it's time for you to go now."

Something moved at the far end of the room, and the other brother, Luther, shambled in, barefooted and wearing bright yellow pajamas. "Whozit?" he demanded sleepily, padding closer.

"The man from Oklahoma," Joseph replied. "Go back to bed, Luther."

Luther blinked, dull eyes uncomprehending. "I'm through my nap."

"Your pill hasn't wore off yet."

Luther grimaced. "I hate the pill. I hate it. It makes my head hurt."

"Go back to bed."

"No."

Joseph turned back to Webster. "We're through. Go. Now."

"Okay," Webster said good-naturedly, forcing a chuckle. "I guess maybe I'll have to look up some of these dates and stuff at the courthouse after all—anything that escaped the fire in the annex building, I mean." He pocketed his notebook. "Just one other thing, though."

Joseph's voice lowered ominously. "I said *go*."

"Right, right. About letting me have a look-see at that burial mound you guys have got out there someplace—"

Without warning, Joseph yelled. It was shrill and deafening, an outburst of uncontrollable rage. He started toward Webster. Webster backpedaled and fell over backward, sprawling on the floor.

"Joseph!" Luther cried, rushing up to grab his brother, pinning his arms. "No!"

"Moron!" Joseph struggled to free himself. "Get out of here! Go back to bed. Let the pill work. Let me take care of this."

Luther kept struggling, managing to half-turn to Webster. "You'd better go. He's bad when he's like this."

Without a word, Webster struggled to his feet and fled for the front door. Some of the dogs came racketing after him. He ran to the truck as fast as his shaky legs would take him, and didn't gulp in a deep breath until he had turned around and started back down the road away from the damned spooky place.

One thing was for sure, he thought dazedly. He would not be going back up here again. Enough was enough, Unc.

But boy, wasn't he going to spend more time at the courthouse now than he had intended. Because, as his head started to clear and he reached the paved highway again, some more things became sure in his mind, too:

Joseph Herman was a dangerous, dangerous man. Quite possibly a maniac. Maybe brother Luther was, too; maybe that was why he took naps in the middle of beautiful afternoons, stoned on some kind of pill that made his head hurt.

But craziness alone could not wholly explain the violence of Joseph Herman's reaction just now. The man had gone positively nuts. Why? What had Webster asked him that so threatened him?

Maybe—the idea hit Webster hard—there was a hell of a lot more than simple family reticence and suspicion involved in the Hermans' notorious secrecy and hostility to just about everyone. Maybe these people had something truly significant to hide.

But what?

This was *great.* Webster had always loved puzzles. He was good at them. Nothing was going to make him quit poking around now, boy.

16

THOUGHTFULLY PUFFING HIS pipe, Randall Dwight Simmons stood on the cantilevered deck of his mountain home and stared out toward the distant sawtooth edge of the Killdeer range.

After a long time, he removed his pipe from his teeth. "It's a damn hard decision, Butt. I never gave a thought to running for public office of any kind until they approached me about it yesterday."

Butt Peabody paused, too, before framing a reply. He was not sure he had made the right decision, coming out here to Simmons's massive contemporary home high on the mountain slope. But this was a good man, an honest one, and Peabody had to learn what he could.

Finally he asked, "The county commissioners came?"

Simmons turned his massive gray head and fixed Peabody with a look of the keenest scrutiny. "Two of the commissioners, yes. The mayor. A couple of others. Do you want all the names?"

Peabody winced. "Nope. Shouldn't have asked anything about it."

"They don't think your lady sheriff is being very effective."

"Huh."

"You do?"

"Yes."

"She's got several bad outstanding cases right now."

"We're working on 'em."

Simmons turned his gaze back toward the mountains and again puffed on his pipe. He was smoking something Peabody was familiar with by the smell: Sir Walter Raleigh. "You think she's a good sheriff?"

"As good as most."

"Butt, if she's a good lawman and doing an honest job, I'm not sure I want to run against her. That's what you came here for, isn't it? To learn my real intentions?"

"What I probably came here for," Peabody blurted, "was to ask you not to run against her, because you could get elected to any office in this valley you set out to get, and I don't want her turned out."

A thin smile tugged at Simmons's lips. "But you can't ask me that, can you? It wouldn't be proper."

"That's right." The words felt acidic in his mouth.

Simmons abruptly changed gears. "This fire at the court-house. I understand the report will suggest the possibility of arson?"

" 'Possibility' hell," Peabody retorted. "Broken window frame, other signs of forced entry, flammable materials sprin-kled around, if you can believe early lab tests. Hell. They even found an empty can of the stuff."

"What about the primitive knife?"

Peabody started. "There hasn't been anything put out about the knife."

Simmons shrugged. "I live here. I'm interested. I have sources."

"The knife was a plant."

"You believe that?"

"Yes."

"Some people don't."

"Some people are wrong."

"You've considered the possibility that the old man who died in the fire might have started it?"

"Accidentally, you mean?"

"Accidentally or on purpose—and then, in either case, got himself caught in it."

"No. He was in his office, and it looked like he never woke up. Smoke got him first. Or carbon monoxide."

"Do you have a suspect?"

"We pulled in a couple of guys we knew had a grudge against the county or the judge or somebody. They checked out okay. We really don't have anybody."

"The man from Alamosa."

Peabody reached for his tobacco and papers. "Tomlinson."

"Yes. The one killed by an arrow."

"I can tell you a new angle we're working on. Of course, it's confidential."

Simmons nodded, and Peabody knew the nod was better than most men's oath on a Bible. He explained about the possible sale and transport of a small quantity of explosives through Tomlinson's salvage yard.

"Find the buyer, find a suspect?" Simmons said, eyes narrowing.

"We hope."

"Why would someone go through a junk dealer in Alamosa to get explosives? You can buy those things through legitimate channels if you're on the up and up."

"Right," Peabody said heavily. "*If* you're on the up and up." He stuck his cigarette in his lips and lit it.

"Tell me why Sheriff Baker hired one of the Ute radicals as a deputy," Simmons said, shifting subjects again. "From what I can judge, there are a lot of people perturbed about that." He paused. "A *lot* of people."

"We need help down in that part of the county. I'm not saying I would have done what Johnnie did, but she had her reasons."

"She's tempting fate."

Peabody sighed. "Yeah, she's good at that."

"What is it with this man Webster? A shard-hunter?"

"He's trying to investigate some of the burial mounds. So far, he's got the Keepers and the Herman family both bent out of shape by his persistence."

"Is Johnnie helping him?"

"No."

"Has she warned him about the Hermans?"

"I think so."

Simmons nodded. "She'd better. They're dangerous people. You know about the murder years ago. The insanity."

Peabody studied the other man's face with keener interest. "All I ever heard was rumors."

"One Herman brother murdered another, long ago. He might have killed old Lincoln Herman, too—the old mountain man who came in here and cheated the Utes out of thirty thousand acres at the earliest day. Or possibly the Utes killed that one, no one can be sure."

Simmons paused to pull an old Zippo lighter out of his pants pocket. "You know, of course, about that lawsuit way back, the one the family settled. I've often tried to find out exactly how much was paid, but it's the best-kept legal secret in history, seems like. I know this much: the family had a lot to hide *somewhere*. They must have paid millions to settle. It ruined them."

Simmons applied fresh flame to the bowl of his pipe. "Now you've got old Elmo out there, living with that Aggie woman. Not his wife. What happened to his wife? I'm not sure. And those two boys. Joseph, the older, is wild. Luther is retarded . . . more of the family curse, down to the present generation."

A slight breeze carried away a fresh puff of smoke from

Simmons's pipe. "If this man Webster is fooling with them, he might be very, very sorry. If Johnnie is helping him in any way, she could be in danger, too. You might want to tell her I said that, Butt."

"I'll do it," Peabody said. Simmons's story had given him fresh things to worry about.

Simmons puffed contentedly. "I've got a while before I have to decide about filing. I don't intend to hurry this decision. But I certainly would not enjoy getting the office because the incumbent turned up dead."

"I better go," Peabody decided.

Simmons walked him downstairs to the door. "One more thing, Butt."

"Yeah?"

"I don't particularly like some of the people who came here to see me about this. Oh, I'm not questioning their sincere interest in Tenoclock and this valley. They're just . . . not my sort. So if I do end up running . . . if I happened to get elected . . . there's one thing I want to assure you about. If I get in there, I'm nobody's man. I'll be fair. And I'll kick ass."

Peabody flipped his cigarette into the gravel of the driveway. "I hope you don't have to do it."

Simmons slapped him lightly on the shoulder. "Me too. But I like this place, Butt. It's where I decided I want to live out my life. If I'm convinced I'm really needed, I'll file. That's just the way I am."

"Understood."

"And remember what I said about this man Webster and the Hermans. They're poison, Butt. Real poison. Unless she wants more mayhem, she'd better keep that sucker away from them."

Peabody got into his truck and drove down the mountainside, passing other big homes back in the trees. He wished he could dislike Randall Simmons, but he couldn't. He wished he could dismiss his warning. But he couldn't do that, either.

THE MAN WHO supervised the operation of Tenoclock's
only currently active cemetery, the sprawling IOOF facility on the
far north edge of town, made his office in a double-wide trailer
on a lot next door to the main gate. His name was Twine, he was
about thirty years old, and he obviously took pride in his work.

After listening to Noah Webster's questions, he had jotted
a few lines on a notepad, gone into an adjacent room, and come
back about three minutes later with two large hardcover books.
One contained area maps of the cemetery, each plot neatly numbered, along with listings of the numbered plots, showing who
owned it, who had been buried there, and when. The other book
was composed of two sections, one alphabetically broken down
by names of people buried in the cemetery, the other divided
into months and years of interment from the earliest records
extant.

"No listing for the original Lincoln Herman," Twine muttered, running his index finger down columns of dates and
names. "Not unusual, though. People buried kin on the home
land sometimes in those days, and records for the early graves
aren't very good prior to about 1934, '35. . . ."

He flipped pages and studied columns again. "Yes . . . yes
. . . here's a real early listing for a Luther Herman, age twenty-
two, looks like it was in 1919. But you can't tell where in the
old, old part of the cemetery that grave might have been—most
of those gravestones fell down, or the graves caved in long ago."

"Mary Alice Herman?" Webster prodded.

Twine kept poring over pages of columns. "Don't see her yet
. . . wait a minute, wait a minute, here's the old man's son,
Lincoln Herman Jr. Section nineteen. Interred July 7, 1969.
And here's somebody named Lucy Herman, died June 4, 1978,
interred in the same family plot November 7 or 8, can't tell for
sure, the ink is smudged—"

"Mary Alice Herman," Webster insisted. "Her maiden name was Sturdivant, and she's the one I'm most interested in. She ought to be buried here."

Twine fumed through pages for fully another fifteen minutes before looking up with a sigh of resignation. "I don't find her, Mr. Webster. Sorry."

Webster groaned. "Well, find me the date of death for Elmo's first wife, Ernestine—died in 1978—and I guess I'm out of here."

Twine looked blank.

"What?" Webster prodded.

"There's no Ernestine Herman buried here, Mr. Webster. I don't even have to look for that one to be sure. I spend a lot of time with these more recent records, and I'm all over this cemetery every day of the week. She isn't buried here. I have no idea where she might be interred."

IN THE BIG living room, the family had a meeting.

Old Elmo Herman stood in the center of the room, suspenders off his shoulders and drooping down around his knees on either side. His white hair stood wildly on end, and tears streamed down his face. Facing him, his son Joseph glared with bright, pitiless rage. The old woman stood back nearer the entry door, her face wet too, helplessly wringing her hands. The remaining family member, dull-eyed Luther, sat in one of the battered easy chairs, staring with mute fear.

"Leave it be!" the old man pleaded, weeping. "Just leave it *be!*"

"We can't, you crazy old bastard!" Joseph said. "Do you want all of it to come out? All the shit? God damn you! You've known some of this for years and years, and you've done your share to keep it hidden. Now just because you're old and you've lost your guts, do you think we're going to give up everything we've got left?"

Sobs wracked the old man. His words were almost indistin-
guishable. "You shouldn't have done it, you needn't have done
them things—"

"What were we supposed to do? Sit here in a hole and wait
for everything to come out? Wait for them to come with their
shovels and guns and handcuffs, and haul us off? Just shut up!
Just shut up! We'll take care of it, Luther and me. We've took
care of it so far."

In his chair, Luther made a sobbing sound. "I don't wanna,
Joseph. Please—"

The old woman cried, "You don't have to, boy! You can stay
right here!"

"Oh, Momma," Luther wailed, heaving himself up from his
chair. "I'm so scared, Momma, and—"

"She's not your momma, you idiot. You'll do what I say."

"Joseph," the old woman moaned. "Please, just—"

"Be quiet!" Joseph's voice, like a whiplash, made both her
and the old man flinch spasmodically. The room fell silent except for the sound of choking tears.

Joseph began pacing, waving his arms, almost out of control.
"We don't just sit here," he told them in a shaky voice. "We
watch. We keep watch. That's all I said we do. Maybe we don't
have to do anything more than that. But we have to *know* what
he's up to. Then—Luther and me—we'll take care of it, whatever comes down. Just like before."

"You just keep going on and on," the old man sobbed,
"and—"

"And it's for your ass!" Joseph shouted in his face. "It's for
your worthless ass, Poppa!" He turned and flung himself at the
old woman, who shrank back against the wall. "And it's for your
ass too, you old whore!" He turned again and brushed against
an old table with a fringed lamp on it. His arm swung out, and
the lamp and shade hurtled halfway across the room to crash
against the fireplace wall in an explosion of glass shards. "God

damn you! God damn both of you! God damn this whole crazy, blighted, lying, sick, ungodly fucking miserable thing we call a family! It's been going on forever! Forever! One generation after another! Luther and me, we'll handle it, I tell you. We have no choice—right, Luther?"

"I don't wanna," Luther blubbered. "I'm scared, Joseph. I ain't smart. All I want to do is have my little garden and catch me a rabbit to eat sometimes and go fishing. Why you got to make me help you do all this bad stuff, Joseph?"

His brother's stupidity seemed to have a bizarre calming effect on Joseph. His shoulders went round. His face became a smooth, emotionless mask.

"We're going now," he announced. "Get up, Luther. *Now.*" He turned to the old couple, who now clung to one another. "Poppa. Aggie. You stay here. You don't talk to anyone. You don't know anything. You keep your yaps shut. You understand me?"

They stared, quaking.

His voice bellowed: *"You understand me?"*

"Yes," Elmo whispered brokenly.

Joseph looked back at his brother. "Luther. I said come on." He strode toward the front door.

Tears still silvery on his cheeks, Luther took three stumbling steps. As he moved, he singsonged a soft little chant, almost inaudible, like a very small, very frightened child murmuring protest to himself: "I can't . . . oh, no, I don't wanna . . . I won't . . . ." But he followed.

Moments later the front door slammed, and the brothers were gone.

IT WAS ALMOST dark when Johnnie and Butt Peabody climbed the stairs from their office and walked out into the fast-chilling night air of the back parking lot. The sky overhead, still only dark gray rather than fully black, already shone with more stars than sea-level dwellers ever saw in their lives. A sky this clear meant a hard freeze before morning.

Johnnie pulled up the collar of her jacket and shivered. "Cold!"

Peabody looked down at her, thinking she had never looked better than she did now, with the starlight on her pale hair. "Want coffee before heading home?"

She shook her head. "Thanks, Butt. I'd better not. I'm real coffeed out, after drinking about ten cups while we made all those phone calls."

Peabody nodded. He wasn't much in the mood for more coffee either. He just wasn't quite ready to go home alone yet. "In the morning our friend Purser Welles ought to be hearing back from Alamosa. Maybe they'll have something for us."

"Yes, and I don't care what George Bonfire says, in the morning I'm hauling the Coyote kid in and talking to him a long, long time."

After Peabody had returned from seeing Randall Simmons, he had found Johnnie in the office working on a list of every known friend or business connection of Big Gully junkman Billy Kickingbird. She explained to Peabody about the money found in the tobacco tin at Kickingbird's place, and her idea that there had to be *somebody* who could suggest where the money had come from, or might have heard him say something potentially useful about a streak of recent good luck.

"Butt, we're going to go back through every name we can come up with, only this time we're going to ask about big sales and big money and dynamite. We're going to contact every bank and savings and loan in every town within two hundred miles of here, and see if we might not turn up another checking or savings account for Kickingbird personally or his yard. It's *possible*— not likely, but possible—that that dough came in here on Western Union or a money order he might have cashed locally, and we need to check on that, too. We need to get our friend from Alamosa, Mr. Welles, to pass this info down there so they can look for any withdrawals or anything else in Tomlinson's books that might jibe with this amount of money—thirty-five hundred dollars. We can start a lot of this stuff by phone. Can you give me a hand?"

He could, and he had. But now, several hours later, and after an interruption for a reported brawl at a county-line tavern, the initial excitement over finding the cash had subsided.

"Are you sure hauling Coyote in is a good idea?" Peabody asked now.

Johnnie frowned. "I'm not sure of anything. But he worked part-time for Kickingbird, Butt, and if anybody knows more than he's told so far, I think it's that kid. If we're on the right track here, the dynamite from Alamosa went through Kickingbird's yard. I can't believe the Coyote boy wouldn't have had a clue about it."

Peabody nodded. "Sure. But he would protect Kickingbird, dead or alive."

"That's why I'm going to bring him in."

"But you heard what Bonfire said. People down there will call it harassment, all that good stuff."

Johnnie set her jaw. "I'm doing it."

Peabody sighed. "About that warning on Webster and the Hermans?"

"I'll track Mr. Webster down in the morning, or have Dean do it, and tell him I intend to jail him if I hear of him being near those mounds down south or around the Herman property again."

"Good."

Johnnie stifled a yawn and stepped off the parking lot curbing beside her Jeep. It was dark enough, and she was tired enough, that she stumbled. Peabody's hand shot out and caught her arm, steadying her. Her movement swung her around against him.

"Wow! Almost fell. Thanks, Butt. I—"

She stopped, catching her breath. She was close against his chest and was tall enough that their faces were quite close together, and his grip on her arm squeezed so tightly it hurt. Her heart started to hammer, and she felt an enormous, incredulous surprise.

He released her and stepped back. "Sorry," he said gruffly.

Rubbing her arm where his grip had made it numb, she climbed into her Jeep. He slammed the door and turned away to walk with his characteristic shambling limp toward his pickup. Her heartbeat still felt uneven. "Oh, my gosh," she whispered to herself in shock and disbelief.

In his pickup truck, Peabody started the engine and turned on the lights and waited to watch her vehicle back out, headlights blazing, and pull behind his parking place on the way to the exit ramp. Then he backed out.

"Dumb bastard," he told himself. "Dumb old fart."

It was just past eight o'clock.

PROMPTLY AT 9:00 P.M., a soft electronic chime sounded over the loudspeakers in the ceiling of the Tenoclock public library. The librarian, one of only four people left in the main reading room, stood up from her desk and glared across the empty tables at Noah Webster.

Disappointed but excited too, he gave her a wink, stood, closed the old newspaper file books, and shoved his notebook into his shirt pocket. The librarian, a short woman of about fifty, with blue-gray hair, came across the room, her low heels rapping an impatient staccato on the tile floor.

"Are you *quite* finished, sir?"

He pulled on his coat. "What time do we open in the morning?"

Irritation flitted across her face. "Nine o'clock, sir."

"Then I'll see you at nine o'clock in Tenoclock," Webster said with a wink. "Yuk yuk yuk."

Stony-faced, she hefted the heavy newspaper file books.

"Must have heard it before," Webster said. "Can I help you carry those things?"

"I'm quite capable, sir." She turned away, staggering under the awkward weight of the big books.

With a sigh, he left the main reading room and went out to the lobby, where he passed through the electronic pillars that checked to make sure you weren't trying to carry out an unauthorized volume. The old-fashioned revolving door made a whooshing sound as he went out into the night.

A blast of cold air enveloped him. Shivering, he turned up his coat collar and lengthened his strides, walking toward his pickup. Several cars remained in the lot, which was dimly lighted by a single security pole more than a hundred feet away. He got into his truck and backed out, pulling onto the empty side street, turning left. The headlights of one of the other vehicles in the lot flashed on, and another pickup trundled out onto the pavement a half block behind him.

Steering with one hand, Webster awkwardly punched the button on the side of his Timex Indiglow to verify the time. 9:06.24. Maybe the lady sheriff worked late, he thought. It was worth checking out.

He did not have all the pieces to his puzzle yet, but the late afternoon and evening had produced some remarkable results. Armed with the information provided by his uncle Jack, along with the Xerox of the old deed map and the dates he had gotten at the IOOF cemetery, he had come up with enough already to interest the sheriff or anybody else with an inquiring mind. It was amazing, he thought, that no one had ever put two and two and two together this way before. Of course, the bits of information had been scattered over decades. You had to look for it. If Tenoclock hadn't had a good little newspaper back in earlier times—one that printed every personal item and tidbit of gossip it could come up with—some of these things could have been lost forever.

The lady sheriff would want to give him a medal, Webster thought. And he wasn't through yet at the library; not by a long shot. And a few things might need to be checked further here at the courthouse, in whatever records might have survived the annex fire.

The narrow street in front of the courthouse was dark and vacant. Two yellowish globe lights glowed on either side of the front steps. Webster turned to go around the block. Seeing an Employees Only sign pointing into an alley, he turned again. Headlights of another vehicle moved past his rearview mirrors, going on at a crawl.

In the back he found an empty asphalt lot walled in by construction-type board fence on one side, buildings on the others. He parked against the side of the courthouse and hurried to the door, following signs.

The front door of the sheriff's department was at the foot of some concrete steps. Opening it, he walked into a small, grubby reception area facing a long wooden counter. The bright fluorescent lights hurt his eyes. The lone occupant of the long, dismal room, an elderly black man sitting at a desk behind the counter, looked up from some kind of old, leather-bound book. "Can I help you, sir?"

Webster walked over. "I guess the lady sheriff has gone home already?"

"Yessir, about an hour ago. What can we help you with?"

Webster briefly considered asking the old guy to try to locate her. But maybe this was fate: by noon tomorrow he stood a great chance of having more info, and *really* blowing her hat in the creek.

He dug one of his business cards out of his wallet. "You might just tell her I came by, if you would, please?"

The old guy limped to the counter, took the card, and studied it. "Any message?"

"Well, you might just tell her I've been having fun and

games over at the library, and I'll be in touch tomorrow. I've got some info for her."

Back outside, Webster hurried back to his truck and drove away from the courthouse. He turned north onto Gunnison, crossing side streets until he reached the east-west road. At this hour traffic had thinned considerably. He rolled down his window and readjusted his side mirror, canting it to shunt the glare of headlights behind him. Coming to the highway junction, he turned again.

About forty minutes later he reached his destination. A sliver moon glittered on the water near his selected campsite.

He parked and got out. Opening the back of his camper shell, he hauled out his tent. Dumping it on the ground, he retrieved the blue plastic tarp that always went down first. He carried the tarp to a flat spot, dense with pine needles, and carefully spread it out. Nobody would bother him here. He felt sure of that.

Turning, he walked back the few steps to get his tent.

He was tired. It had been a hell of a day—an incredible day. If *half* his current suspicions could be borne out, he thought, the little lady sheriff was going to have the case of her life. In the process, one Noah J. Webster, Ph.D., might get access to all the burial mounds he had ever dreamed about. Oh boy, oh boy.

He bent over to pick up his small, rolled tent. Something behind him moved, making a quick, rustling sound in the high brush. Surprised and alarmed, he started to rise and turn. Something awfully hard smashed into the side of his skull. It hurt really, really bad, he thought. Then he didn't think anything at all.

17

WHEN JOHNNIE WALKED into the office at seven-forty-five Thursday morning, County Commissioner Madison Blithe was there waiting for her. His western-cut suit today was pale lavender, his boots white lizard. As Johnnie walked closer to him, she entered a cloud of something like Canoe.

"Johnnie," Blithe announced with his sincerest solemnity, "I've been waiting for you."

"Good morning," she said coolly. "Please wait." She turned to Deputy Billy Higginbotham, looking half asleep at the counter. "Anything, Billy?"

Higginbotham blinked a few times. "Quiet night, Jason said. Here—somebody came in and left a card for you."

"I'll look at it in a minute." She turned back to Blithe. "Give me five minutes, and we'll have some fresh coffee."

"No, no, Johnnie." He produced a folded copy of Teno-clock's weekly, the *Frontiersman*. "I assume you've seen this week's edition?"

Her stomach tightened. "No, but I think I know what's in it, thanks to you and all my other friends upstairs."

Faint pink splotched Blithe's cheeks. He unfolded the paper

and handed it to her. The top story ballyhooed plans to expand
the Rocky Point ski resort northeast of town. Just below the fold,
a headline read SHERIFF TO GET CHANCE TO FACE COUNTY
VOTERS. She glanced at the first paragraphs of Niles Pennington's
bylined story:

> Sheriff Johnelle Baker has earned the right to run for
> the office she has held only on the basis of a special
> appointment up until this time, county commission-
> ers decreed earlier this week.
>
> Sheriff Baker will, therefore, be accorded a chance
> to run for reelection to a full term on her own merits,
> commissioners voted.
>
> The special election will be held July 7 in conjunc-
> tion with other voting scheduled for that date.

She refolded the paper and handed it back. "I guess I should
be grateful, right?"

His expression became funereal. "No one wants this,
Johnnie."

"Then why did you vote for the special election?"

"We had no choice! Don't you see that? All this violent
crime, people scared half to death, clear-cut evidence of threatening unrest among an increasingly lawless minority element,
and what do you do? You go beyond the bounds of your proper
authority and name one of those radicals a special deputy, when
you *know* all it will do is inflame opinion on both sides."

"I knew about this decision. You didn't come here as a paper-
boy. What do you want, Madison?"

"I have it on good authority that a respected resident of the
valley has been approached by certain persons and asked to run
against you. But I understand that decision has not yet been
reached. Believe me, feeling is running strong on this George
Bonfire issue, and the failure of your office to take steps on the

fire and the two recent murders. Yet if you would just take the proper steps, the election might become a cakewalk for you— you might find everyone on your side again."

Johnnie's lips felt stiff. "And what would I have to do to get all that support back, Madison?"

"It's very simple, Johnnie. Reevaluate your recent staffing decisions. Find someone else to appoint as a special deputy. Someone like Billy, over there. Let this troublemaker Bonfire go. And isn't it time, really, for poor old Butt Peabody to be put out to pasture once and for all? The commissioners would support that, too. We might find the votes—Carl and I might find the votes—to increase your departmental budget a few hundred dollars a year if we saw signs you were taking hold of the job with greater competence and spirit of cooperation."

Johnnie walked to the coffeemaker, yanked the glass pitcher off the heating element with a small, angry clatter, and dumped the contents into the rusty metal sink nearby. "I never have been 'cooperative' enough, have I, Madison?"

He walked closer. "Johnnie! It's just a matter of good public relations! We *must* prove to the world that the Tenoclock Valley is safe, secure, and relatively crime-free. We can't have any more of this damaging publicity. Show us you mean to get along, and we'll support you 100 percent."

"All I have to do is fire Bonfire, and let Butt go, and appoint a couple of deputies that you would pick out for me? Is that what you're saying?"

"It would be a start," Blithe responded solemnly. "A new spirit of cooperation. New hope for the end to this crime wave."

"We're not having a crime wave!"

"We *must* act to protect our valley's public relations image."

Johnnie was so angry and frustrated she felt hot tears quite close behind her eyes. She turned her back on him and fiddled with the coffee holder tray. Her fingers trembled.

"Well?" Blithe said. "Will you at least think about it?"

"No. Sorry."

His voice went flat with anger. "You're a stubborn girl. You never did know how to get along around here. The only other way you have a prayer of keeping this job is by solving both these murders, and probably the annex fire, too. And we both know how much chance there is of that, don't we?"

She stayed with her back to him. "Thank you for coming by, Madison. Now, if you'll pardon me, I have work to do."

There was a pause. Then in his dullest tone he said, "Yes. I see that. Making coffee. Good for you, Johnnie. Good day." His boot heels clicked on the ancient green asphalt tile, and then the front door slammed.

BUTT PEABODY LOOKED down at the card in his hand, the one from Noah Webster that Johnnie had just shown him. "What did he want?"

She handed him a cup of coffee. "I don't know." She hadn't mentioned the visit by Madison Blithe. "He said he would be back, according to this note from Jason. I hope he isn't planning another trip to the burial mounds or something equally dumb. I'm not in the mood for another set-to with George Bonfire this morning."

"You going to wait around for Webster to show up?"

"No. I'll have Dean start searching for him. I need to hit the Ace High salvage yard and the little one over there on the east road, the one with the derelict Volkswagen on a pole. Then I'll get down to Big Gully and look up our young Mr. Coyote."

Peabody scowled into his coffee for a minute.

"What?" Johnnie prodded gently.

He looked up. "You've seen the paper, have you?"

"A glance."

"They're going to railroad you out of office and make it all look like they're doing you a favor by giving you a chance to get reelected on your own, rather than serving out another two years on an appointment."

Johnnie didn't say anything.

"I would do anything to make this different," he told her.

He was such a dear man, such a curmudgeon. She had spent two restless, worried hours at home last night, shaken by the surprise of feelings that had gone through her in the moment he grabbed her to keep her from falling. But in broad daylight, with him grumpy like this, she saw that he felt nothing beyond a kind of family devotion. She had been exceptionally silly in that moment last night, and he had guessed nothing. Good. Now they were back to normal, and she could stop worrying about *that*.

As she raised her coffee mug to her lips, the desk telephone jangled. Halfway across the room, Billy Higginbotham picked up. He said something, listened, and waved at Johnnie.

She walked to her desk and lifted the instrument there. "This is Sheriff Baker speaking."

"Sheriff?" She recognized George Bonfire's voice, although it was higher-pitched than usual with painful tension. "You'd better get right down here."

PALE MORNING SUNLIGHT dappled the yellowed brush and scattered aspen along the creekside in the mountain valley. Near the end of the pasture path, the dusty Chevrolet pickup truck with the battered aluminum camper shell on back sat empty and alone, both side doors standing open. A crowd of nearly a dozen young Indian men stood far off to one side near the aspen grove, shuffling their feet and whispering to one another.

George Bonfire hiked back up the slight slope from the parked pickup, carrying a folded piece of paper in his hands. He reached the spot where Johnnie and Butt Peabody waited beside their vehicles.

"It's his, all right," Bonfire said. "I knew it was." He handed over the paper. His hand shook slightly, betraying how upset he was.

Johnnie examined the registration certificate he had retrieved from the truck's glove box. It showed Noah Webster as the owner. "You say one of the guys over there found it this morning?"

Bonfire nodded. "Less than an hour ago."

"No sign of Webster?"

"Nothing."

She pocketed the registration paper. "Let me talk to him. Butt, why don't you go over the truck and see if you can spot something George might have missed."

Without a word, the grim-faced Peabody lumbered down the slope. Bonfire hurried across to the group of onlookers, spoke with them a moment, and started back with one of them in tow. Johnnie felt her pulse running too swiftly after the high-speed drive out from town and the beginnings of shock setting in. If Noah Webster was dead, she thought, good God.

Bonfire reached her side. The man with him was in his late teens, skinny, dark, with traditional long hair in a braid down his back. His blue work shirt and faded Levi's had flecks of weeds and brush stuck on them. His face, pocked by a bad childhood case of acne, looked tight and sullen with worry.

"Sheriff, this is Davy Lorenzo. He's the one who found the truck."

"Hi, Davy," Johnnie said. "Suppose you tell me about it."

Lorenzo's thick eyebrows knit. "Nothing to tell. Came down here early to check the area out. Truck was sitting there. Nobody around. I looked a few minutes and headed back to the gas station, called George."

"Davy, are you one of the Keepers?"

Lorenzo's lips went tight. "Dunno."

"He is," Bonfire put in quietly. "It's no crime," he added.

Johnnie tried to maintain eye contact with the boy, but his eyes darted everywhere else but her face. She asked, "And the truck was not here last night?"

Lorenzo looked startled at that. "We didn't have nobody on during the night."

"Somebody was 'on' earlier in the evening?"

"Yes."

"Who?"

Lorenzo looked at Bonfire.

"Tell her," Bonfire said.

"Jimmy Job."

"Is he in that group over there?"

"Yes."

"I'll want to talk to him in a minute," Johnnie told Bonfire. "Now, Davy, look. I'm not trying to pin something on somebody. I'm just trying to figure out what might have happened here. I know this truck belongs to a man named Noah Webster. He was at my office around nine last night, so he must have come out here well after that. And you say there wasn't one of the Keepers around at that hour?"

"They was at a dance at the Methodist Church."

"Last night, you mean."

"Yes."

"And your guys were all there?"

"Most."

Bonfire interjected, "It's not like the Keepers have a duty roster. It's voluntary. One tells another when he plans to come around . . . check."

Johnnie looked down the slope, where Butt Peabody had opened the back of the camper shell and was poking around inside. "Okay. So sometime after nine last night, Webster drove down here and nobody was on duty. Then this morning, at— what time? Eight?"

"Maybe," Lorenzo grunted. "Maybe a little after."

"A little after eight, you walked down—"

"Rode my bike." He turned to point toward the aspen grove, where a lightweight motorcycle leaned against a boulder.

"—you rode your dirt bike down," Johnnie resumed, "and found the truck just like it is now."

"All except the doors. I opened the doors. I thought he might be inside."

"Did you open the back hatch, too?"

"I looked in. I could see he wasn't in there."

"Then what?"

Lorenzo glanced nervously at Bonfire, who nodded encouragement. "I run to the mounds. I thought he was over there. I couldn't find him. I looked acrost the crik. He wasn't over there, neither. That was when I went back to town."

"You didn't find a sign of him anywhere."

Lorenzo turned and pointed a skinny arm south, in the direction the creek meandered out of sight. "I run down there. They's one little mound down thataway. I didn't find him, but they's some fresh tracks."

"Let's go look," Johnnie ordered.

With Lorenzo in the lead, they crossed the gentle sidehill, walking close to the silent group of male onlookers and down the far side, moving out of sight of the pickup truck. The brook murmured along briskly, tumbling over fist-sized round rocks and an occasional snag that made whitewater. On the far side, steep rock came down almost to the water's edge. Here the pasturelike character of the land became rougher, studded with tumbled boulders and, possibly, glacial till. Young aspen marched out of the older fir forest, reseeding themselves, and in some places nearly reached the water. Lorenzo moved along with sure-footed speed, and Johnnie felt her shirt start to get wet from sweat as she hurried to keep up. The sun felt hot on her back, and she wished she had left her coat behind.

Lorenzo led her and Bonfire around the small ceremonial

mound he had mentioned, then down a sharp embankment. The sound of roaring water began to grow. Moving past a small clot of willows that had blocked the view, they came to a wide, rocky area where another stream entered. The two creeks, their combined volume of water heavy, became a single narrow, swift-moving, deep-looking cataract. The rock walls on the far side were joined by others on this side to form a tight vee. The newly formed little river plunged over a ten-foot waterfall and barreled into the vee, foam boiling against boulders, and out of sight.

Lorenzo jumped down the embankment to the edge of the water. He pointed. "Here."

Bonfire holding her hand, Johnnie clambered down. The pebbled dirt all around had been washed repeatedly by errant waves from the confluence of the two streams. It was yellow and muddy. Just beyond where Lorenzo stood, his boots stained dark by trickling water, the mud was smoother and deeper.

Johnnie walked closer. She saw at once that something—or someone—had torn up the mud in this area. Deep indentations welled full, others had half drained. The slanting morning sunlight sharply shadowed the tread design of somebody's boot soles. Jutting from the rushing water just beyond, several smooth, football-sized rocks caught the flow and formed angry white foam.

"This is recent," Bonfire said unnecessarily. "Another hour or two and all this will have been washed smooth again."

Johnnie bent low for a closer inspection. Except for the deep footprints filled with water and the shallower boot tracks, there was nothing to see. "I'll get pictures."

Bonfire's eyes narrowed. "What good will that do?"

She paused, looking around, upstream and down, toward the waterfall and the boiling, angry vee beyond. She fought the dismay that rose up.

The pictures were not likely to do any good whatsoever. It was only in fantasyland where the pattern of a boot tread clearly matched one—and only one—set of boots anywhere in the area. With her first glance she had seen that the sole pattern was the most common around for ordinary work boots: deep vees, joined in the center, fanning out.

Besides, Noah Webster was gone. Everything pointed to his driving here after leaving the courthouse last night, walking down here in the dark—God only knew why—slipping, falling in. He could have hit his head on one of these nasty protruding rocks and been stunned. The swift current would have carried him over the waterfall in an instant. Beyond, even the craziest whitewater addict would not have stood much of a chance of surviving.

But maybe it hadn't happened that way at all, she told herself. Good lord, maybe somebody else—a fly fisherman, someone like that—had made these marks. Maybe no one had fallen in anywhere. Maybe the silly man from Oklahoma had waded across the brook higher up and gone off into the mountains on some nutty wild-goose chase of his own.

She made some decisions. "Let's get back to the others," she told Bonfire. "Davy, please come along. There are a few more things I want to ask you. We'll get some pictures here regardless."

They walked back along the creek. Butt Peabody was still down beside the abandoned truck, and Johnnie led the way to join him.

"He might have fallen in down there," she told him.

"Shit," Peabody said.

"Anything here?"

"Nothing. All his stuff is on board. It looks like he just drove down, got out—and vanished."

She thought about it. "We need to mount a search. Why don't you get on the radio and have Billy get in touch with the local CB folks in REACT? They love emergencies like this. They can get two dozen people into the rocks on the far side over there, and start combing the ravines."

Bonfire said, "My people can do that."

She turned, surprised. "You can get them to help like that?"

"Of course." His eyes went lusterless with a hint of his old hostility. "We don't need white people trampling all over the mounds and leaving piles of trash."

"Okay, then," she decided. "Do it. Butt, walk back down there with me to get some pictures. Davy, thanks for the help. Don't go away. I still need to ask you a few more things."

She hurried upslope to where her Jeep was parked. Grabbing her ancient Canon out of the storage box, she checked for film and then trotted back toward where Peabody waited for her. Behind her, Dean Epperly's old car hove into view, portable red light flashing on top.

As she ran, she was struck by incredulity. Anyone watching would have surely thought all this looked well-organized and professional. In reality, she felt completely helpless, and this time the feeling was accompanied by a pang of remorse. For if Noah Webster was dead, he had died because he came back here after she warned him against it. She had not made the point strongly enough. And now maybe he had paid the price for her shilly-shallying.

18

BY EARLY THURSDAY afternoon the pickup truck registered to Noah Webster had been photographed on-site, searched, and checked for fingerprints before the county's commercial wrecker service came in to tow it to the lockup lot beside the courthouse. By this time, too, Johnnie and Butt Peabody had taken statements from all the Big Gully men gathered at the ceremonial mound area, while George Bonfire had circulated around the community, drawing a blank on his questions about anyone who might have seen the Webster vehicle in the vicinity the previous night.

The sky clouded over as work proceeded, another cold front rippling in from the northwest, and when Johnnie conferred with her deputies beside the creek shortly after one o'clock, the first flakes of dry, bitter snow had begun to swirl.

Bonfire spread a county map out on the hood of his truck and showed them the plan for the search now underway. Two men had started out on this side of the creek, working downstream through the mound area into the willow brushlands below. Eight had now crossed the creek to start into the desolate mountain ravines on the far side, while five others were driving the long way around into the next county to loop back and start searching well downstream of the creek confluence where Webster might have met his fate. Meanwhile, Hobe Springer, the sheriff in adjacent Silver County, had also entered the search from over there, sending out two deputies and eleven members of his volunteer alpine rescue squad to mount a systematic search, one section at a time, until the two counties' search parties met.

Two small aircraft from the local field occasionally droned overhead, the private pilots also volunteering. Johnnie did not put much stock in their chances of orbiting around up there and managing to spot a lone man in the woods, but the effort was comforting.

Niles Pennington had appeared from the newspaper and was walking all over the place, taking roll after roll of pictures and generally making a nuisance of himself. After word of the missing man had spread, a small traffic jam had developed in Big Gully as curious motorists tried to get in on the excitement; Johnnie had sent Dean Epperly back into town to divert nonlocal traffic back in the direction it had come from.

"And that's about the size of it," Bonfire concluded, sloppily refolding the map. "I've put the word out for more help. I think I can keep eight to ten men in the field right through the night, if need be."

Peabody stuck a freshly made cigarette between his lips. "Night search wouldn't stand much of a chance, George."

Bonfire nodded. "I know. But these boys are good. You needn't worry they might get lost, anything like that."

"Sure, sure, I know that. But there wouldn't be much need for night search anyway, would there, now?"

Bonfire's eyes narrowed.

"Because?" Johnnie prompted.

Peabody's expression was bleak. "With this snow it's going to get a lot colder. All Webster's blankets and all were in his truck. If he fell into that water and somehow managed to get back out—or even if he just wandered off someplace like the blamed fool he is—he'll never survive the cold tonight. If we don't find him by dark, he's a goner."

No one said anything right away. Not far away, Niles Pennington had climbed up on a mound in order to point his camera back this way, long lens catching dull cloud light as he rotated for better telephoto focus. A few spectators who had somehow eluded Dean Epperly's roadblock stood not far from him, pointing, conferring, and eating candy bars.

"We'll find him before dark," Johnnie said finally.

"Sure," Peabody rumbled.

"I'm going back into town and make sure his truck gets sealed up properly," she added. "Then I'll wait for the crime lab boys to get here again. God, they must know the way by heart by now. I'll have my radio on, Butt. You can let me know if anything develops here." She looked at Bonfire. "I know you said you wanted to get into town to round up some more help. Why don't you do that? I can give you and your guys four walkie-talkie radios so you can keep in touch with each other."

"No need for that," Bonfire said expressionlessly

She hesitated an instant and then laughed. "What are you going to do? Send smoke signals?"

To her surprise, his teeth gleamed in a genuine grin. He reached inside his heavy coat and pulled out a slim gray Motorola cellular telephone. "Ma Bell works best, even out here in the boonies these days." He hesitated, then added with a somber wink, "Honest injun."

DRIVING BACK INTO Big Gully alone, Johnnie mentally reviewed the morning's events. The disappearance of kooky Noah Webster felt like the last straw. Dammit, she had *warned* him about crossing the local Indian population and trespassing on their sacred land. What was wrong with the man that he wouldn't listen to common sense?

She remembered the warning Butt Peabody had relayed late yesterday. She should have taken it more seriously—set out searching for Webster right then and there. She could have locked him up overnight, given him time to think about it.

If she had, he would be alive and accounted for right now.

She couldn't definitely suspect anyone of causing whatever had happened to happen. The creek site where Webster had disappeared was not even individual property in the normal sense; it was part of the area owned by the local tribe, held in some kind of informal trust by a hundred names, used a bit like white society used public park land. The only difference being that nobody was supposed to camp—or do anything else—on this property. It was supposed to be held holy for the spirit world and those who had gone into that kingdom long ago.

But damn Noah Webster just hadn't been able to resist, she thought disgustedly, driving past the first poor houses on the edge of the settlement. Had he paid with his life? As each hour passed, she felt more like that was the case.

She drove slowly past the dilapidated old schoolhouse that the valley board of education amazingly managed to consider equal to the new twelve-million-dollar junior high plant just finished in Tenoclock. A handful of kids ran around the bare dirt playground. One of the swings had an old tire lashed to its chains for a seat. The other positions didn't even have chains. She saw pieces of cardboard in some of the building's windows where they had cracked or broken.

As she neared the gas station corner, she felt her anger growing. Noah Webster's disappearance could fan new flames of the old latent racism. She could expect more crank calls, more Confederate battle flag window stickers in ratty-looking pickups, more fights at places like the Eastside. Webster's latest—and possibly final— trick would make a lot of lives more miserable, including her own.

Seeing her gas gauge nearing the empty mark, she remembered she should have filled up at the county yard yesterday. The Big Gully station was just ahead on her left. She wheeled in. She paid for her own gas part of the time anyhow, subsequently submitting expense vouchers that seemed to get misplaced during processing about 50 percent of the time.

Pulling up beside the regular no-lead pump, she got out and started the gas going in. Aware of two or three faces watching her from inside the office, she kept her back turned to them. She felt mad at everybody.

It wasn't until the voice spoke close behind her, startling her, that she turned. Old Abner Wakinokiman stood there, a blanket draped over his battered felt hat and wrapped around his skinny body like the shroud for a mummy.

"What?" Johnnie said nervously.

Wakinokiman licked leathery lips and spoke louder, but his reedy voice still was hard to pick up over the mutter of the gas pump. "I said, have you found the missing man yet?"

"No. No, we haven't."

The old man nodded. "I did not expect you would." He started to turn away to go back into the station building.

"Wait a minute," Johnnie called after him. "What do you mean, you didn't expect us to find him?"

The wind made tears well in his pale, narrowed eyes. "The man chose to risk the curse. He will never be seen or heard from again."

Despite her sympathy for traditional beliefs, Johnnie's fatigue and worry made her blurt out a very white reply: "I don't believe in curses."

His wizened face stiffened. "Yet you claim Indian blood."

"My people were Choctaw, yes."

"So a small part of you may still believe, and that is why you react so strongly."

She shook her head vehemently. "No. Oh, look, Mr. Wakinokiman, I don't want to offend you or anybody else on what they choose to believe. But Mr. Webster was not carried away somewhere by some ghost or goblin. Either he wandered off, or he died somehow in an accident, or some person did something to him. Magic—a curse of some kind—is not part of it."

"Yet a lion walked. The earth shook."

"Those were *not* parts of a curse."

"Are you so sure?"

Behind her, the gas pump chunked off, the Jeep tank full. She turned, replaced the nozzle, and closed her gas cap. "Look, I've got to get going. I'm sorry if I can't buy into this stuff about a curse."

Wakinokiman stepped stiffly aside to let her pass. "You do not believe in the power of a holy man to gain favor from the Great Spirit? You do not believe that ordinary men may act under control of the Prankster?"

She smiled nervously, embarrassed for the old man. "No. Sorry!"

Wakinokiman suddenly spread his arms out wide and looked up at the sky. His eyes, closed and his lips moved, although she could not hear his words over the stiff, snowy wind. He trembled.

"What—?" she began.

The wind stopped. Instantly.

The snow drifted down in perfect stillness. Moments earlier Johnnie had been aware of the distant racket of a radio playing inside the station, but now that sound too had vanished. She felt like a cocoon had descended over her and Wakinokiman, still motionless in his posture of supplication to the sky.

As if a switch had been thrown, the snow stopped. Nothing moved—nothing existed except the vast, eerie silence. I am not on earth, she thought, dazed.

Only the swollen gray clouds hanging low overhead were in motion. They churned, and a rent opened up. For an instant

188 / JOHN MILES

bright sunlight beamed down, warming her face. Thunder
rolled.

Wakinokiman lowered his arms and bowed his head. The
sound of the radio came back. The wind whipped Johnnie's coat
collar, sifting brittle snow down her neck. She shivered.

Wakinokiman turned and shuffled toward the station shack.
Johnnie hurried after him, touching his arm. He looked at her.

She stammered, "Maybe I ought to, uh, maybe it wouldn't
hurt—I mean—whatever I happen to believe about a curse, or
anything like that—is there more to it than you told us that night
when the lion got loose? What makes you think Mr. Webster's
disappearance could be curse-related?" Then she began to get
her bearings again, and a new thought lanced into her mind.
"Do a lot of people here believe in the curse? Do they worry that
it might fall on them? Could somebody around here have thought
they were working to prevent the curse from falling on them,
maybe, by stopping Mr. Webster from disturbing the mounds?
Anything like that?"

"I do not believe any person in human form harmed the man
you seek."

"Somebody in *nonhuman* form, then?" She felt like a fool
for asking, but the magic only moments ago had shaken all her
usual logic.

Wakinokiman bowed his head. "Come inside. We can talk."

She pointed at the sky, wincing as the heightening wind
made snowflakes sting her face. "How did you do that?"

"Come inside. I can smoke."

"Will you tell me a little more about the curse?"

"Will you buy me an RC Cola?"

IT WAS MORE than thirty minutes before Johnnie left the
sweltering little station office and returned, teeth chattering, to
her Jeep. The snowfall was heavier now, making the nearby

mountainsides look like slabs of smoke. She started the Jeep
and headed back toward Tenoclock.

Of all the stuff she had ever heard, she thought, the old man's
meandering story had been one of the strangest. She felt silly
for having listened. He hadn't helped her at all, and she had
been foolish in the extreme to think he might.

Or not.

After watching her pay for her gas and buy him a cola,
Wakinokiman had solemnly borrowed a cigarette from the boy
running the station, then sat back in a creaky rocker in one
corner near the potbellied stove and talked through his swirling
tobacco smoke.

He repeated the story he had told on the night of the lion,
telling how the old people, possibly Anasazi, had had a great
chief who was crippled in a manner similar to Kokopelli, the
Anasazi flute man. That chief, Wakinokiman said, set the curse
on the valley after having visions of doom for the Indians, pes-
tilence, and strange white people multiplying like ants.

"The great chief of the old people said all Indian people
must protect the burial sites and other holy places, and if they
did so well and courageously, he would see that they were spared
whatever doom might come to pass on the white people as a
result of the curse."

The chief, Wakinokiman told Johnnie, had gone to the sky
in both body and spirit when he died his human death, and it
was his deformed, broken back that caused the curve of the stars
through the heavens, and made the moon wane at times when
his pain grew extreme and he had to go into a cave and so could
not see to it that the lazy moon shone as brightly as she could.
But the one thing the old chief had always done was watch over
his people and this valley, which was the center of the universe.

"Sometimes he comes down out of the sky and tests us,
sometimes with funny jokes and other times with great suffering,
and at such times he is often seen as the Prankster, a wolf

sometimes, but sometimes too a chicken. So the wolf and the chicken are mortal enemies because they are the two shapes taken by the Prankster, and each considers it a great honor, and they contest with one another to see who is the best, so in the future the chief will come only in their form, and not in the form of the other."

The chief, Wakinokiman said, was very wise and very patient. He forgave most things. But there were two things he could never forgive. One was the Indian's giving up of his sacred heritage and following the white man's ways in total forgetfulness of his own. And the other was failure to protect the burial mounds where the bones of the old people slumbered in peace.

Wakinokiman told Johnnie several stories about young men or women in the past who had forgotten their traditions and quickly vanished under mysterious circumstances. He told how the chief had saved the old people in many battles with other tribes, and had even saved their descendants, in a fight with the cavalry, by allowing the people to sprout wings and fly across a great distance, their wingtips beating the earth so strongly that valleys like this one, and even the Grand Canyon, were formed.

At an early day in the pollution by white people, the old man said, the descendants of the People, today's Utes, had been cheated out of their lands by an evil man named Lincoln Herman. This, too, was in the legends. The great chieftain had foretold how a lone white settler would bring tears and despair to the modern people.

"Today," the old man droned, lighting another Camel, "too many forget. The walking of the lion and the shaking of the earth were signs that the chief is very angry. Then this man of yours, Webster, came and would have violated the mounds. It may be that the chief came as the prankster and killed this man Webster and threw his body into the ocean after devouring his liver. Or it could be that the chief entered into the body of a young man hereabouts and took his revenge on your man Webster in such a way. In either case, he will not be found. The curse cannot be denied. The man Webster is lost forever."

"But your own people—the most traditional of all, the Keepers—are helping us search!" Johnnie protested.

Wakinokiman inclined his head. "Of course. This is a rule of the chief too. Do not expect the white people to be sane, but go along with them and humor them unless they come to destroy your tepee."

IT WAS NONSENSE, Johnnie thought now, driving out of Big Gully, the windshield wipers of her Jeep kerchunking heavily under thick, growing burdens of packed snow. A *spirit* had not made away with Noah Webster.

If he had not fallen into the creek or gotten lost on his own, some very real person or persons had done him in. And the old curse had nothing to do with it.

But Wakinokiman's story—and that frightening moment when he seemed actually to change reality out by the gas pumps—had not been wasted on her. She saw now, as she never had before, how profoundly someone could be affected by the old stories, the old ways . . . the old fears.

She had not wanted to believe it up until now, but now she was forced to face a strong possibility she had earlier tried to ignore. If others in Big Gully—the Keepers most of all—believed in the curse and the spirit world as fervently as Wakinokiman did, then they would have stopped at nothing to prevent Noah Webster from returning to their land and violating the ceremonial mounds.

Despite everything they had said, and George Bonfire's trust in them, they could have been lying. One of them might have been out here last night, found Webster foolishly trespassing again, and taken steps to make sure he would never violate this or any other sacred site, ever again.

19

BACK AT THE courthouse it was quiet. Some employees were being released early because you could never tell about a late storm like this; the worst in the recent history of the Teno-clock Valley had been considerably later, in early May of 1919, when twenty-seven inches of snow fell in less than twenty-four hours, trapping two parties of hunters and killing eleven of them, along with more than forty people found later, frozen in their homes.

Johnnie found clerk Hesther Gretsch morosely sorting meaningless correspondence and sent her home, too. Back in the jail, Jason Ramsey was already back at work.

"Mr. Ramsey, you didn't need to come in this early. Maybe you ought to get on home in case this storm gets worse."

Ramsey looked up from a book whose pages were cluttered with Greek lettering. "The storm is why I came in early. It's warmer here than at my house."

Returning to the front, Johnnie called Butt Peabody on the radio. He reported no progress at the search site. The only good news was that the snow seemed to be letting up out there, and the weather office at Denver said the front was sliding back north again as a warm front, which ought to moderate temperatures by morning.

But Noah Webster, if he was out in this, was not likely to last until morning.

Johnnie went back to the jail office. "Jason, your report about Mr. Webster said he came by, asked for me, said he would be by today sometime, and walked out again. How did he look? Are you sure he was alone? Did he say anything else at all?"

Ramsey thought about it. "He looked tired, but okay. The man was sort of . . . hectic, you know?"

"That's normal for him. Anything else?"

"Well, he gave me the card—which I left for you—and he said he would be back in the morning. Or maybe he just said tomorrow." Ramsey paused again. "Wait a minute. He did say one other thing. He said . . . let me recollect and see if I can get it almost word for word . . . he said, 'Tell the sheriff I've been having fun and games at the library, and I'll be in tomorrow because I've got some information for her.' "

Johnnie rubbed aching eyes. "The *library?* Are you sure he said the library?"

"Positive. I didn't write it on my note because it didn't seem like it meant anything at the time—"

"Is there anything else?"

He thought about it. "That's all."

"Good Lord," Johnnie breathed, "what would he have been doing at the library?"

"I think that's safe to assume," Ramsey said, surprising her.

"What?" she demanded.

"You told me how fascinated he is by Anasazi culture, and how he was in touch with the Herman family. I should think it obvious that he would want to investigate the Herman family background, especially as it relates to the present-day Utes."

———

THE LIBRARY READING room librarian's name was
Hunzecker, according to the discreet name tag on the lapel of
her pastel dress, and she had just come on duty minutes before
Johnnie arrived.

"He's a small man," Johnnie told her at the reading room
counter. "He wears eyeglasses, and he was probably wearing
jeans and a heavy shirt, with work boots, probably—"

Mrs. Hunzecker's eyelids flipped up and down in rapid irritation. "I'm quite sure I know the man you mean, Johnnie. He
was here most of the evening, and when it came closing time, I
practically had to run him out. A most irritating man, I might
add. He kept asking me for all kinds of help, as if I didn't have
lots of other things to do."

"What was he looking for? What kind of things did he have
you bring out?"

Hunzecker's lips tightened with indignation. "Everything!"

Johnnie smiled patiently. "Like . . . ?"

"Well, that was part of it, don't you see. He didn't know
exactly *what* he wanted. First he asked for county records—
deeds and leases, that sort of thing, as if we had things like that.
Well, I tried to accommodate him, lord knows. I dug out our files
of county histories, the Smith book, the two volumes by my uncle
Fred, the series put out by the genealogical society, and he fumed
through those for a while, flipping pages too loudly—honestly, my
regulars were all looking across the room at him and practically
staring *daggers* at him for all the noise he was making—and then
he wanted local biographies, so I sent him to the computer terminal
to look for those, and he came back with about twelve cards, some
for books we haven't taken off the shelf for *years*, and then he wanted
to know what we hold in the way of local periodicals, magazines,
pamphlets, things of that nature. It was just a *fishing expedition*, he
didn't have any idea what he was looking for!"

Hunzecker paused, out of breath, eyelids snapping.

"He never gave you a hint what more specific subject matter he had in mind?" Johnnie probed.

"Well, next he wanted old newspaper files. I showed him where the microfilm is stored and explained the indexing system. But we have only two microfilm readers, don't you know, and they were both being used. So there was no help for it but he had to have me go all the way down into the basement and start hauling up those *huge* bound volumes and laying them out on that table over there for him. I *told* him there was a limit to how much time I had for him, but he kept asking for more."

"Did he have particular years in mind," Johnnie asked, "or what?"

"Well, of course he reeled off subjects at first, but I stopped him on that fast, you can be sure. We have no indexes set up like that. Heaven knows the genealogical society would *like* for us to have everything on God's green earth cross-indexed by names, but until somebody like the Mormons come in here and do it for us as part of their worldwide cataloging, it just isn't going to be done. Do you have any *idea* how long it would take to go through more than a hundred years of old newspapers and copy out every name and create an index of all of them? People just don't understand our problems. On our salary scale—"

"You say he mentioned names or subjects?" Johnnie interrupted as gently as possible. "Do you happen to remember any of those?"

"Well, yes, some. . . ." Hunzecker frowned, a tic starting to jump in her forehead. "Those old Indian mounds down southwest. He wanted to know about those. And pioneers. He wanted anything to do with the earliest settlers. Then, as for the years, he wanted the earliest papers. Then he wanted *all* of 1969, and before he was through he asked for almost all of every year since then. Then after riffling through some of those he put them aside and came back and said he wanted 1919. *1919!* Is the man

crazy? What difference does it make now, something that might
have happened in 1919?" Hunzecker paused to gasp for breath
again before resuming. "Then he had a whole *pocketful* of those
dreadful little yellow things—you know, Post-its—and I saw
him making notes in a notebook and sticking those yellow things
on some pages in the 1919 volumes. *Then* he came back to me
and wanted to know what we might have on local cemeteries.
Well, by that time I had about had my fill, so I told him I didn't
have time to help him any more that night. So he went back to
those big old newspaper books and kept on poring over them,
and he was still at it when it finally got to be nine o'clock and I
finally got him to leave."

Johnnie thought about it while the librarian caught her
breath. Noah Webster was an eccentric, but he was not crazy.
He had been searching for something specific, and it would
seem that he had found at least some of what he had been after.

He had found enough before library closing time, she
thought, to go directly to the courthouse searching for her. And
he had promised to be back "with information."

Had he then decided to act on the information, and had that
somehow led to his disappearance?

The thread seemed impossibly thin. But it was the only one
she had.

"Mrs. Hunzecker," she said, deciding, "would it be possible
for me to look over some of those newspaper books Mr. Webster
examined last night? I know it's a terrible amount of trouble for
you, but—"

Hunzecker harrumphed. "Not as much as last night, I can
assure you. We haven't had time to drag them all back to the
basement yet. They weigh a ton, after all." She turned and
pointed down between the stacks. "They're all piled on that steel
table back there in the back. You can help yourself if you want
to, Johnnie."

Johnnie decided she had time for a preliminary look-see.

She tiptoed down between the stacks, fearful of the librarian's ire. At the back of the long room, where the light was dimmest and individual footprints could be seen on the dusty tile floor, she found perhaps a dozen large gray ledger-style books stacked haphazardly on a metal table.

There was a steel chair nearby. Taking a deep breath, she pulled the chair over, sat down, and started looking over the books of old newspapers, searching first for protruding yellow Post-its.

The first one she found was in a volume marked "Apr-May-Jun 78." Carefully folding back the decaying old newspaper pages to the place marked, she scanned the narrow columns of faded type for the edition of June 17, 1978.

There had been a light snow. A traffic light was to be installed at Silver and Gunnison. With school out for the summer, residents were urged to watch out for children playing in the streets. Wickley's Department Store planned a Crazy Days Sale. The city commission planned to study the budget for the fire department. A hiker from Texas had broken his legs in a fall near Anvil Mountain. Stray dogs were again a problem. Lucy Herman—*wait a minute*—

It was the only item on the page that Noah Webster could possibly have been interested in. Johnnie read it quickly.

Lucy Herman, only daughter of Lincoln and Mary Alice Herman, of Tenoclock's pioneer Herman family, had died in a hiking accident. Lucy, forty-three, was not married. She was survived by her brother, Elmo, of the home. Her father had died in 1969. Her mother had predeceased him in 1937. Burial was scheduled Saturday at 10:00 A.M. in the Herman family plot at the IOOF Cemetery, Rev. John Mock presiding.

Puzzled, Johnnie looked carefully but did not find anything else in the edition. She closed the book and continued her search of others. She saw that all four volumes for the year 1937 were stacked together, but there were no Post-its in any of them.

One of the 1969 books had two yellow tabs protruding from it, both in September of that year. The first story was not hard to notice, since it had led the Sunday edition's front page. Lincoln Herman, son of the pioneer Herman who first settled in the Tenoclock Valley, had died after a long illness at the age of seventy-three. He was survived by a son, Elmo, and a daughter, Lucy.

Lincoln Herman's father, the first Lincoln Herman, had come to the valley in 1888, the story said. He purchased 29,000 acres of prime pastureland and mountain forest in a transaction connected with the transfer of Ute tribal lands to the United States government in that year. Purchase price was said to be ten barrels of whiskey and an undisclosed amount of tobacco.

Despite a reputation for a fierce temper and occasional spells of what was called in those days "peculiarity," the original Herman had later sold off an estimated million dollars' worth of timber to the railroad and once was an important stockholder in the Denver & Rio Grande Railway Co.

After expanding his empire through a series of land negotiations and sale of Indian bones and relics to several national museums, the story said, the first Herman had become an elder in the Presbyterian Church around 1912 and led the drive to fund and build the Redeemer church building, which remained one of Tenoclock's architectural marvels. In 1916 the pioneer Herman was shot and killed in an incident that remained unexplained to the present day, and the younger Lincoln Herman took command of the family.

Under leadership of the second Lincoln Herman, the family accumulated additional wealth by supplying horses to the cavalry during the Great War. Tragedy continued to dog the family, however, and in 1919 Lincoln's younger brother, Luther, died in a hunting accident.

It was said that Lincoln himself had carried the gun that accidentally killed his brother, the story said, and he was reported plunged into melancholy that plagued him all the rest of his days. His wife, Mary Alice, died in 1937 after bearing him two children, Elmo and Lucy. He would be remembered as a great man.

It didn't make a lot of sense to Johnnie, and she failed to see how it could possibly constitute information that Noah Webster might consider significant. Frowning, she turned to the second marker in the book, only a few pages later.

A class-action lawsuit brought by more than ten thousand members of the Ute nation against Elmo and Lucy Herman, and John Doe and Mary Roe, whereabouts unknown, demanding twenty million dollars in damages, had been settled out of court.

The suit, the story said, had alleged that certain transactions involved in the Herman family's original acquisition of Ute lands had been based on fraudulent representations and forged documents. Judge Julius Weaver, in accepting the settlement and closing the case, noted that plaintiffs had failed to produce any documentary proof of their allegations, and "no living person remains who might testify as to the veracity or falsehood of said allegations of wrongdoing." The judge hailed the defendants for their good-faith bargaining in an attempt to resolve long-standing hard feelings.

Terms of the settlement were not divulged. Plaintiffs were represented in court by Jones and Jones, attorneys-at-law, Breckenridge, Colorado.

Johnnie made a couple of notes on this one. She began to see that Noah Webster was fixated on burial mounds, and the Herman family evidently had made a great deal of money at an early day by looting a mound on their property and selling everything they found. That information, combined with this story about a settlement with the Utes, might have sent Webster off looking for more information about the Hermans' history—why, she could not quite be sure.

But Webster had said something once about genealogy, family history . . . some link between someone in his family and some branch of the Hermans. Did he imagine these stories helped with that line of inquiry? And if so, why would he think the sheriff's department would be interested? Had he possibly imagined that the Hermans could still have records about the old burial mound exhumations that could help him in his Anasazi investigation?

Johnnie walked back to the front of the library with a nose full of library dust and a head full of confusion. Webster had seen something in this mess that she couldn't see at all. She didn't have a clue about what it might have been, but she was quite clear about something else.

She needed to see the Hermans, and now.

Thanking Mrs. Hunzecker and getting a glare in return, she went back outside. The snow had let up, the sun was trying to break through, and little bands of tourists had appeared on the streets here and there. A cement truck rumbled by, probably headed for the new condominium development just getting underway over east.

She climbed into the Jeep and reached for the mike. "Sheriff's department base, this is unit one."

"Unit one, go ahead."

"Any messages?"

"Negative, one."

"Ten-four. I'll be en route the Herman ranch."

"Ten-four."

20

AS A CHILD, Johnnie had been among legions of Tenoclock
grade-schoolers who secretly went on the adventure of taking a
hike onto the Herman ranch. It had been deliciously scary.

In those days there had been a massive black iron gate over
the roadway leading back into the property, and many acres of
virgin timber had not yet been clear-cut in a make-money operation that some early-day environmentalists decried even then.
It had been easy, once you raced through the open gate, to dart
into the black woods and with your heart in your mouth sneak
all the way up the mountain to the place where the ghostly old
mansion brooded over a once-magnificent lawn now turned to
trash-strewn weeds.

Nothing ever happened to any of the children who made
the spooky journey—at least not as far as anyone knew—but
the stories told were wonderful. The old man had been crazy,
the stories said. There had been murders here. There was a crazy
woman in the house even today, the old maid that some kids
once reported seeing out on the front balcony over the porch,
wearing a white nightgown and singing at the sky. The dogs who
roved over the property were man-eaters—or kid-eaters, too,

unless you took along a bone from the butcher's shop or an old doughnut or something to toss at them when they discovered you and came barking bloody murder. Sometimes the barking of the dogs brought out Mr. Elmo, and sometimes he stalked around, limping on a bad leg, with a shotgun in his hands.

When Mr. Elmo came out like that, you ran like maniacs back down through the woods and out the front gate and lay gasping in the weedy ditch across the road, hidden, sure you had escaped with your life only by a miracle.

Johnnie hadn't been back up here on the property since the last time she made her second—and final—spook incursion at the age of eleven. This afternoon she didn't feel the kind of stomach-aching fear she had felt in those old days. But as she turned her Jeep into the road where the gate used to be, she did not feel entirely calm. She didn't expect ghosts or crazy women to scream at her, as she had as a child, but she didn't exactly expect a very friendly reception either.

Driving slowly up the long, narrow dirt mountain road, she saw that the property had gone drastically downhill since her childhood forays. Aspen and lodgepole pine had begun to re-claim the stripped slopes, but much of the thin topsoil evidently had been lost to erosion following the clear-cut, and the new growth did not look healthy. Deep gullies interlaced the land, and she saw no sign of wildlife. There were few cattle. The land had a dying quality, a sadness, about it.

The Hermans had come into all this land and wealth unethi-cally, if not illegally, she thought. They had incurred the enmity of the modern-day Utes by cheating them out of land worth many millions and then desecrating at least one sacred burial mound in order to sell the pottery and other Indian artifacts found inside it. One death in the family—at least—had been under myste-rious circumstances.

Thinking about it, she felt a shiver down her spine. Possibly it was nothing more than an adult version of the childish fear she had enjoyed so long ago. But perhaps it was a wiser intuition. Perhaps the Herman family had all kinds of things best left hidden . . . and Noah Webster had tried to pry into almost all of them.

This was what she had to find out, if she could.

Turning through the thin woods as she neared the crest of the slope, she brought the old house into view. It loomed blacker and bleaker than she remembered. A new garage building had been built off to one side, and there were trucks in it, but everything else looked neglected and run-down.

Several of the Hermans' ever-present dogs loped out to bark and growl at her as she parked near the front of the house. Looking out at fangs and crazy eyes, she was wondering whether she dared risk getting out when a movement at the front of the house caught her eye and she saw the front door open. One of the Herman brothers—at the distance she could not tell them apart—stepped out onto the small front stoop. He put fingers to his mouth and emitted a piercing whistle. The dogs turned and obediently raced up to him.

Johnnie got out and strode up to the steps. Some of the dogs growled at her, but they stayed close to the man's side. She saw now that it was Luther, the younger brother, who hadn't struck her as very bright.

"Hello!" she said, smiling bravely. "I'm Sheriff Baker. I guess you remember me."

Luther Herman's thick, stolid face did not change expression. "What do you want?"

"I think a man named Webster visited you guys the other day. I wanted to talk to you about him."

To her great surprise, Luther nodded and stepped back, opening the way to the door. "Come in."

Most of the dogs rushed in ahead of her. She entered a tall, dark entry foyer with a big staircase spiraling up into the gloom. Straight ahead was the bright open doorway into a large room with sun coming in the windows. Luther pointed her in that direction, and she entered it.

Sitting at a card table near the dead fireplace, old Elmo Herman and a woman who must be his wife looked up from a game of dominoes. Johnnie had not seen Elmo for years and was shocked by how he had aged. His wife appeared drawn and tired. Both of them struck Johnnie as edgy and suspicious.

Just getting up from one of two old armchairs half a room away, Joseph Herman gave her a furious, challenging look. "What do *you* want?"

"Friendly visit," Johnnie assured him, walking deeper into the room. She tried to appear as confident and relaxed as possible. "I hope I'm not disturbing you too much."

"Disturb us?" Joseph snapped. "Is this the way you always work? Drop in unexpected?"

"I'm not here to cause your family any trouble, Mr. Herman."

"Then what is it you want, barging in like this, surprising us?"

"I'm looking for a missing man, and I understand he visited you here recently. I thought he might have said something to you that would give me a hint about where he might be."

Elmo's pinched, deeply lined face became more suspicious. "Who would that be?"

"His name is Noah Webster, and—"

"That fool?"

"He's missing."

"I'm not surprised. He was meddling in everyone's business."

"Now, now, Joseph," Elmo said quietly. "The sheriff has a job to do. What's past is past. Let's let her ask her questions."

Joseph growled and sat back down. His brother Luther lumbered over and sat in the other chair. Elmo motioned Johnnie to a spot on the couch and took a place at the opposite end. His wife left the card table and shuffled over to sit on the footstool near her husband.

"What can we help you with?" Elmo asked.

Johnnie hesitated. There was a curious rehearsed feeling about their movements and the way the old man had asked the question. She wondered if she was imagining things and decided to dismiss her uneasiness. "When did Noah Webster visit you?"

"That would have been yesterday," Elmo said.

Joseph put in, "Had a lot of dumb questions about family history. We don't take stock in that kind of stuff. We couldn't tell him much."

Elmo's wife spoke for the first time in a low, tremulous voice. "He seemed like a nice man."

"Oh, yeah," Joseph said. "We did what we could to help him, get him off our back."

"Did he happen to say anything about his plans for later in the day, or this morning?"

Joseph looked blank and innocent. "No, not that I can recollect. Do you remember anything, Pop?"

"No, I surely don't," Elmo said.

"Me neither," Luther rumbled.

"He seemed like a very nice man," the old woman repeated.

In order to give herself time to think, Johnnie unbuttoned the pocket of her jacket and took out her notebook, slowly riffling back to a blank page. Her earlier uneasy feelings had sharpened. She was being given a performance. Whatever they knew or didn't know, they were not about to tell her anything.

"So you can't think of anything that might help me?" she asked, smiling at Joseph.

He shrugged in silence.

"Didn't Mr. Webster ask for information about some member of your family who was related to him?"

Elmo jerked back as if she had struck him across the face.

"No. Certainly not. Nothing like that." His lower lip began to tremble.

Joseph said, "He talked about looking at some of the burial mounds down by Big Gully. If I was to guess where he might be going next, I'd say he was headed down there."

"That's right," Elmo chimed in eagerly, his voice quavering. "I hadn't put much stock in that. But you're right. I imagine he was planning to go down there."

"Did he ask to visit the mound you have back on your property?" Johnnie asked.

"On our property?" Joseph repeated with another blank look. "There's no mound on Herman property."

"I thought there was. I must have been mistaken."

"Was," Elmo said.

"Was?" Johnnie studied him. A sickly film of sweat glistened on his face.

"Got destroyed," Elmo said. "Dug up. Fell down. All signs of it gone now, long ago. Too bad. Grave robbers, I guess."

She decided to attack, just a little bit: "I had always heard the Herman family made a lot of money by digging up that mound and selling the artifacts to museums."

"That's a lie!" Joseph said.

"The Herman family would of never been a part of anything like that," Elmo put in solemnly.

"Where was the mound?"

Elmo pointed north. "Out there, someplace."

"You don't know the exact site?"

"It's a big country. I don't get around much of it since the horse fell on me and broke my hip."

"I'm sorry."

Quite suddenly tears sprang to his eyes. "Is there anything else? Will you go now? Leave us in peace?"

"Okay, Pop," Joseph growled. "Okay, now."

The old man's shoulders quaked, and he began to sob brokenly. "I can't do this anymore. I don't know how much more I can take. I never wanted anything but for people to leave us alone."

"Shut up, Pop," Joseph said sharply. "Shut up."

"He ain't well," Luther protested. "Don't talk mean to him."

Joseph whirled on his brother with a killing glint in his eye. "You shut up too!"

Johnnie got to her feet. "I'm sorry I intruded. I guess there's nothing else you can tell me."

The old man's sobs made an ugly, choking sound in the room. His wife went to him and bent over him, hugging his shoulders. He clung to her like a man whose life was destroyed—a man broken.

Joseph stood and took Johnnie's arm. His hand felt big as a banjo. "I'll show you out, Sheriff. No hard feelings. But he isn't well. You can see that."

Luther sat staring as she let the older brother direct her toward the front foyer. As they passed a half-open doorway at the far end of the room, she had a moment to glance into the adjoining room, a littered office of some kind with a rolltop desk and worktable and piles of old newspapers on bookshelves. A small, bright row of winking red lights caught her eye, and then she was into the hallway and beyond.

"Thanks for your help," she told Joseph on the porch.

"Don't mention it," he said stiffly.

He stood there, arms folded across his massive chest, while she climbed into the Jeep, started it up, and backed away. He was still standing there when she drove into the woods and out of his line of sight.

It had been a strange and puzzling performance, she thought, by all of them. Possibly only at the end—when old Elmo broke down—had anything been honest or spontaneous.

She had had the intuition that their words and actions felt rehearsed. But it hadn't been until she left that she realized they truly had been. It had all been an act, especially their protestations about how surprised they were by her visit.

The glimpse she had had of a row of blinking lights in the office room proved that. She knew a Bearcat scanner when she saw one. The gain had been turned down during her visit. But she would have been willing to bet a month's wages that it hadn't been turned down earlier. They had heard her call to the courthouse, announcing her intentions. *Then* they had turned the scanner gain down and prepared for her "surprise" arrival.

And they had done very well, she thought, until old Elmo broke down.

She reviewed the conversation around the time that tears appeared in the old man's eyes and he seemed on the verge of breakdown. They had hustled her out fast after that. What had she asked that so stressed him?

She remembered: she had turned to asking about the old newspaper reports of the family's selling artifacts from the burial mound on their property. Elmo had denied that, vehemently. Then she had asked where the mound was located, he had been vague, and at that point the tears had come.

Suspicions began to crystallize as she drove on.

She had no idea why Noah Webster had marked old newspaper items about Herman family history; possibly all of that had been for what seemed his unrelated search for genealogical information. But he clearly had a passion about the burial mounds. He had marked the item about the Herman site, too. . . .

She reached for her microphone. "Sheriff's unit two, this is unit one."

Nothing came back for about thirty seconds. Then the squelch broke, and Butt Peabody's gravel voice sounded clearly: "Unit one, this is unit two, go."

"Ten-twenty?"

"Search location, over."

"Anything to report?"

The flat tone of his voice underscored the single word: "Negative."

"Is our special deputy on-site?"

"Affirm."

She poised her thumb on the mike button, reconsidering her intuitive impulse. She decided to trust it, dammit; nothing else had been working. She squeezed the mike. "Two, this is one. Request you report to headquarters, over."

It was Peabody's turn to pause. She could imagine how his forehead must be furrowing as he worried over her unexpected request. Ordinarily he would have stayed at the scene until Webster was found or the search was called off because of darkness. He had to be wondering what was on her mind.

When he came back, however, it was with no hint of the uncertainty she knew he must be feeling. "Roger, one. Unit two will be in transit to headquarters." He delayed a second or so, then added, "Unit two to base, did you copy that, over?"

Jason Ramsey's voice came back promptly. "Ten-four."

"Unit two out and rolling."

Johnnie keyed her mike one more time. "Unit one out, en route headquarters."

IT WAS ABOUT forty minutes later when Butt Peabody limped into the basement office, his coat and hat dusted heavily with snow and his face angry red from the cold wind. Johnnie gestured for him to join her in the small, seldom-used interrogation room.

He studied her with obvious scowling concern. "What's up, Johnnie?"

She briefed him on her visit to the Herman mansion.

He snorted when she finished. "You're lucky they didn't try to scalp you."

She chuckled mirthlessly. "Better not try to scalp an Indian, boy."

"What do you make of what happened out there?"

"Butt, until I went out there this afternoon I was feeling pretty sure that Noah Webster went back down to the mound site outside Big Gully last night, and somebody—one of the Keepers, or maybe someone else—did him in."

He licked wind-cracked lips that had to hurt. "But now you're not so sure?"

"Now I'm not so sure."

"Because?"

"Webster is a nut on those mounds. One of the things he marked in the old newspapers was about a mound on Herman property. It was when I mentioned that that Elmo started to crack up. Maybe Webster didn't go to the Big Gully mounds last night at all."

Peabody's forehead wrinkled twice as deeply, and he fumbled inside his heavy coat in the unmistakable gesture of fishing for tobacco. "What's the bottom line?"

"I'm wondering if there could be anything about that old, desecrated mound on the Herman ranch that they don't want examined. One of the other newspaper stories Webster had marked told about settlement of a class-action lawsuit brought by some Utes back in the sixties in regard to that particular piece of property. That cash settlement must have been huge. I think that must have marked the time when the family's fortunes started downhill. Butt, I don't know *what*, if anything, that mound might have to do with Noah Webster's disappearance. But I want to check it out. And I want to dig into the old records here at the courthouse and see what else we might find about the Herman family history, too."

Peabody rolled paper around fine shards of tobacco. "Won't find much old stuff. Records prior to 1935 were all in the annex, remember?"

"Oh, hell. Right. Well, then, this mound . . . ?"

"I've never seen it. No big deal to me, and you know how

pissy—pardon—sensitive the Hermans have always been about trespassers."

"I want to see the site," Johnnie repeated stubbornly.

"Yeah, but I don't know where it is, exactly, and I can't think of anyone who would."

Johnnie had been thinking about this, and she had a ready answer. "I can," she told him.

Peabody looked up from his half-made cigarette. "Who?"

"Wakinokiman."

21

LIGHT SNOWFALL COVERED the ground and denser evergreens around Abner Wakinokiman's weathered old mobile home. Inside it was steamy hot. In a tattered red-and-black flannel robe and worn, fur-lined moosehide slippers, Wakinokiman spread wrinkled fingers over the county map that Butt Peabody had just unfolded on his kitchen table.

The only sound inside the cramped trailer was the bubbling of a Crockpot on the sinkboard as the old man peered down the length of his nose through drugstore reading glasses and strained to orient himself to the map's depictions.

His long index finger started to trace an area colored greenish yellow, depicting the rise of higher ground west and slightly south of the mountainside Johnnie recognized as the site of the Herman mansion.

"It is here," Wakinokiman said slowly, continuing to move his finger. "I have not been at this place for forty years or more. But I remember it. There was a logging road once, long time ago. The river can be seen here. This area"—his finger made a small circular motion—"was great forest, but the Herman family sold it and made it like death. On beyond . . . here . . .

against the side of the cliffs that build up to the mountain, is where the sacred place is located."

Johnnie studied the map, seeing how it might be reached after an easy hike overland from the abandoned west mining road. "Mr. Wakinokiman, could you find someone—one of the Keepers, perhaps—who could lead us there?"

"My people do not go to that place."

"But you guard all the others near here—"

Wakinokiman's voice shook: "That place has been desecrated. The bones of the old people were dug up—scattered—and their holy things taken away, so that the spirits of those dead walk in the night, never to enter the spirit world." He looked up at Peabody, then at Johnnie, and the anger in his eyes was so bright it seemed like a fire. "The place is cursed. None of my people will go near it. None here has seen it in many, many years."

Johnnie sighed and turned to Peabody. "I guess we can find it."

He frowned and glanced at the small, sweaty window over the sink. The glass was quite gray. "It's too late tonight, Johnnie."

"We'll go first thing in the morning."

Peabody nodded. "I'm going to go check on how the search is going. Then I'll meet you back at the office in an hour or so."

"Okay, Butt. Fine."

Thanking Abner Wakinokiman, they left the trailer and walked to their vehicles, parked side-by-side in the snow and frozen mud of the front yard. Darkness was falling faster, and the cold had intensified. Johnnie hesitated at the door of her Jeep, and her eyes met Peabody's.

Neither of them said it, but she knew they were thinking the same thing. This kind of night cold was deadly. Hope for Noah Webster was fading as swiftly as the remnants of daylight.

Thirty minutes later, the search was called off for the night.

————

JOHNNIE WAS IN the kitchen of her house at 5:45 the next morning, Friday, when the sound of an approaching vehicle broke the vast dark beyond the thick log walls. Looking out the kitchen window over the sink, she saw headlights coming up her road from the highway a half mile down. Butt Peabody was a bit early; they had agreed to meet between 6:00 and 6:30 for their trip out to search for the burial mound on Herman property.

Aching all over after about four hours of restless, worried sleep, she hurried to pour water from her teakettle into two mugs primed with instant coffee. Hers was black, Peabody's laced with a heaping teaspoon of powdered creamer. Poor Butt, she thought, would need it. He had to have gotten up at 4:30, latest, to be here so early.

Johnnie was fully dressed—jeans, wool Pendleton, heavy socks, and leather hiking boots. She already had her blond hair tucked up under a faded red stocking cap. The outside temperature gauge beside the kitchen window read 24 degrees.

She stirred the coffees, watching Peabody's turn chocolate-yellow. Outside, the headlights of his pickup became blinding in the dark as he pulled up in front of the house behind her Jeep. His engine racket ceased, and his headlights went out. In the pale illumination of her porch light, he was barely visible as he climbed out stiffly and limped toward the front.

Johnnie carried the mugs to the big coffee table in front of the wood-armed sofa in the living room.

She had already called downtown and gotten the same information Jason Ramsey said he had given Peabody when he called just a few minutes before that. The searchers out at the Big Gully site planned to start again with first light, and George Bonfire had already called in on his cellular phone to say he was there and waiting to get started.

As reported the previous night, searchers had exhausted possibilities within walking distance in the shallow canyons and gullies immediately west of the spot where Noah Webster's pickup truck had been discovered. Two men had explored north, along both sides of the creek, with no results. A recheck of the immediate area had turned up nothing new.

This morning, three or four men would work their way farther south, beyond the spot where muddy tracks had indicated Webster might have fallen—or been dropped—into the icy water above the waterfall. According to plan, the main search party today would follow the river's course on downstream to the west beyond the confluence, checking every nook and cranny as far as they could make it. They expected to meet other search parties working in the other direction out of Silver County by early afternoon, latest.

The mountain canyon area extended about two miles beyond the waterfall. At that point the earth leveled out somewhat, breaks between the mountains forming small, mostly grassy meadows where ranchers sometimes put in cattle. At this time of year the cattle were still in lower pastures, and the only life in those breaks was in the form of deer, black bear, and small wild animals.

The wind often shrieked down those narrow meadows, accelerated by a venturi effect as air was squeezed between canyon walls and then ejected with great force into the broader areas. It was god-awful country in there; most of the time only the hardiest hunters went in, and always on foot.

Johnnie did not see how Webster could have gotten that far. If he had, she harbored little hope that he could have found any kind of shelter that might allow him to survive the night. She was trying to hang on to hope. But reality spread black tentacles through her mind.

The sound of Peabody's loud knock on the thick front door intruded on her thoughts. She hurried to open up.

Wearing a tattered leather bomber jacket and Levi's, Peabody hurried in, slapping thick arms around himself for warmth. "Morning! It's almost like winter again out there!" After what had to have been a night shorter than her own, he looked amazingly normal: ruddy, stubble-bearded, wide awake.

He also looked worried.

"Nothing new out there," he said, spying the mugs on the coffee table and limping over to them. "Guess you know that."

"I called right after you did."

He sat heavily on the couch and sipped his coffee. "Um. Good." His face went sad. "Poor silly bastard."

"You don't think there's any hope."

"I don't see how there can be, now."

"Unless he isn't down there at all."

He squinted at her. "You mean he didn't fall and wasn't dropped in down there? Somebody just set it up to look like that?"

"Butt, I've gone back and forth a dozen times on a lot of stuff. The things in the courthouse annex fire looked like plants to me. So did the arrow in Tomlinson's throat. If I'm right about that—that someone is trying to put it all off on the Ute community to divert suspicion from themselves—then planting the pickup and obvious signs at the creek down there would fit into the pattern exactly."

Peabody sipped more coffee and thought about that. "The Hermans?"

"God, I don't know. It's far-fetched. I don't see a motive. They're miserable, violent people. But are they even smart enough to hatch this kind of plot? And if so, what's in it for them? Why would *anyone* go to desperate lengths like this, for that matter?"

"Maybe, when we find Webster's body, we'll get something that could give us an answer."

"Shit, I hope you're wrong!" she burst out.

He looked up, startled. "What say?"

"About Webster. I keep trying to think he might be okay somewhere."

Peabody's barrel chest heaved. "Are we ready to roll?"

"Sure. Let me turn off a couple of lights."

He stood. "Okay if I take the cup in the truck?"

"Sure."

She turned off lights in the bedroom and kitchen, leaving the one on in the living room. Peabody watched in silence as she took the belt holding the holstered .357 Magnum off the coat tree beside the door and strapped it on. A trip to the kitchen counter added her walkie-talkie. Everything else she might need was already in the Jeep, as it always was: flashlights, extra ammo, shotgun and shells, handheld spotlight, first-aid kit, blankets, the rest of it.

She picked up her coffee mug from the table. "Ready."

"You lead?"

"No. You. You know that backcountry out there better than I do."

They went out into the dark. To the east, over the ridgeline spiky with the silhouettes of big firs, the sky showed its first faint signs of another day. An owl cried. Peabody climbed into his truck, and Johnnie into the Jeep. Using the hand-choke she had had installed at the county barn, she got her motor started instantly. Headlights came on behind her, and then Peabody's massive, mud-splattered pickup trundled slowly around her to go first. She turned on lights and radio but did not reach for the microphone. Thinking of all the scanners merrily flashing their rows of lights in homes around the valley, they would maintain radio silence except in emergency.

Peabody's truck moved away from the house, heading downslope toward the road. Johnnie put the Jeep in gear and followed.

By the time they reached the two-lane asphalt road below, the eastern sky had already begun to pale just a bit more. Peabody's truck turned right, west, and she followed. They drove a few miles, passing the gates to the Banner ranch, and then the clutter of two dozen mobile homes down in Shadetree Acres on the left. Beyond, the bright lights of an all-night convenience store competed with the growing light of dawn. By the time they reached the west river road and turned north onto the dirt, it was possible to see everything in faded gray on all sides: scrubby country, arid clumps of sage and an occasional tumbleweed, a broken-down bit of fence along here, a weedy side turnout into a pasture on the other side farther along. Johnnie spotted a puff of smoke come out of the driver's-side window of Peabody's truck. He was smoking up there. She almost wished she hadn't sworn off.

They rattled over a pipe cattle guard, dipped down into a gully that probably flooded with every good spring rain, and had to slow down drastically because the road became nothing more than a humpy, rock-studded path that twisted meaninglessly along the side of a barren hill. On the far side there was a downhill, and then along the edge of aspen groves on the right, tumbled volcanic boulders and sage on the left, low cliffs beyond. It was light enough now that the sun had to be up, but high cloud cover prevented seeing it.

After another thirty minutes, Johnnie followed Peabody's pickup more closely because she was absolutely unable to see what hints of a "road" he must now be following. They were down to ten miles an hour, often less, rolling over rocks and into holes, constantly up and down, pitching side to side. A glance at her watch said it was almost 7:40.

The terrain, unbelievably, got rougher. Peabody led the way closer to the creek meandering along on the left side, skirting young aspen and avoiding the worst holes, his left tires sometimes splashing in the water of the creek itself. A grassy promontory on the right descended sharply toward the creek, blocking off the view on that side. On the left, the cliffs had mounted higher now, more than sixty feet, slabs of eroded granite shattered by slanting fault lines, vertical breaks as if a giant had attacked them with an ice pick.

After a while Peabody's brake lights flared, and he came to

a stop. His lights went out. His door popped open, and he climbed down, shotgun in hand. Johnnie looked ahead of his truck and saw that further progress was blocked by fallen rock.

She shut down and got out too, walking forward to join him. He was making another cigarette. "Got to hike the rest, Johnnie. Not far, I think."

They worked their way through boulders that seemed to have fallen from the cliffs overhead, tumbling through the creek to come to a rest here at the foot of the promontory that still blocked a long view to the right. Beyond the boulders they came to a stand of young ponderosa pines intermixed with spruce and an occasional fir or, at the edge where more sunlight might penetrate, baby aspen. The sweet smell of the conifers was strong. The creek burbled along. A hawk soared far overhead, turning, looking for breakfast.

Peabody stopped and hauled out his county map, partly unfolding it and looking close. "It's got to be right in here."

They moved in through the light woods. The space between the high ground on the right and the cliffs on the left narrowed until it began to feel as if they were walking into a keyhole. It was dimmer in here, the wet smell of decaying vegetation growing.

"Uh-oh," Peabody grunted suddenly, stopping.

"What?" Johnnie stepped up beside him.

Just ahead, the narrow gap widened sharply. The creek angled across their path. On the left side, close in beside the cliffs, a gentle, grassy hillock began. But most of it had been buried. There had been an enormous collapse of rock from the overhanging formation: gravel, fist-sized rocks, boulders and broken slabs and shards of every size piled high, a grayish mess twenty feet or more tall in some places.

"I think we've found it," Peabody muttered.

Johnnie pointed. "Butt, that collapse and landslide is *recent*."

"Better believe it is. See? Nary a weed or blade of grass sticking out of the powder, anywhere."

She looked up at the towering rock walls. Even in the poor light it was quite easy to see how a great cup-shaped indentation had been scooped out of the face partway up, bringing down countless tons of debris.

"I think we've found what people out thisaway felt," Peabody said. "This would shake the ground all around. This was *big*."

"Lightning, maybe?"

He shrugged. "Maybe a natural fault."

"Or maybe," Johnnie said softly, "dynamite."

"Why?"

She didn't bother to reply, because she had no idea.

Taking the lead, she walked around the edges of the mess, picking her way between boulders the size of an automobile, boots slipping in shale, pebbles, and rock dust. It was sixty feet or more to the other side of the buried mound, judging by a slight rise in the dirt at the edge of the pile of fallen rock. Peabody worked around the other side, out of sight. She heard his boots splashing in the creek. When they met, he was slightly out of breath.

"I don't know what the hell to think about this," he admitted.

"Butt, I don't think this was a natural fall."

"Well, maybe."

"I think this is where the damn dynamite went."

He touched a football-sized rock with the toe of his boot, and it tumbled off several others, making a hollow clatter as it tumbled to a new resting place. "But *what for?* You got an idea about that, too?"

She had no answer. "Let's look around just a little more."

After another twenty minutes or so, however, there was nothing new to be found. They stood back on the edge of the fall, where they had first seen it, and looked back at it again.

"We got to get people out here," Peabody said. "Dig."

Johnnie looked at him in dismay. "Butt, my God! It would take a month to get a backhoe in here."

He opened his mouth to reply, but the squawk of the walkie-talkie on her belt startled both of them. Jason Ramsey's voice. "Base to unit one or two."

She pulled the small radio from her belt. She had explained she would not check in and should not be called except in direst emergency. She depressed the transmit button on the side of the unit. "Base, this is one, go ahead."

"Public service this office, ten-four?"

She looked at Peabody, whose wrinkled forehead showed he was as puzzled as she was. She could not comply with Ramsey's request: the nearest telephone had to be twenty miles away.

She thumbed the radio again. "Negative, base. Unable public service. Go ahead this frequency, over."

The radio fell silent for ten seconds or so. Then: "Report subject Webster located."

The radio went silent as the squelch tail dropped. Johnnie continued to stare at Peabody while the shock sank in. Then the overwhelmingly important single question came out of her mouth even as she pressed the transmit button again. "Alive, Jason? Is he alive?"

"Affirmative, one. EMS unit en route."

She breathed again. "Units one and two will be en route headquarters. Estimate arrival . . . uh . . ."

"Hour and a half," Peabody rumbled.

"—sixty to ninety minutes," Johnnie said. "One out."

"Base out."

Johnnie clipped the radio back on her belt. Peabody led off without conversation. They stumbled along as fast as the brush and rocks allowed.

22

WHEN JOHNNIE AND Peabody hurried into the emergency room of the Tenoclock hospital, they found George Bonfire and several of his tired, bedraggled searchers in the waiting room, along with Deputy Dean Epperly and a city cop.

Bonfire stood to meet them. His face was suffused by a fierce pride. "Didn't think it would happen."

"What happened?" Johnnie asked. "How is he? How did you ever find him?"

"They think he's all right," Bonfire said, shaking his head in amazement. "Fatigue, maybe a little frostbite, maybe a touch of shock. If talking is any indication, he's definitely in shock. That man is a world-class talker, in case you hadn't noticed."

Johnnie chuckled. "I noticed. Where did you find him? What happened?"

"They found him in a yurt up there in the high country. He must have crawled in after crawling out of the river. How, I don't know."

None of them had thought of the yurts—primitive shelters scattered here and there through the high country to provide safe haven for hunters or others who might be caught by bad weather. She said, "He spent the night in a tent?"

"I called it a yurt. That's what the snowmobile club calls it. Actually, this one is a deserted mine shack they gave a new tar-paper roof and some minimum provisions. Luckily including a wood stove. There was still smoke coming from the chimney when my men passed nearby. Whether they would have checked it without spotting the smoke, I don't know."

"How did he—"

The doors into the emergency treatment rooms swept open, and a male nurse pushing a gurney hurried through. On the gurney, blanket-swathed and as white as the pillow behind his head, Noah Webster swung hectic, dazed eyes around and saw them.

"Hey!" he called hoarsely. Then, to the nurse, "Hang on a second! Whoa! Park it, man, please!"

The nurse raised eyebrows to heaven and stopped. Johnnie, Peabody, and Bonfire went over.

"Hey, there!" Webster said through puffy, cracked lips. "Man, I don't know your name, but like I said before, your fellows did a hell of a job finding me. I was kind of afraid nobody would. It's a long ways up there, even riding most of the distance in the river, like I did. Quicker, but I don't recommend going that way. I felt pretty puny, no kidding. I wasn't sure anybody was going to get to me in time, and then when I passed out—at the time I just felt like I was going to sleep, but from what the doc said in there, probably not—"

"Mr. Webster," Johnnie broke in, "will you stop babbling for a minute and just tell us what happened to you? How you got there?"

"Sure! I left the library and went by your shop and left you a message, and then I went out to that state park on the west road, and I got there and I was just starting to set up my tent when somebody clobbered me."

"Clobbered you?"

"Clobbered me. Clobbered me. Hit me in the head."

Johnnie exchanged glances with Peabody. "Go on."

"Okay, fine. Well, the next thing I knew, I was in the back of a pickup or something with a camper shell on, and I was really messed up, only about half there, but then I figured out it was *my* camper shell. You should smell some of that stuff back there. I mean, after you've been on the road, camping—"

"Stay on the point, will you?"

Webster giggled, definitely giddy. "My wife used to say that too. That was before she decided to throw me out—all right, all right, I'll try. Well, the pickup stopped bouncing me around back there, and I passed out again for a while, and when I came to again I was less there than I was before. I think I upchucked. Anyway, somebody was carrying me, like, man, over their shoulder like a feed sack. Whoever it was, he was strong. I'm not fat, but I'm stouter than I look. The last time I had a physical—"

"What happened *next*, dammit?"

"I blacked out again. Then—this was the scary part—the next thing I knew, I hit what felt like the bottom of the ocean, only a lot colder, and the current swept me along, bumping me into rocks and stuff. I was gasping for breath and taking in water and having a hell of a time, and I do not exaggerate. For once. Anyway. I went over a waterfall or something, and the water got deeper, and there I went, bobbing along like a cork on a fishing line, and I thought I was a goner."

Webster's eyes seemed to go out of focus for a moment.

The nurse growled, "He's had an IV."

Webster's eyes shocked open. "What? Oh. Right. Well, as I was saying, I went bob-bob-bobbing along, and I really thought I was a goner a few times because even deep as the river was wherever I was by then, there were still some boulders sticking out here and there, and naturally I creamed into every one of them, seeming like.

"Anyway! After a long time I was about turning into ice myself when I hit this one especially big rock and it kind of threw me around to one side and lo and behold I felt my feet hit bottom, and then the current sort of swept me in shallower, and the next thing I knew I had crawled up out of the water.

"Well, I spent about sixty seconds being thankful to be alive, but it was a lot colder out of the water than in it, even. Do you know how hard the wind can blow up there wherever I was? It felt like standing behind an airplane with its motors running. I've never actually *done* that, but—"

"How did you get to the yurt?" Johnnie cut in again.

"Yurt? Oh. Right. Well, I just sort of was stumbling half-ass along in the snow and all, and I practically bumped into that old shack. Was I glad to see it! Anyway, I got the door open and went in, and kind of fumble-farted around in the dark, and I found some stuff on a shelf, and one of the things was a metal box with matches in. I finally got one lit—I was shaking so bad I didn't have to scratch it, all I had to do was kind of get one shaking hand with the match in it up against the other shaking hand with the scratcher-pad on it—and then I saw the place had a stove and some firewood inside and everything else.

"I got some wood and paper in the stove and got 'er fired up. Do you want to hear how good that felt, when the heat started coming out of that stove? Never mind. Anyway. Then I got out of my wet clothes and wrapped up in all the blankets they had in a cabinet, and I still had a Snickers bar in my coat. It was pretty soggy and yukky, but I couldn't work the plastic bags on the emergency rations they had in there, still shaking too bad. So I ate the Snickers and then I caved in, more or less, and that's where I was when this guy's people found me."

The talk had worn Webster out. His eyelids drooped, and he began to snore softly. The nurse prepared to push the gurney away.

Johnnie gently shook Webster's shoulder. He opened his eyes again. "Huh? Oh. Hi. How long did I sleep?"

"Who did this to you?" she asked.

His eyes closed. "Don' have a clue. . . ." He was going out.

"You saw the Hermans earlier. You marked papers in the library about them."

His eyes half-opened again. "Big lawsuit. *Big* lawsuit. They settled. Something about that mound out there. Too anxious to keep me away from it. My second cousin twice removed . . . or whatever she was . . . Mary Alice . . . s'posed to be in IOOF . . . not there . . . where? How come . . . way back . . . old Lincoln . . . died in hunting accident? You believe . . . that? What . . . happened . . . these guys' mom? Nod in cem'tery either. . . . Crazy. All of 'em. . . . Oh! One more thing . . ." His chest heaved. "That old lawsuit . . . if you ask me . . . I know, you didn't ask me . . . anyway. Lots to hide, those people. Bad stuff . . ." His eyes slowly closed.

"Do you have *any* idea who did this to you?" Johnnie demanded.

His eyes opened. "Sure. Gotta be them—Hermans. Hide stuff. Oh, my . . . I think I'm going to sleep now. . . ."

His eyelids slid shut again, and he began snoring.

"Sorry," the nurse said grimly. "That's it." He pushed the gurney away from them, heading fast down the tiled hallway toward the elevator.

"Jesus Christ," Butt Peabody muttered. "You talk about luck. Did he say one time there he was 'a little scared,' or something like that? It's a miracle. The man ought to be dead."

Johnnie addressed Bonfire and his men. "I want to thank you. You did a great job."

They nodded. A couple of them smiled in acknowledgment.

Johnnie asked Bonfire, "You're going back out now?"

"Yes. Don't know what else to do, though."

"If that shack hasn't been sealed up, I would like you to do that. Butt or I will have to get out there and look everything over—just make sure there isn't something that might help us."

Bonfire nodded and turned away. He and his men walked to the exit doors and went on outside.

Johnnie turned to Peabody.

"Where?" he asked.

"Isn't it obvious?"

He took a deep breath. "Guess so. Let's get going."

23

THEY WENT IN Peabody's truck.

"They've got a scanner," Peabody said on the way. "They'll know he was found alive."

"I know," Johnnie replied.

"They'll have their stories ready again, just like when you were out here before. We don't have enough to pin anything on them."

"Butt, that cliff was *blown*. The mound was buried on purpose."

"Maybe. But we don't know—"

"It takes dynamite to do a job like that."

"Doesn't mean they did it, or if they did, they got the stuff from Tomlinson."

"Dammit, then, what about that woman Webster mentioned? Old Mary Alice? What happened to *her?*"

"None of it proves a thing, Johnnie."

"Where there's this much smoke. . ." She left it unfinished.

"Thanks for reminding me," Peabody said. He reached for his tobacco.

They rode the rest of the way in silence.

AFTERNOON SUN HAD pierced the clouds by the time they reached the Herman property. When they drove up to the front of the decaying mansion, everything looked as it had before, except that the dogs did not larrup out to greet or intimidate them. Johnnie and Peabody walked to the front door of the house. They were both wearing their sidearms.

Peabody knocked.

Dogs started raising hell just inside. Moments later, a male voice could be heard yelling at them. Their racket died down, and the door opened. Joseph Herman stared out at them.

"You again?" His narrowed, bloodshot eyes betrayed lack of sleep. He was barefoot, stubble-bearded, his hair unkempt, wearing jeans and a tattered sweatshirt.

"Joseph, we need to talk," Johnnie told him.

Joseph gave Peabody an antagonistic look. "What do *you* want?"

Peabody shrugged. "I'm with her."

Joseph's lip curled. "Yeah. I heard how she'd put you back on the county charity list."

"Can we come in?" Johnnie snapped.

"No. What do you want?"

"Can we come in?"

"I said no."

"Mr. Herman, we're giving you a choice here."

"Choice? What choice?"

"We come in, or you go downtown with us, and we talk there."

Muscles leaped as he clamped his jaw. He stepped back, letting them in.

Johnnie entered first. She experienced a strong sense of déjà vu. The dogs were all inside and milled around her as they had before, roughly nudging her with their big snouts, their thick

230 / JOHN MILES

bodies bumping against her legs. One of them snapped. The entry hallway stood dark and grimy, with only the brighter doorway into the big back living area open. Joseph slammed the front door and gestured toward the back.

Johnnie and Peabody went in. There was no fire in the fireplace, only one very old metal floor lamp lit over the far end of the shaggy sofa. The room smelled strongly of stale cigarette smoke. It felt dank, chilly, deserted. No one else was in sight.

Joseph padded around them and turned to face them in front of the coffee table. Hands on hips, he looked ready to fight. "Spit it out. I'm busy."

"We'd like to have all the family in here for this," Johnnie said.

"Why?"

"We've got some questions, and we want answers from everybody."

"Maybe I'll just tell you to fuck yourself."

"Son," Peabody intervened in a deceptively quiet tone, "I think it would be a whole lot smarter for you to just cooperate, you savvy?"

Joseph's big hands curled into fists. He froze, his face twisting as he fought an almost overpowering rage. Then some muffled obscenity burst from his mouth, something Johnnie couldn't understand, and he hurled himself past them on the way to the far door.

Peabody cocked an eyebrow. "Real nice folks, these Hermans."

"Butt, I think he really is crazy."

"Yep. Maybe I should have told you a lot more of the bits and pieces you pick up about these folks, living here year after year, keeping your ear to the ground. The old, old man was crazy, old-timers have said. There was a son way back that was a maniac—maybe he was killed in a hunting accident, maybe he was shot by his own brother. That was after his father was shot, too." Peabody's mouth turned down, sour. "Another accident. Of course, in those days the Hermans owned everything in these parts. You didn't cross 'em. Sheriff back then did what they said. People stayed away. Nobody crossed 'em."

Loud voices approaching from another part of the house cut him off. Joseph could be heard shouting angry words. A voice not much softer—old Elmo's—retorted. Joseph shouted again. A crashing sound, a table or something being overturned. Luther, the other brother, in a pleading tone, and Joseph again, this time close enough so that the words could be made out: "Just say what I told you! Just tell the story and shut up! You understand me?"

Footsteps echoed in the hall. Luther Herman, a faded, frayed bathrobe wrapped around his body, walked in unsteadily, his eyes dazed and uncertain. The old man, Elmo, limped in behind him, his wife clinging to his arm. Joseph, in a towering rage, followed them.

"Sit there," he barked at Luther, pointing to a chair. "You two. On the couch." He swung back to Johnnie. "We're all here. Say what you want to say."

She had been mentally rehearsing how to handle this, but uncertainty made her voice sound tentative: "The man who was here to see you, Mr. Webster? He's been found. He's alive. He's going to be fine. He's been telling us . . . a lot of things."

On the couch, the old woman gave a sharp, keening wail of despair and bent over from the waist, her head going to her knees. Elmo's face twisted in pain as he put his arm around her. "It's all right, Aggie, it's all right—"

"Shut up!" Joseph said sharply. Luther started rocking back and forth in his chair, head down, like a child on a hobbyhorse.

They were on the edge, and although she didn't completely understand why, Johnnie's intuition told her to attack, and fast. "Why did you have to blow up that cliff to cover up the ceremonial mound out there?"

"Blow up a cliff?" Joseph made a weak attempt at a derisive laugh. "What are you talking about?"

"You blew up the cliff, Joseph. We know that. We've been out there, and the evidence is obvious. Did you buy the dynamite from the man from Alamosa, or was Billy Kickingbird a middleman for you?"

"You're crazier than hell! We don't have to take this kind of crap. Get your ass out of our house. Now. Both of you."

"Did Kickingbird kill Tomlinson—or did you?"

The old woman wailed again. His arm around her shoulders, Elmo shook her. In the chair beside him, Luther made a little moaning sound and rocked more spasmodically.

But to Johnnie's amazement, Joseph suddenly seemed to go calm. His shoulders slumped. He shook his head in every appearance of defeat. "No use, I guess—right?"

"Right," Johnnie said, and held her breath.

Joseph threw his arms out to his sides in a gesture of resignation. "People were digging out there. Tearing up our property. The Utes, too. Looking for bones or something. Who understands a bunch of Utes?"

"So?" Johnnie prodded.

"Back before the explosion, we saw a truck coming out of there one day. We ran him down—stopped him. It was Kickingbird. He said he was looking for stuff he could sell. We scared him real good and let him go. Right, Luther?"

Luther looked up, eyes wide with fear. "Right. Right." He watched his brother with a mute fascination.

"Right after that," Joseph resumed, "that night, we felt the house shake. We went out next morning. He'd tried to blow up the mound to uncover stuff—that's what we figured—but by accident he made the rocks come down instead. And that's the truth."

He was not entirely unconvincing. Johnnie paused, forming her next question.

Peabody stepped in first. "How come he got killed, Joseph?"

Joseph raised his eyebrows in a very good simulation of puzzlement. "We have no idea. But what I think, myself—I told Pop about this—is, whoever down there was paying him to steal stuff from us, when he messed up the demolition, they got mad. Real mad. They got him for it."

"And the other one? Tomlinson?"

"Maybe he was the one that supplied the explosives to Kickingbird. Maybe, before he got killed himself, Kickingbird had to kill him to keep him quiet."

Peabody's tone lowered sarcastically. "And the annex fire?"

Joseph went blank and spread his hands. "How should I know?"

"So," Peabody said, "Kickingbird blew up the cliff by mistake, trying to steal relics, and then he had to kill Tomlinson to keep it all quiet, but then somebody killed Kickingbird for messing up."

Joseph again spread his arms and shrugged.

"Joseph, do you really think anybody would buy that yarn?"

"If that isn't the explanation," Joseph said with eerie calm, "then I don't have any answers at all for you."

Johnnie turned to the younger brother. "What did you say to Billy Kickingbird when you caught him, Luther?"

"Don't say anything, Luther," Joseph warned.

"What did you say?" Johnnie repeated.

"We—"

Joseph's voice had a strident urgency: "Don't say anything, Luther!"

Johnnie moved closer to Luther and bent over him, trying to force eye contact. "Tell me about Tomlinson, the man from Alamosa, Luther."

Saliva drooled from the corners of Luther's trembling mouth. "We . . . I told him . . . I said . . . you shouldn't ought to come rob our mound—"

"*Tomlinson,* you said that to, Luther?"

He shook his head in despair. "No. I mean the other man—"

Elmo said suddenly, "Leave him be. Please!"

Johnnie ignored him. "Luther. Where did you get the arrow?"

"We—"

"Be quiet, Luther!" Joseph warned. "She's trying to mess you up."

"We—"

"Shut up, Luther!"

Luther looked up at Johnnie with bloodshot eyes filling with scared tears. She felt sorry for him. But she couldn't stop now. She was on the verge of breaking him. She hated it, but it was the only way to go. She pushed on blindly, grabbing on to one of the dozen theories that had gone through her head at one time or another:

"Did you get the dynamite from Billy Kickingbird, Luther? Did he get that arrow for you, too? Is that why you had to kill him when he got back from Denver, just the way you had killed Tomlinson before?"

Luther's lips trembled. "I said get off our land, and then Joseph said, if you come back we'll kill you, and he said—I can't remember what his name was, it was dark—"

"Luther," Joseph growled.

Luther turned spasmodically toward him. "I can't remember! Oh, Joseph, I can't remember what you told me to say!"

"You idiot! Just be still!"

Luther's face went all to pieces, and he began sobbing.

Suddenly Elmo said, "Joseph. We can't keep it up, son."

"Keep quiet, old man," Joseph said.

Elmo shook his head. Slowly he removed his arm from around his wife's shoulders. His demeanor and posture changed, as if a great weight had dropped onto his shoulders.

"No," he said quietly. "We can't lie anymore. We've lied forever. We can't do it anymore. It's over with."

"Shut your face," Joseph warned. "They can't prove anything—"

"The boys got the dynamite from Kickingbird," Elmo said hoarsely, tears beginning to roll. "It was the Alamosa man that brought it—Kickingbird was a middleman—the Alamosa man got cheated out of most of the money we sent for him, and the boys—they didn't want to do it—they had to kill him, he was going to talk—and then Kickingbird knew—he *knew*, don't you see—"

With a growl, Joseph launched himself at his father. He moved too swiftly for anyone to intervene. He grabbed the old man, both hands closing around his neck, and shook him like a doll. The old woman screamed. Johnnie tried to pull him off. Luther erupted from his chair and rushed across the room, toward a massive old armoire on the far wall.

Peabody violently tossed Johnnie aside and grabbed Joseph around the top of his head with a convulsive, wrenching movement. Thrown to her knees, Johnnie saw Joseph pulled loose from his father and knocked off balance to the floor. The action pushed Peabody off balance too, and he sprawled half under the coffee table. Elmo fell backward, choking for breath. Joseph scrambled to his feet and went for Peabody.

Across the room, Luther cried, "*Joseph! Don't!*"

Johnnie whirled to see Luther poised beside the old cabinetry. In his hands he had some kind of semiautomatic rifle— short barrel and stock, foreign, the kind terrorists used, probably illegal. Tears streamed down his face. He aimed the rifle at his brother.

Seeing the gun, Joseph stopped dead. For an instant Johnnie thought he was quitting. She started to reach for her service revolver.

"No, Joseph," Luther said, his voice almost inaudible, half fearful but with a strangely calm certainty in it. "No, Joseph," he repeated. "I won't let you—no more."

Joseph made a low, growling sound and threw himself down at the other side of the coffee table, tearing at the edge with both hands. Johnnie saw too late that there was a drawer under there—saw it open—didn't yet have her revolver clear of the snap-flap holster. She saw Peabody rolled wildly to one side, his hand clawing for his own weapon.

Joseph's hand came out of the drawer with a revolver in it. He started to raise it—aim it at his brother.

The rifle in Luther's hands erupted in a shattering cannonade of shots. Everything seemed to happen at once: burst of smoke from the muzzle, little coppery shower of ejected shell casings, incredible staccato roar of noise, savage hammering of objects into Joseph's chest, throwing him sideways and backward in a shower of red.

The sound stopped as abruptly as it had begun. Through the tremendous ringing in her ears Johnnie heard Elmo crying out and his wife screaming, and then the sound of a heavy object hitting the floor. She saw Luther falling to his knees. He had dropped the rifle.

Gun in hand, Peabody went across the room with a quickness that would have done justice to a twenty-year-old athlete. In what seemed like one continuous movement, he kicked the rifle toward the far end of the room, knocked Luther down, rolled him over, and reached for the handcuffs latched to the back of his belt.

Johnnie rushed over to where Joseph had been hurled half behind the couch by the fusillade of bullets. One look was enough for her. She turned back to Elmo and his wife, still on the couch, horror twisting their features almost out of recognition.

"I'll tell the rest," Elmo sobbed. "I'll tell you all I know. I know almost everything. I can't stand hiding it all anymore."

24

W H E N   S H E   W E N T to his hospital room two days later, on Sunday, Johnnie found Noah Webster in a robe and slippers, sitting up in the bedside chair in his room. He looked considerably better after a full two days of sleep and medication.

"I hear you're getting out this afternoon," Johnnie said.

Webster had been reading some kind of scientific journal. He tossed it onto the bed. "I'll say so. I'm ready. I mean, it's kind of neat, you know, being in a place like this, having people wait on you hand and foot. But there are always trade-offs, like they come in at three in the morning—three!—to draw blood, and then at five—five!—they come wake you up again to weigh you. How important can it be, what I weigh today compared with what I weighed yesterday? And why all the blood tests, anyway? I asked the doctor. He's a nice guy, graduated down in New Orleans, likes Dixieland jazz a lot, you can't find a lot of people that do, these days. Anyway. He said something like, 'Well, we have to make sure all your levels have stabilized,' and I said to him, 'How significant, chemically speaking, can a little change be at this point, when I obviously feel a hundred percent?' He didn't have an answer for that. So I'm outta here. Hey. Listen. You *said* you'd finish your investigating and interrogation and all today, and fill me in on the whole deal. At long last, I might add. After all, I'm the body that didn't get found dead, right? So what's the deal? Do you tell me now, or not?"

Johnnie sat on the edge of the bed. "I might, if you would shut up long enough for me to get a word in edgewise."

Webster put a hand over his own mouth.

Johnnie told him what was now known, after four interrogations of Elmo Herman, the addition of what poor, stupid, dazed Luther had been able to supply, along with preliminary screening of some of the crumbling old documents and letters, many dating back more than forty years, that they had found strewn over a half-dozen hiding places in the mansion.

Some of it—unless the continuing search turned up even more evidence—might never be known.

Fragments of a few letters found in the house went back as far as the teens of the century. They made clear that the original settler, the first Lincoln Herman, had been a strong, violent, unstable man; there were hand-scrawled notes threatening neighbors, references to lawsuits, and senseless, raging notes and sketches that seemed to have been produced and then never sent to anyone.

Sometime in the mid-teens, however, Lincoln Herman had undergone a strange religious conversion. He threw himself into the life of the church, if many scraps of paper showing donations could be believed, and there was a small pasteboard box containing portions of his original land deed and transfer papers indicating he might have been preparing to give over virtually everything to his religion.

It was at that time that he had been reported killed "in an accident."

His son Lincoln took over family affairs. In 1919, he killed his brother, the first Luther, in a "hunting accident." Other papers found in the moldering files included billing and correspondence from a mental hospital—called an asylum in those days—in Kansas. Luther, apparently quite mad, had been home for a visit at the time of the alleged accident.

The record was even more fragmentary after that. The interviews with old Elmo had supplied most of the details for later times.

Elmo had been born in 1934, his sister Lucy a year later. At an early age it became apparent that the streak of mental instability in the family had been passed down to the girl child. Elmo's father and his wife—Noah Webster's lost relative Mary Alice Sturdivant—had sheltered the mad young girl, and the family had increasingly cloistered itself.

Mary Alice had tried hard. But the second Lincoln Herman was a violent man, driven to drunken rages. When, after years of torment, she had learned that her husband was a murderer and that her own children must carry the gene of madness, she had sent a long letter to her sister back home, including the part of the original land deed she knew was proof of the family's dishonesty in procuring all their land.

Then she had tried to flee. But her husband had caught her.

For a very long time Elmo believed his mother died of natural causes in 1937. For a long time he did not know why she was not buried in the Tenoclock Cemetery.

In 1969 Lincoln Herman fell ill. On his deathbed, heavily sedated, he told his son everything he knew, or had guessed, about the earlier family history.

He also blurted out to Elmo what really had happened to his mother.

The shock to Elmo was extreme. But there was nothing to do about it. After a period of near-paralysis, which people attributed to simple grief over the loss of his father, he picked up the pieces. He took responsibility for his sister. Later he married his wife Ernestine, and their sons Joseph and Luther were born four and five years later.

In 1978 the usually clannish family had taken on a handyman named Clerkson. He had quickly started a relationship with

Lucy, now forty-three, confused as she had been all her life, given to flights of hysteria, night-walking, visions, and periods of eerie peace and isolation.

"He was after our money," Elmo said in one of his taped statements. "Poor Lucy. She was never right. I had to protect her. If he had stayed, he might have found out the old secrets. I beat him up. I told him I would kill him, the son of a bitch. He went away. But then—" Elmo at that point in the interrogation had broken down again.

Lucy had hanged herself in her room less than a week later.

In the aftermath of the latest tragedy, Elmo himself had been plunged into despair. It was already apparent that the Herman curse had come down to his children, too—through his genes. Joseph was given to violent outbursts of uncontrollable temper, and Luther was retarded.

Elmo took care of them as best he could. He knew, now, much of the old history, what his father had told him and what he had learned on his own, digging through chaotic family records. The original deed to all the property was imperfect, fatally flawed by lies, misrepresentation, and extortion. Later transactions might also have been illegal. If any of the details ever came out totally, the family might still lose everything.

At some point his wife Ernestine learned enough of this—or was so overwhelmed by the madness and turmoil in the house—that she ran away. Elmo had never been able to find her. Years later he met his present companion, Agatha, and she moved in with him. They had never been married.

As the years passed, Elmo slowly allowed his sons to learn some of the past. He explained the fragility of their claim to the land and other properties. It was a secret the family had to keep forever, at all costs.

The lawsuit brought on behalf of Ute descendants, originally cheated out of their land, had required expenditure of virtually all the money Elmo could lay hands on. He had thought that settlement—at long last—meant the past would be buried forever.

"But that," Johnnie told Noah Webster now, "is where you came in."

Webster stared. *"Me?"*

"Your first letter."

"What did *I* do? I just said I wanted to come visit and ask about Mary Alice Sturdivant, and maybe muck around the burial mound."

Johnnie nodded. "But they couldn't let you do that. What if you dug into old records at the courthouse annex and found something that might uncover all the old cheating? They tried to tell you to stay away."

"Yeah, but I wrote again, telling them the little I did know about old Mary Alice, and said I was coming anyway. Which—"

"That was when Joseph panicked, you see. That was when he and Luther had to burn it down to make sure nothing remained that you might find useful."

Webster's eyes sagged. "Oh, boy."

"And then they had to get the dynamite and blow up the mound, but they paid Billy Kickingbird to get it for them, and he got it from Tomlinson, down in Alamosa. Then—this is not entirely clear because poor Luther gets so hysterical every time we get him to this part—it looks like they blew up the cliff, but Kickingbird tried to cheat Tomlinson out of his payment, and Tomlinson came back, raising hell to the Hermans, and they had to kill him to keep him quiet."

"Geez," Webster breathed. "And Kickingbird?"

"Well, he had to go, too, of course, as soon as they could find him—when he got back from Denver. He knew the Tomlinson-Herman connection. He was too dangerous."

Webster thought about it. Johnnie waited to let him catch up. Outside in the hospital hallway, somebody pushed a cart of equipment past the door, bottles and metallic objects clattering.

"The old man did it all?" Webster asked finally.

"The boys did. Joseph. He bullied Luther, and Luther went along like a big, cowering hound, just like he always did on everything."

"But Elmo knew."

"Yes. He guessed some, got the rest out of them. But he was as scared of Joseph as Luther was—as Aggie and everybody else who ever met him was. He had to go along. He was helpless. I mean—my God, the things he wanted to keep hidden."

"Lord," Webster said after a while. "All because they thought I *might* find something in the old files in the annex that would bring out some of this stuff?"

"They didn't know what you might already have. They thought you might be able to put two and two together when no one else had."

"I didn't *have* two!"

"But they didn't know that."

Webster shook his head. "And they blew up the mound just to spite me? So I would get discouraged and probably go away?"

Johnnie shook her head. "Oh, no. I'm afraid not, sir. I wish it was that simple."

Webster stared at her. "I don't feel at all sure I want to hear this, whatever it is. If it's what I think—"

"Way back there," Johnnie said, cutting him off, "in 1937—"

"When Mary Alice mailed the partial deed, and tried to bug out?"

"Yes. But her husband caught her."

Webster groaned. "He killed her?"

"Yes."

"But she wasn't buried in—oh, shit!"

"He secretly hauled her body out to that mound, and he dug a hole in the side, and he buried her in it."

"And that's what Elmo found out years later," Webster said, "and the boys finally learned about it too."

"Yes. So they could hardly let you poke around that burial mound, you see, because—"

"Mary Alice was in there."

"I'm afraid so, Mr. Webster."

Webster leaned back and stared at the ceiling. "Oh, boy. Poor Uncle Jack. This is not going to look good in the family history."

TWO WEEKS LATER the weather had warmed, and it was a perfect spring day. Out in the remote mountain ravine, they had finally hacked through enough of a pathway to get the trucks in. Three pickup trucks and a loaded flatbed truck were there. They had pulled in not far from where Johnnie and Butt Peabody had parked their vehicles near the mountain of rock rubble hiding the old ceremonial mound. Another old truck was nearby.

Standing halfway up the side of the weedy promontory overlooking the site from the east, Johnnie and Peabody watched the backhoe operator cautiously back his big yellow machine off the rear of the flatbed. Three drivers and seven laborers stood nearby, ready to assist. A lot of other equipment, including portable generators, compressors, air hammers and hosing, and hand tools of all kinds, lay scattered on the grass.

Not far away, three other men stood silent. Johnnie had conferred intensively with all of them. One, a criminal forensics expert from Denver, was among the best at directing an excavation aimed at locating an old crime scene, or the remains of a crime victim. The second man, an archaeologist from Boulder, had overseen exhumations at a number of primitive burial sites in Colorado, New Mexico, and Arizona. The third person in the group, a representative of the Ute people, had veto power over everything that might be done, to assure respect for whatever historic materials might be disturbed in the search.

"Mr. Herman was once shown the mound area where the woman supposedly was buried in a shallow grave," Johnnie had explained to all of them, using a hand-drawn map to illustrate. "We're hoping, once the rock rubble has all been

244 / JOHN MILES

removed, the hand-digging won't have to be extensive."

"All ancient remains and artifacts that might be disturbed must be restored to their original location," the distinguished Ute told her.

"We understand," Johnnie assured him. "And the court's order verifies it."

"Perhaps it will not be possible to identify that white woman's bones even if bones are uncovered."

The forensics man spoke up with quiet firmness. "Oh no, sir. I can assure you. We can distinguish modern remains from ancient ones. Furthermore, with any luck whatsoever, we will be able to establish the woman's identity with a high degree of accuracy."

So they were all here now, ready to begin.

The backhoe operator finished backing his machine off the truck. Its smokestack belched black diesel as he engaged a forward gear and crept it around its carrier and nearer the mound. The operator brought it to a halt.

Another pickup truck, this one with an old camper shell on back, appeared through the trees and brush to the left. It pulled in along with all the others, and Noah Webster hopped out, cameras flopping around his neck. He spied Johnnie and Peabody, waved, and trotted up the hill to them.

"You said I could watch," he reminded her.

"That's all," she told him severely.

"And take pictures," he added.

"From a respectful distance."

"Sure. That's cool."

"And keep quiet!"

"Um."

Below, the laborers and experts waited. The man on the backhoe idled his engine back, dropping its note to a low, lurching rumble.

The doors of the old pickup opened. George Bonfire got out on the driver's side. From the other came a tall man, very old, wearing a robe of red and black and purple that draped from his lean shoulders all the way to his ankles, and carrying a small, handcrafted leather bag. It looked as old as he.

Wakinokiman walked slowly, probably in some arthritic pain, from the truck to the one edge of the burial mound not obscured by rock debris. Bonfire stayed near him, but a respectful half-step back.

Wakinokiman bowed his head, then looked up at the flawless sky and began a low, unmelodic chant. Johnnie could hear only the alien sound, not the words, if there were any.

After a minute or two, Wakinokiman reached into his leather bag, took out some shards of stuff, and began working his way around the periphery of the rock pile, strewing bits of tobacco, sage, and corn. The faint sound of his chant continued.

It took a long time for him to make a complete circuit of the mound, purifying it for the work that had to be done, reconsecrating the site, placating the spirits, promising them that these men meant no harm.

Finally the old man was through. His chant died away. He said something to George Bonfire, and the younger man steadied him by the elbow as they walked back the way they had come.

When they reached the truck, Wakinokiman turned and looked back, tilting his head as he searched for Johnnie's group. Their eyes met over the distance. Johnnie felt a sharp tingling of *something*, some archaic stab of emotion, half fear and half recognition.

The old man almost imperceptibly bowed his head, granting permission.

Johnnie signaled the excavation crew foreman below. He called something up to the man on the backhoe.

The operator moved handles, the big machine snorted noise and dense black smoke, and the bucket lowered, digging in to move the first scoop of rock debris, beginning the job of uncovering the past.